Kinundrum

Piney Falls Mysteries

Joann Keder

*For Meghan, Mackensie, Laura, Piper, Jayden and
Lauren
May your stars always shine bright.*

The joy of siblings is the connection of heart and soul. The misery of siblings is the inability to release it.

— F.T. Glennon

Characters

Cedar Hill–Cosmo's sister
Obie Lumquest—Piper's boyfriend and Boysie's son
Sterling Truth—Owner of Sterling Hotels chain
Harmony Gregory—his girlfriend
Rusty Mellow—new delivery driver for Cosmic Bakes
Trigger Jarvis—stranger in town
Jim Winterkorn—Trigger's partner
Meea and Aurielle—new in town

Chapter One
Lanie

"Cos, your sister isn't going to arrive any sooner whether you're watching for her or not."

My salt-and-pepper-haired hunk of a husband has been glued to the window for over an hour.

It always amuses me when the little-boy-who-never-was emerges from the adult skin of my husband. His sister, Cedar, called last week from San Diego and asked if she could spend some time with us. Without asking the reason for her unplanned visit, he gave her an enthusiastic yes.

"She said one and it's two-fifteen," he replies mournfully. "Why didn't she just let me pick her up from the airport?"

I take his uneaten grilled cheese from the kitchen counter and set it down beside him. "I'm sure she still loves you dearly. Maybe she wanted to take in the scenery on her way. You know what a pretty drive it is from Portland. Though she should understand how it's killing you to wait. You haven't seen her in months," I say, rubbing his back as I scoot in beside him.

"Six. It's been six months and she barely talks to me on the phone anymore."

"We knew when Cedar moved to San Diego to be the marketing manager for the Sleepy Sounds corporate offices that she would have less time for us."

"You're right." Cosmo takes a big bite of sandwich and leans his head on my neck. I can feel his warm breath as I drink in his familiar woodsy scent. It is my favorite way to hold the man dearest to me.

The sound of gravel under tires alerts us to the long-awaited arrival.

"She's here!" Cosmo says, jumping up and flipping his sandwich on the floor. Before I can argue, he is out the door and waiting impatiently for her to exit her rental car.

I watch with amusement from the picture window. She opens the door, looking every bit the stunning woman I remember. Her silver hair is still cut in a bob at her neck and her face is round, cherubic. Cosmo lifts her in the air and they spin in a circle of sibling bliss.

We haven't seen Cedar since Christmas and though her makeup, hair and dress are all the latest fashion, she has definitely lost weight. Studying her further, there is something off about her smile too.

"You're being ridiculous, Lanie," I remark, forcing myself to move away from the window. They deserve some brother-sister time without my prying eyes. Moving to the kitchen, I doublecheck that the coffee is hot and the Mission Control Marionberry Scones, the ones she requested, are warming in the oven.

"Lanie, guess who I found!"

His joyous voice is infectious.

Peeking my head around the corner, I see Cedar's face. I'm always thrown when I see them together. They share the same breathtaking, ice-blue eyes.

"Cedar! We're so happy and surprised to see you!" Bringing her in close for a solid hug and kiss, my worst fears are confirmed. She's nothing but bones. "Your scones are ready! Come into the kitchen."

She looks down at her shoes, which are covered in pink dust.

"Vem was showing off last night," I explain. "She's purchased all sorts of new gadgets under the auspice of 'weaponry' and this one shoots pink sparkles into the air."

"That nut talked Truman into helping as well." Cosmo shakes his head as he maneuvers around us in order to reach the kitchen first. "My good buddy is a sucker for a good firework."

He pours three coffees and plates the scones with smooth, quick, efficient motions only found in those who work in the food service industry.

"Thanks for letting me come," Cedar says softly, bringing her mug to her lips. She closes her eyes and takes a journey somewhere in time. "Just as good as I remembered. Bumpy Ride Roasters could compete with any roaster in the world."

"How was your flight?" Cosmo asks, leaning in a little too close to her. If I were the jealous type, this fawning might upset me, even though it is his sister. Their overly-close relationship was part of the package when I signed on as his wife.

"It was fine. I had...a lot on my mind." Her long, dark eyelashes flutter as she looks away.

I pat her leg, bringing her back to the safety of our kitchen and her family. "Tell us all about your job! You always have good stories from the Sleepy Sounds corporate headquarters!"

The Sleepy Sounds Corporation is the owner of our local Fallen Branch Inn and Resort. They have three levels of hotels, beginning with the Groan Inn, for the budget-conscious traveler. Towels and air conditioning are add-ons. Next comes the Snore More, a medium level establishment that, in addition to complimentary towels and air conditioning, offers a free breakfast, a gym and a nice pool.

The resort-level is the Hi Sigh chain. Our Fallen Branch Inn and Spa (where I work as the marketing manager) falls into this category. It's got all the perks and the price tag that comes with it. None of the rooms go for less than $300 per night. We are proud to be one of the crown jewels of the company, and even prouder yet to have Cedar working in their corporate offices.

"Oh, things are going so good!" Her face brightens. "We're planning sixteen new locations in the next year!"

"That seems kinda ambitious, doesn't it, sis?" Cosmo has thankfully moved away from Cedar and leans back in his chair, relaxing his posture, but his eyes remain trained on her. "I mean, you've got three locations in Denver alone."

Cedar breaks off the tiniest piece of scone and places it on her tongue like she's taste-testing professionally. "I don't make those decisions, Cos. I'm in the marketing department for the corporation, remember?"

"Thought you might be running the place by now." He winks at me and I wink back.

"Not yet."

Usually, his teasing brings a smile to her face. Today is different.

"Cos and I are so happy to see you. We were just a little surprised. Last we knew, you were planning some big trip to Europe with your vacation time."

Her eyes dart away from the window, wide and

full of fear. "What else did I tell you?" Cedar wiggles in her chair.

Patting her arm comfortingly, I say, "Nothing at all, Sis. Just that you were coming."

"This is a safe space. You can trust us with whatever Sleepy Sounds secrets are rolling around in that brilliant mind.Now the yak-fest living next door, she's another matter." My husband's thumb juts in the air in the general direction of November Bean's home. He still hasn't caught on that his sister isn't in a good space.

"I'm sorry, guys. You know that I trust you both. Work has been terribly stressful, that's all." She takes another tiny nibble of her scone.

"We can't wait to hear all about it. We're going to spoil you rotten this week. That's what family is for!" Cosmo's eyes twinkle as his voice rises. It would be so cute if Cedar's current situation wasn't so concerning.

Cedar nods and bites her lip. More than anything, I want to take her in my arms and hold her close, removing the pain that's weighing so heavily on her boney shoulders.

"When are we gonna meet that boyfriend of yours?" Cosmo asks, continuing on his I'm-not-reading-the-room path. At least he's consistent.

"We...we...we broke up." She jumps up from her chair. "I'll go get my luggage."

Cosmo rises with equal gusto. "Now, what kind

of a host would I be if I let my sister carry her own bags into the house?"

There isn't a word for what happens next; shocking doesn't even come close.

Cedar shoves Cosmo out of the way, causing him to lose his balance and fall into my lap. "I have to get it myself!" she shouts, rushing toward our front door.

When I hear it slam shut, Cosmo and I stare at each other in disbelief.

"Not that I don't love you in such close proximity," I begin.

"Nor do I hate this position," he replies. "But that was so—"

"Out of character," I finish for him.

"I was going to say weird, but that covers it. What do you think is going on? This isn't like my sis at all!"

Before I can answer, Cedar returns to the kitchen, carrying a large suitcase. "I'm sorry. I guess I'm just really stressed out from work. Can you forgive me?"

Cosmo bounds off my lap. "There's nothing to forgive, Sis. Now that you've done the hard part, I'll take your stuff to the guest house. We've got all the smelly soap and—"

"I'd prefer to stay here with you guys, in the main house. Would that be an imposition?"

Once again, we're left speechless. Cedar, while loving her brother, is fiercely protective of her privacy. After growing up in a cult, she savors that time to herself. She was the whole reason he and his best friend, Truman worked so hard to finish the guest house in the first place.

"The guest bedroom is all ready to go," I reply. "The bed isn't as comfortable, but it's still nicer than sleeping on the couch."

I tilt my head toward Cosmo, hoping he understands my cue to take her suitcase and give us some girl time. Thankfully, this cue hits its mark.

"I've got to make sure the grill is ready for our steaks tonight after I drop off your suitcase, so I'll leave two of the most beautiful women in the world alone. Sure you can find something to talk about."

He kisses both of us on the cheeks before disappearing with her suitcase.

When he's gone, I give her my sternest gaze. "Okay, Cedar. All of this is really strange. You called two days ago to ask if you could stay with us. Not that we mind, but you're a very schedule-oriented person and this is very last-minute. On top of that, you clearly aren't yourself. My goodness, you're a two scone girl and you ate the equivalent of four ants. Spill it."

I cross my arms and try to keep my face serious so she knows I mean business.

"I didn't want to tell you yet. Let's enjoy some family time first. And I want to enjoy my niece. I haven't seen her for —"

"You saw her at Christmas, just like us," I interrupt. "Come on, girlfriend."

She sighs and runs her fingers through her thick, silver hair. "I suppose you're right. I need to rip off the Band-Aid and get it out in the open."

Cedar moves to our living room with me following behind. When we're both seated, she sighs again before beginning. "It all started in the fall. That's why I didn't come home for Thanksgiving; I couldn't concentrate and I cried at the drop of a hat.. I started seeing a therapist, trying to deal with left-over cult stuff."

Most of Piney Falls, including Cedar, November Bean and Cosmo, grew up in the Fallen Branch Cult. They've come so far.

"It's the gift that keeps on giving, isn't it?"

She nods. "My therapist strongly encouraged me to make some new friends. 'Find a hobby,' he said. When I failed at tennis, golf and bird watching, he suggested I try just getting out of the house instead, meeting up with people. It just so happened my office was hosting a get-together that week."

Cedar pauses, drumming her fingers on her chair. "There were so many new faces my anxiety went through the roof. I turned to leave and bumped into the most gorgeous man I'd ever seen."

As I remain stoic, I remember the last person she described this way. I love this woman with all of my being, but the 'most gorgeous men she's ever seen' always turn out to be bad news.

"Sterling was taller than me, with chestnut hair and big brown eyes. He said he'd been watching me and could tell I hated these things as much as he did."

Cedar is lost again, in some movie I wish I could see.

"Evidently the small talk was short-lived," I quip.

Cedar blushes. "He told me he was working with our company in hopes of placing some of line of luxury care products in our Hi-Sigh hotels. They have a nice goat soap and a moisturizer that makes your face feel like butter." She pauses, touching her hand to her flawless face. "His family owns the Truth Corporation."

"I've heard of them! They name their hotels after family members. Cos and I stayed in The Gregory last year. Very impressive."

"They are. And Sterling was very proud of them. We talked all evening and then continued our conversation the next day, over lunch. We agreed on everything, from business practices to television shows, even what kind of food we liked. It was like this perfect man just dropped out of the sky."

"And you're going to tell me that wasn't the case."

As we've been speaking, I've noticed Cedar getting progressively more fidgety. In a seminar I attended, entitled, "Don't Show 'Em Your Hiney," Jebb Winch taught us that every single movement is a cue. I slept with him, and let me tell you, that guy didn't give off any cues to his lack of mobility.

"I should have known," Cedar continues. "We spent every moment of every weekend together, either at one of his estates or in one of his hotels. Then, just as abruptly as it began, he stopped taking my calls."

"Oh boy," I reply, not sure where this is going.

"I scoured the internet, trying to find a secret phone number for him. All I wanted was a reason. That's normal, right Lanie?" she asks tearfully.

"Of course it is, hon. A guy who would treat a woman like that doesn't deserve someone like you."

"That's when I hired a local private investigator." As if reading my mind, she adds, "Sorry, Lanie. I didn't want anyone in the family to know about this until I was sure."

"Sure of what?"

Cosmo enters the room without either of us hearing. "Are you in some kind of trouble, sis?"

She doesn't meet his concerned gaze. That is a bad sign. "I was telling Lanie about my boyfriend and how he disappeared out of nowhere."

"Yeah, I heard that part. What did the P.I. tell you?"

"That Sterling was surrounded by the Starfish Syndicate Crime Syndicate. Even his security had ties to that organization."

Cos bursts out laughing. "Doesn't sound very ferocious to me. Do they deal in illegal gas pills?"

"Cos!" I snap. "She's in the middle of her story. If you don't want to listen, go play with your power tools in the garage."

After the door closes, I lean over and take her hand. "Oh, Cedar. I'm so sorry!"

"I told my boss, of course, and he ended talks with the Truth Corporation. The next day, Sterling showed up, or I should say, stormed into my office with his barrage of men. He pounded on my desk and demanded to know what I'd said about him."

Trying to imagine sweet Cedar being confronted by this overpriced thug brings tears to my eyes. "I hope you called security and had him thrown out!"

"I reminded him of all the plans we'd made and the good times we had together. That was when... that was when he threatened to kill me."

I can hear knuckles cracking behind me and my insides tighten at the implication. "I don't have a problem getting rid of him. Where is this creep? We can take care of this today." Cosmo Hill will do whatever it takes to protect his family, even if it involves using his gentle baker's hands to rearrange someone's face.

Impulsively, I stand and grab my husband's arm. "No, Cos, that's not how to handle—"

"Neither of you have to worry about him," Cedar whimpers. "I killed him."

Chapter Two
Piper

For some reason, everyone in town wanted to try her cauliflower cheese soup special today.

"Thanks for your help, babe!"

Piper waved to a slim, dark-haired man with green eyes and a smattering of freckles across his cheeks. He had a boyish charm that belied his almost-thirty years of existence.

Officer Obie Lumquest, also known as her "dreamboat," very generously offered to help her through the noon rush at Cosmic Cakes and Antiquery. Doris, their longtime employee, called in sick. Since she rarely missed a day, both Piper and Cosmo knew poor Doris wasn't doing well.

The only other full-time person at the downtown Piney Falls location was her father, Cosmo, and he was at home, anxiously awaiting the arrival of his sister.

Obie pulled a small orange cloth from his pocket and rubbed it on his face. One of his numerous quirks that no one questioned, though the first time they met, Piper was curious.

"You want to know why I'm carrying around this ridiculous orange cloth, don't you? It comforts me. I've got two, both made from a blanket my mom made when I was four. It's one of those things I have to do a certain number of times every day, touching it to my face. I can't explain it. I come with a lot of baggage. And handkerchiefs."

Obie worked for the Piney Falls Police Department as a deputy, and as luck would have it, today was his day off. Normally, he would sleep until noon. It was his way of coping with too much time around other people. He loved his job, but at the end of the day, he was ready to curl up in bed next to his favorite person in the world.

"Could you come help me?" a tearful Piper pleaded. "I'm all by myself and the line is out the door!"

"Of course. No payment required, though I wouldn't say no to one of your world-class shoulder massages later."

When he arrived, just as she'd described on the phone, customers were lined up down the block.

"Hello, Officer Lumquest!" A small child hollered as he fought his way through the crowd.

Obie paused, recognizing her from one of his public outreach trips to Flanagan Grade School. "Hi there! Come for some soup today?"

The girl's mother nodded. "I wasn't sure why people were standing out here, and I figured there must be something good on the menu today. Oh, Officer Lumquest, I've been hearing about a new drug, called Glamour? Do I need to worry about my daughter?"

Obie placed his hands on his hips. "It's called Glitz. And yes, we've been seeing an increase in activity, but me and my dad and everyone else on the force is doing our best to keep our young folks safe."

They worked together like a well-oiled machine, Obie taking orders and Piper filling them. He wasn't fond of the potential for mess that came from dishing up soup, so it worked out just fine.

As they served the last customer, Obie wiped his hands on the last of the clean towels. "You didn't exaggerate when you said there were a lot of people! The next time we want to round up local thugs, you'll have to make your soup to lure them in!"

Piper wiped a tiny speck of soup from Obie's chin. "Do I ever lie to you, Obie Lumquest?"

He lowered his face to hers, kissing her passionately. When they'd finished, he smiled. "You're a bad influence on me, Piper Moonlight Hill. I planned on washing my cruiser this morning after I picked up this week's uniforms from the cleaners. Now my schedule is off for the whole day."

"I know. You're a wonderful guy to come and help me like that, especially when a plot twist in your schedule is so hard for you." She stood on her tip toes and kissed him one more time. "You have my permission to finish your activities. Dessert tonight? At my place?"

"Counting on it. I'll bring the new Sassy Lasses Radical Rose and my best smile."

Piper crinkled her lavender eyes. "I still wish you'd come with me to our family dinner. You know my Aunt Cedar won't mind."

Obie shrugged. "It's my day without extra people. There's only one beautiful woman I'd like to see tonight."

Piper wiped down the last table and plopped down in the nearest chair. She'd grown used to the rhythm of Cosmic Bakes (the second location of Cosmic Cakes and Antiquery), the commercial bakery located on her farm home. The only sounds were those of the neighboring cows or the occasional car on the lonely highway. For a girl who'd spent her childhood dreaming of stability, her life was the closest thing to heaven she'd found.

Piper allowed herself the luxury of closing her eyes. The last time she attended one of November Bean's Moaning and Meditation sessions, November told everyone that the first thing they saw when they closed their eyes was the most important thing in their lives.

As she began to relax, visions of those she loved danced in front of her. To her right, her beautiful mother, Lanie, a carbon copy of 1940s screen siren Tulip Sloan. To her left, her ruggedly handsome father, Cosmo. Straight across the table sat her soul-mate, Obie. They talked and laughed, reliving They reminisreminisceded about the oddities of Piney Falls, both recent and from times past

It was the experience she'd only dreamt of as a child, when her then-parents dragged she and her brother from town to town, ostensibly to keep them safe from former Fallen Branch cult members.

It had all been a lie.

She smiled and her shoulders relaxed as she pictured herself sitting at the dinner table with the family she'd created, where she belonged. In addition to Cosmo, Lanie and Obie, the entire town of Piney Falls had taken her in. November Bean, local entrepreneur, Urica Jollopy, artist, and grumpy octo-genarian Gladys Petrie all played a role in her current life.

The next thing she knew, someone was tapping her on the shoulder. She jerked upright, both confused by her current whereabouts and embar-rassed to be caught sleeping in a chair.

"What? I'm sorry. I thought the place was empty."

"I want a coffee and a sandwich, if you have them."

She knew all of the regulars by their voices now: Boysie Lumquest, police chief and Obie's father, by his nasal upper register pitch; Cosmo by his loud, reassuring sound. It wasn't anyone on her current rotation.

Piper stood, smoothing her dark hair and wiping the drool from her face before she turned.

He was tall, though everyone in Piney Falls felt taller than Piper, save the fifth grade class that came in the week before last to watch her make five-hundred Pluto Peach Scones.

This person appeared to be roughly her age, with brown, curly hair and hardened dark eyes.

"Sure, I can get you a menu—"

"Just make whatever's easiest. I'm not picky."

Though his words were meant to ease her burden, his presence was making her uncomfortable. She could feel the anger emanating from his body.

As she began constructing a ham and cheese sandwich, she decided the wisest thing to do was to call someone she knew. Just having another person in the building would help her feel more comfortable.

She watched as he walked over to the antique side of the building before she stepped inside the walk-in freezer and pulled out her phone.

Going through a quick list of friends who hadn't succumbed to illness, she found one and dialed. Obie would come right away, but she'd already disrupted his schedule enough.

"Truman? It's me, Piper. I need your help."

Her father's best friend didn't hesitate when she explained. "I'm in town. I'll be there in approximately two minutes. Do you need me to be armed?"

"No, just come and be another presence here. That's all I need."

She returned to the kitchen and finished his sandwich. While it was heating in the panini press, she made his coffee. November would tell Piper to add one of November's homemade sleeping pill concoctions, which included animal excrement and some weed she found on a hike. Something that made Piper roll her eyes. Now she was just being paranoid.

She finished making his meal and brought it over to the table, where he was sitting with his head resting on his hands. When she set it down, he didn't acknowledge her. Afraid to upset him, she returned to the kitchen and waited for Truman's arrival.

When the bell over the door jingled, Piper was relieved.

She waited like a coward, just out of sight while Truman did his thing.

"Hello there, young man. Hope you don't mind company."

Truman grunted as he lowered his body onto the chair. Piper peeked around the corner, dismayed to see the strange man continuing to eat without acknowledging Truman. Maybe he was deaf? If so, she would feel horrible, siccing her friend on him.

"I'm a presidential expert. You may not know this, but you are the approximate height of our tallest president, Abraham Lincoln. Six-foot, four-inches, to be exact."

Truman waited for a response. When there was none, he drummed his fingers on the table.

"I 'spect you know what it's like to be an outsider. I can tell you've spent most of your years on the fringe of society. There's no shame in being different. It's what makes our country great, if you ask me."

The man's shoulders tensed. He shoved the last bite of his sandwich in his mouth and stared outside, where a light rain was falling.

"Yessiree. This is good place to start over if you're looking to do just that. Small town, friendly folks, we all take care of each other. That's why I gotta ask you to move on, now that your belly is full."

For the first time, he looked up, surprised.

"What?" he asked through a full mouth.

"We're a good place for earnest, hardworking newcomers to start over." Truman cleared his throat. "I've lived enough years to know the scent of someone who's got less-than-honorable intentions. You, young man, have that scent."

He poked his finger into the chest of the stranger and Piper held her breath. The last thing she wanted was for Truman to force an altercation. Her elderly friend wasn't likely to win that battle.

The man stood, sticking out his chest in a threatening manner. He leaned over the table and whispered, "I've taken down men twice as strong as you, old man. They didn't live long enough to fight back."

Truman smiled. "Don't doubt it. You know how I mentioned I'm a presidential expert?"

The man didn't seem to know what to think of that, so he stood his ground, still too close.

In one motion, Truman grabbed the stranger's arm and thrust it behind his back while using his other arm to collar the stranger around the neck.

"Four presidents knew martial arts, starting with George Washington. Maybe instead of spending your time scaring this young lady, you should find yourself a table in the library."

Piper's mouth dropped open.

"Piper, call Boysie and tell him we've got a guest at the county jail tonight."

Piper nodded and picked up the phone to call.

"Wait!" The man called from the table, where his head was now resting, just shy of his empty plate.

"You've got more threats to make, do you?" Truman taunted him. "This old man can wait, but I doubt the police chief will be so patient."

"Piper, tell him to stop!" He begged.

"How...how do you know my name?"

Truman tightened his grip as he struggled to stand. "Not going anywhere, son. At least until the police get here to straighten things out. Hurry up and call Boysie now, Piper."

She picked up her phone again. Her hands were shaking as she dialed. "Boysie? It's me, Piper. We've got a situation at the bakery. The one downtown."

She hung up and tried to steady herself. It wouldn't do anyone any good if she panicked. "He's on his way."

Piper folded her arms and leaned against the doorway. "You're lucky I called Truman. If I'd thought of her first, November Bean would probably have broken your neck by now."

Truman chuckled. "Ain't that the truth,"

Boysie Lumquest, an older, heavier version of his son, rushed in, completely out of breath. He surveyed the situation and then pulled out his hand-cuffs, snapping them around the man's hands before Truman released him.

"Okay, fella, what exactly is going on here? You bothering the nice lady?" he asked in his official policeman voice.

"No, I just ate. If anyone is bothering anyone, it's this old man. He just attacked me for no reason."

Piper stepped forward. "I asked Truman to come. This guy gave me the creeps. But he's right, he didn't do anything wrong."

The man let out a frustrated laugh. "Unreal. Just unreal."

"What, son?" Truman asked. "That we small town folk know how to protect our own?"

"It's more a matter of who 'your own' might be."

He glared at Piper so hard she felt like he was boring a hole in the middle of her chest.

"Your precious baker here is pretending to be someone she's not."

"What?" she asked, surprised by this turn of events. "I don't know what you're talking about."

"You're Piper Moonlight." He smirked. "Your parents thought you were the next person to lead their cult. Turns out you didn't quite live up to their expectations."

She squinted, trying to remember him. There had been so many former cult members in and out of their lives. At the time, she had no idea who they were but it was all part of her then-mother Olivene's master plan to turn her into a cold killing machine. Thankfully, she failed.

"I'm sorry. I don't remember you. Both of my parents are dead, and I'm no longer Piper Moonlight. I'm—"

"Shh!" Boysie warned. "Don't give the boy more than he needs. We're going down to the police station to have a nice talk. Then he'll be on his way."

As they moved to the door, the man put his hand

on the door frame, trying to prevent Boysie from removing him from the bakery.

Truman, seeing the struggle, began pushing on him from behind.

"I'm not leaving until I talk to my sister! In private!" he yelled in frustration.

Boysie let go and whipped him around. "What are you—"

Now she remembered where she'd seen him before.

"Sawyer?" Her voice rose an octave. "Is it really you?"

Chapter Three
Lanie

I'm currently re-thinking my decision to invite my best friend, November Bean, to our family dinner, along with Truman Coolidge and our daughter, Piper. It isn't that she wouldn't be supportive, but November has a knack for rooting out a hidden trauma. She's annoyingly accurate too.

She dresses monochromatically, tonight wearing a sunshine yellow one-piece jumpsuit with a matching headband and glasses frames. Her shoes, I'm sure, match as well, but she has removed them and set them by the front door, so that if she gets a case of the "jumpies" she won't damage any of my furniture. Despite all of her oddities, she is the most loyal, loving, frizzy-haired gal I've ever met.

After Cedar's startling revelation about the death of her boyfriend, she abruptly stood and went to the bedroom. We didn't see her for the rest of the afternoon. Several times, Cosmo paced back and forth outside her door with his hands in his pockets. I was relieved when she agreed, through the closed door, to join us for dinner.

"Lanie and me are going to Charming next week to try a new restaurant," November says, her mouth full to the brim with macaroni salad.

"You should come with us, Cedar," Vem continues as she leans forward and sucks the first piece to escape from her mouth right off her plate. "I keep hearing that's where all the single men on the coast are hiding." She pokes Cedar's side. Another mistake I made: seating them beside each other.

Cedar doesn't respond, nor does she look up from her plate.

"Aunt Cedar, you have to come out to the farm and see my new place!" Piper says excitedly. I smile at her, both relieved at the change of direction and proud of all she's accomplished.

"Sis, I know I gave you the run down on our new set up, but you need to see it for yourself. Our Piper has expanded our business. Heck, she's doubled business by providing homemade pastries and rolls to local restaurants."

"We're a family of business men and women now," I add, pleased by our successes.

Cosmo grins. "Guess I can brag about you as a proud dad, can't I?"

"Yes, but not every single time we have company," Piper shoots back.

"Piper created a scone at my behest, didn't you Piper-sweetie?" November asks.

"Yeah, we did finally come up with a flavor we could agree on."

There is a sadness in her tonight. Maybe it was just a rough day at the bakery.

"I've got to hear this one," Cosmo says as he fills his plate with the delicious salad Piper brought. She's included hazelnuts, cranberries, cucumbers and goat cheese along with her signature cranberry vinaigrette dressing. There is truly nothing our talented daughter can't cook, create or bake.

"What flavor scone are we talking about?"

"It's called the Nostradamus November. We're testing it out before it goes in the display case." Piper nods to me, a sign I've come to learn means, "this isn't the whole story."

"It's a jellied , pinecone and cream cheese scone," November says proudly. "I wanted to add ground pinecones, but your girl here convinced me the exit process wouldn't be pleasant."

"Is this something you're actually going to sell?" I ask.

Piper opens her mouth to speak, but November jumps in instead. "I'm starting a new class next week. It's a hybrid moan and meditation class I'm calling,

Om My Goodness. I'd like to order my signature scone for everyone to try after the inaugural class."

"So you don't want them to come back?" Cosmo says with a smirk.

November scoops a helping of macaroni salad, thankfully ignoring his barb. "I have sign-up sheets everywhere. It's getting great buzz. And I thought I'd also offer an instruction class on my new weaponry."

"Vem, is that wise? Your trip to the government auction gave you some serious firepower. Do you really want someone to use it on your property?"

She seems surprised by my question. "Lanie, you seem to forget that Truman used the sparkly diversion rocket on the 4th of July and did just fine."

I glance over at Cedar, realizing that all of this cross-table chatter hasn't included her. She's using her fork to pick at her hamburger bun as though it were a complicated salad. Her face is taut and white.

"Cedar, would you like some tea to settle your stomach?" I ask, hoping to snap her out of her funk.

She shoots me an angry glance, much to my surprise. "What makes you think I have an upset stomach?"

"Oh...I'm sorry. I just thought—"

"There's deceit in this one," November says, burying her nose in Cedar's hair. Though it comes in handy often, Vem's ability to sniff out dishonesty isn't a welcome party trick this evening.

Cedar turns her head and shoves November

away. "I don't need your nonsense tonight." She stands abruptly, pushing her chair in. "Lanie, Cos, I'm going to bed early. It was nice to see you, Piper." She nods to my daughter without changing her expression. "We'll go to lunch soon. I'll see you all in the morning."

Our happy little dinner party guests all stare at each other in shock.

"Be patient and calm; no one can catch a fish with anger," Truman states, finally breaking the silence. "Herbert Hoover, of course. Your sister needs our patience. She's obviously going through something."

"Thanks, buddy." Cosmo reaches over and squeezes his friend's hand. "I don't know what's gotten into her. This isn't the Cedar I know."

"Cos?"

How could he forget that she confessed to murder?

"A cow that sleeps in mud only appears to wear a coat of dung," November says matter-of-factly.

"How does that...possibly...apply to this situation, Bean?" Cosmo seethes.

I try and catch his eye to calm him down, but he refuses to meet my gaze.

"It's simple, Cosmo Hill," Vem begins in the sing-song voice that means she'll refuse to back down. "I smelled deceit on your sister. Our beloved Cedar Hill has changed from the sweet, innocent woman we voted Fallen Branch Beauty three years in a row, into a cloud of darkness." Vem makes broad, dramatic motions with her arms, to emphasize her point. "That girl has major poo on her hide."

Cosmo stands abruptly and shoves his chair in, causing the table to jiggle and our glasses to spill. "I need some air. Truman? Could you see fit to join me?"

"I thought you'd never ask." Truman is almost gleeful.

I'm a little hurt that I'm excluded from this group. When they've gone, Piper smiles at me with concern.

"Mom, what's going on?" she asks. "Why is Aunt Cedar acting so strange?"

I glance at Vem, who is now scraping the bottom of the macaroni salad bowl with her index finger. She'll be no help. "Your aunt has been really stressed at her job. They expect too much from her."

I'm pleased to have come up with that one so quickly. "That's why she's visiting," I continue, "so that we can help her relax and find her old self again."

Vem's eyes are like saucers. "No, Lanie, that's not—"

"You're confused, November," I say, cutting her off before she shares what she may or may not know. "I think we have ice cream in the freezer. Shall we clean up and see?"

Without waiting for a reply, I jump up and start grabbing plates. Piper follows suit, while November continues to graze the table for any leftover bits.

As we're loading the dishwasher, Piper touches my arm. "I didn't want to say anything when we were all together."

"What is it, hon?"

She reaches into her pocket and pulls out a business card. "This fell to the floor when Aunt Cedar got up."

I take it from her hand and read: Sonny Pride, Criminal Defense Attorney.

I have to be as red as a beet. "Oh, that's right!" My voice is high-pitched and fake. "Cedar mentioned she's been collecting these from business travelers at hotels in the Sleepy Sounds family."

I relax, proud of myself for this on-the-fly embellishment of the truth. "In a month or two, she'll do a business card drawing for a free night's stay."

Piper cocks her head to the side and gives me a funny look. "Okay, Mom."

November's phone rings with the tune she commissioned, "November Bean, West Coast Queen." In an uncharacteristic move, she jumps up and runs to the bathroom with her phone.

It's unclear whether Piper believes me or not. I hate keeping things from her, but for now, this is what's best.

"What's new with you? We hardly see you now that you're so busy with the second location."

She takes the dirty pot from the stove and begins washing it. "Well, Dad and I bought that delivery van in Tellum last week. I dropped it off yesterday and the logo should be ready by tomorrow."

"Oh yes," I say, handing her rinsed plates one at a time. "Your dad did mention that. He told me that he'd hired a delivery driver. What was his name?"

"Rusty Mellow. He moved here from Blackberry Cove recently. He worked in the grocery store there and is ready for something different."

"Perfect timing!"

She starts loading the dessert plates as she continues. "It will take a load off my shoulders. Making deliveries and baking is too much."

I nod in agreement. "It certainly doesn't give you and Obie much time together. Is that what's bothering you tonight?"

She sticks her tongue in the side of her cheek, something I find adorable and also very sad. After all of this time away from her crazy Moonlight family and the strange ideas they had, our sweet Piper is still afraid to show emotion.

"That's something I wanted to talk to you about. Both you and Dad, actually." Her lavender eyes dart back-and-forth. "I...um..."

It occurs to me there could be a very logical reason for her strange behavior. "You're getting married, aren't you?" I ask excitedly. "How did I miss the signs? You've been uncomfortable all evening. Oh, your dad will be so thrilled!"

She shakes her head, causing her thick, dark hair to fall into her eyes. "No, sorry. Obie and me have both been through some hard times and we want to take this slow and easy for now. We're thinking of moving in together."

"I admire you for that, hon." I can't say that I'm not disappointed, but I understand.

"Yeah, when it comes time for my wedding, I want all the important people to be there, you know."

It takes a moment to realize what she's referring to.

Both Gladys and I offered to help her track her brother down, but she resisted. She's always kept her distance from the prying eyes of Obie's grandmother, but it stung that she didn't accept my offer of help.

"Anyway, what's bothering me isn't Obie. Something happened today at the bakery. I asked Truman not to tell Dad yet."

I turn my body toward her, scanning her body with concern. "What happened, hon?"

She swallows hard. " I had an unexpected visitor at the shop."

I place my hands on my hips. "You're scaring me. What's happening?"

" as I was getting ready to close, someone came in," she repeats.

"Yes, you mentioned that. Who was it?"

"It was...Sawyer. He showed up out of nowhere. He is back at my place. I asked him to join us, but he was too tired from the drive."

My mouth has to be scraping the floor. When I'm finally able to speak again, I ask, "Did he say why he came now? Is he here for a visit, or does he want to make Piney Falls his home? Does he want your share of the inheritance?"

When Olivene, Piper's first mother, died, she had a sizable bank account. Piper and Sawyer split it fifty-fifty. Piper wisely invested hers for her retirement.

"He's pretty closed off. I was that way too, but luckily I had you and Cos to bring me out of my shell. Sawyer didn't have anyone."

There is something deeply unsettling about his sudden appearance. Though I realize he didn't have the luxury of a proper upbringing, Sawyer could have at least called to say he was coming. The only people who show up unannounced are...

"Mom, there's one more thing. Sawyer said he'd been in prison in Ohio. For murder."

Chapter Four
Piper

It was dark when Piper turned down the long gravel drive. She hesitated before going inside, feeling nervous about sharing her private space with someone besides Obie.

"He's your brother, for Pete's sake," she muttered under her breath.

Piper crept up the porch and opened the door as quietly as she could. One of the perks of living out in the country was that she didn't worry about keeping her doors locked. Cosmo told her she was far too trusting, but so far, her only nighttime guests were a noisy family of raccoons and the occasional bear.

The living room was dark, but Piper knew where the lamp was, so she felt her way to the table and clicked it on. She jumped a foot in the air when she saw her brother, seated in the corner.

"Sawyer! You scared me to death! What are you doing sitting there in the dark?"

His face was taut and he was gripping the handles of the rocking chair as though they might fly off.

"I think best when I'm in the dark," he remarked, devoid of any emotion. "How was dinner?"

"Oh, it was fine. My mom—"

Her hand flew up to her mouth. "I meant Lanie." Since they'd been out of touch for so long, she hadn't told him about her adoption.

"Lanie sent leftovers for you and said she wants you at the next family dinner and she won't take 'no' for an answer."

Her actual words were, "Be careful, hon. He may not be the same brother you knew. Bring him with you next time so Cos and I can talk to him."

Sawyer began rocking the chair slowly. Though his face hadn't changed, he didn't seem as menacing as he had when she turned on the light.

Piper flopped down on the couch. "I'm sorry I didn't recognize you today. I guess I just wasn't expecting you to be there, since we've kind of lost touch."

She hated how that came out, but it was true; Sawyer left Piney Falls soon after their mother's death. For months, she tried calling, texting and emailing, but he never responded. Eventually, she just gave up.

"That's funny. I'd never forget your face." The rocking chair squeaked every time his feet pushed off.

"After Mom died—"

"Was murdered," he interjected.

"You left to join Better Branch with other people who were disgusted by the old Fallen Branch cult, and it was like you disappeared into thin air," she continued, unwilling to engage in a discussion about that awful day. "I think you owe me an explanation." Piper frowned before continuing. "It really hurt when you left, bud."

Sawyer stared straight ahead. "Still thinking of life in terms of fairy tales, aren't you?" he remarked, sarcasm dripping from his words. "We were both a mess. It was good we went our separate ways so we could each deal with it on our own."

"And what way would you be referring to? Are you still involved with Better Branch?" She heard an accusatory tone in her voice she didn't like. "I mean, I'd love to hear about where you've been. The adventures of Sawyer Moonlight." She giggled uncomfortably.

He shook his head. "Maybe later. There's too much to tell right now."

She studied his face, trying to remember her sweet younger brother. He shared their father's thick brows and curly brown hair. The shape of his face was just like Olivene's, but the rest of him was pure Hal Moonlight.

"The more I look at you, the more I see Dad."

"Yeah, I guess." Sawyer turned his head away from her and she could see numbers tattooed on the side of his neck.

"Sawyer, what does three-three-eight-four-nine mean? Is that some sort of code?"

His large hand smacked the side of his neck, followed by a chuckle as he replied, "Something like that."

Piper raced to think of something that might connect them. Some bit of their shared history that would bring them together now.

"I remember—"

"I stopped and saw—"

Piper giggled at their simultaneous speech. "You go ahead. What were you saying?"

"Oh, I was just gonna say I went to see my grand-parents. Hal's parents."

It stung that he didn't think of them as hers too. Even though Olivene admitted that Piper wasn't biologically their child, she grew up in the same house as Sawyer, thinking of the same people as her relatives.

"What did they say? Did they know Dad died?"

Sawyer shrugged. "Hard to say. They refused to speak to me."

"Really? Their only grandson?"

"Good old Olivene burned every single bridge. Do you remember the Christmas they spent with us in Rapid City?"

Piper had done a good job of removing those memories from her daily life. She had a new family here, one not entangled in painful tendrils. "Um, yeah, I remember."

"They brought a car full of toys. You got in the back and started opening them and I went and told on you."

It was starting to come back. Dolls, makeup, fancy dresses and nail polish. Everything a girl desired. She'd begun tearing the doll out of the package when her mother discovered her in the back of their car.

"Come out here, young lady." Olivene ordered.

Piper, at times defiant of her mother's strict rules, made her way to the front of the vehicle. She still had a glimmer of hope that Santa was real and she didn't want to do anything to spoil it.

When Piper was standing by her side, Olivene crawled into the back seat and retrieved every gift. She instructed Piper to take them all to the fire pit in the back yard of the fancy place they were renting.

Piper knew Olivene's orders upset her, but at the time, she had no idea that there was a different way of living.

Piper and Sawyer watched as their toys and their fantasies about Christmas went up in flames. "We have to keep our load light," Olivene explained. "Not only that, I expect my children to be disciplined. Time spent with frivolous objects weakens the mind."

Their grandparents never visited again.

"I'd pushed it away, I guess. Life is so much better now."

"Yeah, well, maybe for you. I'm still trying to figure out how to live like a normal person, when my entire childhood was about protecting you from pretend danger."

His gaze hardened.

Piper clutched the collar of her shirt uncomfortably. "What exactly did Hal's parents say?"

"I knocked on the door. When nothing happened, I started banging on it and yelling that I wasn't going away until someone came out."

She pictured two elderly people looking through the peephole in their door. When they saw a tall, angry stranger yelling at them, they must've been terrified. "Did they answer?"

Sawyer shook his head. "Nope. Eventually, a neighbor came over and asked who I was. I explained I was their grandson, and she went back to her home. She returned a few minutes later. I could tell by her expression that it wasn't good. She shook her head and I could see tears running down her cheeks. Poor old grannie."

Piper couldn't tell if he was being facetious, or if he was truly empathizing with this woman.

"They don't want to see you, son," he mimicked in a high-pitched voice. "I called them and they won't budge."

Sawyer grinned as if this was a pleasant memory. "Nice old grannie did send me on my way with two-dozen cookies though. It wasn't a total loss."

"Did she—"

"Say why? Yeah. They were sure I had something to do with Hal's death, given all the time I spent with Olivene."

"Oh, Sawyer," Piper leaned forward, attempting to comfort her brother. Instead, he jumped as she tried touching his arm.

"Sorry," she said quickly.

He rubbed his arm as though she'd hit him with a pipe instead of offering comfort.

"I got used to sleeping a few hours at a time and always being on my guard," he explained.

"Did you...sleep in your car?"

The next question she wanted to ask was what happened to Olivene's money. Divided equally, Sawyer received fifty-thousand dollars.

"Off and on. At least I could lock the doors. Then prison came, and I never slept at all. You never want to turn your back on anyone, or sleep too long."

Now she sat back and put her hand up to her face. "I...don't know what to say." She wanted so badly to ask him about his crime, but decided against it.

"Sentence was ten years. I was out in two for good behavior." He raised his brows and glared at Piper. "Only one of us had a cushy life after our parents died."

"Who says? Why do you think my life was cushy? Is that why you came here, Sawyer? To make me feel bad for the life I've created?"

"I don't know why I'm here, to be honest. I guess I wanted to see it for myself."

"See what?"

He motioned around the room. "This. I shared a cell with someone from Piney Falls. He told me all about your bakery and your new family. Bennie you put on airs like you were somebody. Half the town has no idea who you really are."

His voice had an icy tone that frightened her. "I think you should go. Boysie and Obie are one phone call away if you try to harm me."

Sawyer put his hands on his knees and rubbed his worn jeans. "Here we go again. Poor little victim, Amaris. Always clamoring to be the center of attention. I wasn't going to hurt you. Like I said, I wanted to see who you'd become."

Amaris was the name Olivene gave her as the future leader of their cult. The minute she could, Piper changed it.

Her face burned crimson. "There's no Amaris

here. She was a make-believe girl in Olivene Moonlight's world." She balled her fists and squeezed them hard. "Just Piper Moonlight Hill, a hardworking person with a growing business and people around who love me unconditionally. My brother apparently took his money and wasted it before he landed himself in jail."

Sawyer huffed and she tightened her body, expecting him to lurch forward and grab her.

"I went to jail for attempted murder. They didn't have proof, but my lawyer was a month from retirement and didn't give a damn. As far as the money goes, I'm not comfortable telling you right now."

None of this was going the way she'd worked it out in her head. "I don't have spare time in my life, Sawyer. Cosmo and I just purchased a delivery van and I've got to train the driver tomorrow. I would love for you to stay and we could get to know each other. But if you only came here to show me how miserable you are, then you don't need to stay."

He stared, incredulous. "That's it? After all I did for you?"

It was Piper's turn to be incredulous. "What YOU did for ME, Sawyer? Do you know how many times I lied to Olivene so she would punish me instead of you?"

She hated the tears spilling down her cheeks. It would have counted as a sign of weakness in their home.

"I'm going to bed now. It's been a long day." Without acknowledging her words, Sawyer stood up and stretched. His head almost hit the ceiling fan. Their arguments fell into the same rhythm they had growing up. Each said their piece and then one of them got up and left. The next morning, everything would be forgotten.

She pointed in the direction of the guest bathroom. "There are clean towels under the sink," she mumbled.

"I'll be here for a week, no more. I needed some sea air to clear my head."

She resisted the urge to ask what, exactly, needed cleared from his head.

"Goodnight, sis." He walked out of the living room and up the stairs to the guest room. She heard the creak of the steps as he climbed each one.

Piper felt empty. He was her brother and she loved him. This—whatever this was—didn't resemble the sweet boy she remembered.

As she placed the uneaten leftovers in the refrigerator, she noticed something on the floor and bent down to pick it up. It was a business card that read:

Sawyer Kaine, Handyman
skaine@tickermail.com

"Hmph," she snorted. "Sounds legit for a guy who made a real point of telling me he wasn't."

Chapter Five
Lanie

"Cedar! It's Lanie! I brought you coffee and scones!"

This is the third time I've knocked on her door this morning. She's barely been visible since confiding to us that she killed her boyfriend. Her unceremonious exit from the family dinner didn't help. The Cedar I know would have apologized profusely the next day.

I'm determined to find out exactly what happened and why she thinks she killed Sterling Truth, but it's becoming very clear that it will take more than a few scones to extract that information. "Honey, I'm not going anywhere. I don't have a meeting until four this afternoon, so I can camp out all day."

Still nothing.

"Vem asked if she could come and do her Moan

for Misery outside your door. I told her no, but I'm happy to—"

The door swings open and Cedar appears, dressed in the fuzzy, light blue robe we gave her last Christmas. Her eyes are puffy and her hair hasn't been washed.

"I'm coming in, whether you like it or not, sweetie."

Forcing my way past her, I set the basket of scones and the coffee on the tiny table next to her private balcony. When we built our home, I insisted on a guest room to rival the finest hotels, so that when our friends and family stayed with us, they felt like royalty. "Cos remembered your second-favorite last time was the Lunar Lemon. I hope that's to your liking?"

She is standing behind me. I can feel her breath on the back of my neck and for just a moment, I worry that she is, in fact, a murderer. Then I remember that she and Cos are so tightly woven together that she feels his pain clear down in San Diego. She would never harm me, knowing what it would do to her brother.

"Let's sit down and chat. I promise I won't bother you for long. Then you can go back to your—"

"Sulking You were going to say sulking."

We exchange knowing smiles before Cedar pulls out a chair and sits down at the table, with me following suit.

This morning she actually takes a normal bite. I want to reach over and pat her on the back for mastering the task of chewing, but quickly I decide that's crossing a line.

"You're wondering about my boyfriend," she says with a mouth full of scone. "These are just as amazing as I remembered."

"I'm not here to dredge up painful stuff. If you think you killed him, then Cos and me will do everything in our power to protect you. But we need the whole story. You can't drop a bombshell like that and expect that we're not going to ask for more information."

Her posture relaxes and she takes a lengthy sip of her coffee. Strangely enough, my directness appears to connect with my sister-in-law.

"When Sterling stopped answering my calls, I decided it was something I'd done wrong. I've still got that cult mentality, Lanie. My first assumption is always that it's me who has screwed up."

"Cos has the same affliction," I say with care. "You've both come so far, but there will always be scars. Those take longer to fade."

Cedar nods in agreement. "Eventually, I went on with my life. I asked to visit different chains to see how their advertising could be improved." She rolls her eyes. "That's a job normally reserved for the lower level employees, but I was desperate for a change. In my third week in marketing outreach, I visited a Sleep in a Heap motel, our new ultra-budget offering. The manager turned out to be a complete jerk who was content to collect a paycheck and nothing more. I was sitting in the bar, feeling defeated, when I saw him."

"Sterling? In a cheap motel?"

I'm trying to imagine this blue-blood slumming it in a motel that charges for electricity.

"Right there in the bar. And he wasn't alone."

"Oh boy." I lean back and cross my arms. "He was with another woman, I gather."

Cedar looks down at her empty plate and nods. "Yes. A beautiful redhead. They were laughing and touching each other's faces over cheap beer and nachos. I don't know which one disgusted me more."

"So, you saw Sterling in the bar. Did you confront him?"

"I did. We'd never really had a resolution, since the time he barged into my office."

Cedar breathes deeply. "That's when things got weird. I asked to speak with him alone and he refused. Sterling said I didn't understand him because we were from two different worlds, and that's when he leaned over to his girlfriend and half-whispered, 'met this one at a bar and now I can't shake her.' That woman found it hysterical."

"Cedar," I begin, doing my level best to remain calm, "you didn't deserve any of that. It's only natural that you would have been upset."

"Upset, yes. But I got drunk too." She clicks her tongue in disapproval. "So drunk. By the time I left the bar, they were gone. I went to the front desk and told them my husband left with the key, and his name was Sterling Trust. That's the last thing I remember from that night. The next day, I awoke to the sound of sirens. Since it was a cheaply built motel, I could hear everything happening. They were there because someone died."

"That doesn't mean that you—"

She holds her hand in the air to pause my thoughts. "I went to the bathroom and that's when I saw it. My sink was full of blood, as if I'd washed an entire gallon off my hands the night before. It made me sick to my stomach to think I was capable of that. I left town immediately and came straight here, to Piney Falls."

There are times I'm a master with words. This is not one of them. "You can stay for as long as you like. Down the road, we can discuss all of this with Boysie. He won't turn you in to the California authorities unless he's certain you really hurt Sterling."

"We were perfect together, Lanie."

Her eyes display a faraway dreaminess that makes me both happy and sad for her. She has the worst luck with men.

"He was going to purchase property up here, you know."

"Really?" It sounds absurd to me. He's a wealthy man who can live anywhere. Piney Falls, while idyllic, is not exactly a millionaire's destination.

"Yes. I talked about my hometown and all the people so much that we decided to take a trip up here to look at land. He wanted to build us a vacation home. Of course that never happened."

"Hey," I reach over and rub her arm. "You're entitled to feel sad."

This is her cue to dissolve into tears and reach for me for comfort.

"Shh. Let it out. Let it all out."

Going through a depression with Cos some time back, I worry that Cedar will sink so low that I can't help her.

"You came to the right place. Your family will make you whole, I promise."

She pulls away from me and looks pleadingly in my eyes. "You will?"

"*We* will. We want you to stay for as long as you need. And it's not just for you. Cos is better when you're close by."

Cedar sit up and nods as I wipe her tears away. "Oh, Lanie, I almost forgot the worst of it. When I went into the bathroom at the bar to fix my makeup, his girlfriend followed me. I didn't want a confrontation, so I turned to leave. That was when she grabbed my wrist."

"That's beyond jealousy. That's crazy!"

"She said, 'after all Sterling did for you, this is the thanks he gets? If it weren't for him, you'd be dead by now."

It sounds as if this woman is completely off her rocker, but I don't want to make matters worse. "Were you able to get away after that?"

"Yeah, I remembered my self-defense classes with November and I spun around and loosened her grip. I grabbed my suitcase and left without leaving instructions for upcoming ads with the manager. He probably wouldn't have followed them anyway."

"Yoo-hoo!"

Shoot. On any other day, I would welcome Vem's company. Today, when I'm trying to extract information from Cedar, she is the last person I need around.

"We're in the guest room, Vem!" I call.

She is resplendent in pale pink from head to toe. Even her shoes and glasses frames match. "You didn't tell me you'd be spending the morning in bed," she says with disdain. "Lanie, I'm surprised at you. You may have started here as a Lazy Louella, but I thought I'd whipped you into shape?"

It's very early in the day to use up my eye rolls, but I can't resist. "What's up, Vem? Cedar and I were just discussing her boyfriend. She was telling me about his family."

Vem pulls a banana muffin out of her pocket and begins to eat it. "Yeah," she says between bites, "I was telling my Moaning for Money class this morning about him. They all think he's a crook."

Cedar gasps but then chuckles. I sigh with relief. She knows November, thank goodness.

"Well, this has all been very enlightening. Thank you for sharing, Cedar! We feel so detached from you, living so far away." I stand and motion for Vem to do the same.

"What?" Vem asks. "Did you already ask her about the dead guy? I always miss out on the good stuff!"

"How did you—no, Vem. That's none of our business. Let's go downstairs to my bedroom."

She's recently purchased expensive listening devices and I'm positive she's been using them to eavesdrop. "They have a range of up to one-thousand feet, Lanie. I can't wait to experiment."

"I have a wardrobe question for you." I take her by the arm, hoping she'll come without a fight

"Lanie, if I've told you once, I've told you a million times, you can't wear pink bras after Labor Day!"

"This was enough today. It's all too painful. I hope you'll understand," Cedar says quietly.

"In your own time, sweetie," I reply, holding tight to Vem. "We'll be here when you're ready."

Once Vem and I are out of earshot, I whisper, "Let's not ask her any more about the murder. I'm still not convinced there was a murder. I'm going to do some investigating and see what I find. He's probably enjoying the joke with his nasty new girlfriend."

Vem stops abruptly. There is no way I can keep her moving if she doesn't want to move. She's twice as strong as I am. "Lanie, he's no longer in California; I saw him. And I can assure you, he's as dead as a doornail now."

Chapter Six
Piper

She knocked on the door to her guest room with hesitation. Piper had no idea what time her brother got up every day. A morning schedule, a favorite food, these were intimate family details that she no longer shared with her brother.

The door opened quickly. Sawyer's face displayed a scowl so dark she jumped back instinctively. "What?" he snarled. He held the phone up to one ear and she couldn't tell if he was irritated with her, or the person on the other end of the line.

He motioned for her to enter. When she did, he stepped into the hallway and closed the door. *Not exactly what she had in mind.*

The positive for her was that she was entitled to snoop; given the fact that he shut her inside, he was practically begging her to go through his belongings.

A large suitcase was open on the floor and

clothing was scattered inside and on the floor. "Some things never change," she mused, stooping to pick up a sweater. As Piper brought it to her face, she drank in his familiar scent. Vanilla mixed with cherry, and...it was modeling clay, wasn't it?

"You smell like edible modeling clay," she told him on the days she wanted to get under his skin.

Moving to the dresser, she noticed her brother was still using the same kind of body spray he'd stolen from a grocery store in Topeka. Piper sprayed a little in the air, taking in that smell as well.

The top drawer of the dresser was slightly open. She glanced at the door and heard her brother's deep voice still immersed in conversation. She touched the drawer, pulling it out in tiny increments until the contents were visible.

"One—two—three driver's licenses. It's your face on every one, but different names and states. What have you gotten yourself into, brother?" she whispered. There were two more hidden in the back, both listing his name as Brad Bentley from Columbus, Ohio.

Piper swallowed hard. Did she really want to continue? The more she knew about him, the less likely it would be that she would want to spend time with him.

Everybody has a dark side.

The middle drawer was also open and a large roll of cash was plainly visible. The door to the room opened and she jumped back, simultaneously slamming the top drawer shut on her fingers.

"You always were a snoop."

"Ow!"

"Serves you right. Did you find anything worth the pain?" he asked with a hint of sarcasm. "I'm not gonna explain anything in my drawers since you didn't have any right to be in there in the first place."

Piper nodded. "That's fair."

No, it wasn't. The Sawyer she knows doesn't have any interest in fake identities or secret jobs that pay in large wads of cash.

"Are you planning on stealing my clothes?" Sawyer gestured toward her right hand, where she was still grasping his sweater.

"Huh?" She looked down just as he jerked it away and threw it on top of the suitcase.

"I thought...I thought... you might like some breakfast."

"Yeah. My stomach is still working on the adjustment to real food since prison. Always hungry but struggling to eat."

He rubbed his taut abdomen.

"Come on downstairs when you're ready. I made extra carrot and cream cheese muffins for an order in Tellum, and of course coffee too."

She turned away from him, embarrassed at the relief she felt to be out of his presence. Once she reached the kitchen, her phone buzzed.

Call me when you can. Important!-
love, Your Dad

She chuckled. Cosmo still thought texts were like letters, in that you had to sign off every time you sent one. As Piper pushed the button to call him back, she heard Sawyer's heavy shoes clomping down the stairs. Whatever this message was would have to wait until later.

"When I made out the schedule for this week, I didn't include breakfast with my little brother!"

There was a fake smile plastered on her face. It was uncomfortable but she'd already committed to it, so she was stuck, grinning like a fool for the duration of their conversation.

"Fill me in on your life. All I know is that you went to visit our, I mean your, grandparents."

She poured two mugs of coffee and pushed a plate of oversized muffins toward her brother.

He chuckled as he placed one on his plate. "What you're asking is why your little brother was in prison. Did I get that right?"

Her face turned red as she stammered, "No...that wasn't...I didn't mean..."

Since when was she so tongue-tied around her little brother? This was her playmate and confidant throughout her entire childhood. No one else shared the memories they did.

"Okay, since you brought it up, yes. I would like

to understand why you went to prison. I mean, picturing you as a murderer is not the Sawyer I remember."

He stuffed half of the large muffin into his mouth. Eating his entire meal in one bite was the real reason for his stomach problems.

"After Mom died, I was a lost little puppy," he remarked, chewing with the ferociousness of a wild dog. So much for his stomach issues. "I think I knew that Dad was dead before you told me. That one didn't sting. But Mom, despite her controlling nature and fixation with you, was the parent I related to."

"Oh, Sawyer, I'm so sorry." She moved quickly to his side and remained standing, resisting the urge to tousle his hair.

"That part isn't your fault. You were a kid too." He stuffed the other half of the muffin in his mouth and grabbed another. "But you'd found a nice comfy spot for yourself here, long before Mom died. Do you know what happened when it was just the two of us?"

Piper tensed, waiting for some horrible story.

"Mom was all over me. She wouldn't let me out of her sight. She wanted me to tell her when I went outside or to the bathroom. I felt like I couldn't breathe."

Piper raised one brow. "That wasn't what I thought you'd say. Didn't you want to be the center of attention? Wasn't that why you told on me every time I even committed the smallest infraction of her ridiculous rules?"

"Yeah, I guess I did," he admitted, lacing his fingers together in front of him. "But it became too much. After I was done being angry with you for letting her die, I got really mad at her. She ruined my childhood. After the threat was gone, she still made my life hell."

Piper wanted to ask so much more, but it felt like a minefield and she didn't want to step on anything that might explode in her face.

"After you left here, you went to Ohio." She pictured herself shoving those dark memories out of her head. That was her therapist's idea.

"Like I said, I was confused. Angry one minute, relieved the next. I had no preparation for life. I went back to some of the places I wished we'd stayed —Des Moines, Phoenix, Kansas City. Instead of fixing me, they left a bitter taste in my mouth. I ended up back in Ohio. That's when I got myself into trouble."

He stood and walked over to Piper's shiny new coffee maker, pouring himself another cup. "You want more?"

Piper shook her head no.

Sawyer sat back down, stretching his long legs out in front of him.

"You remember I had friends in Ohio? Broken Branch fell apart when everybody decided it was more important to eat than chase after some crazy cult ideas."

"I'm glad. I was worried when you left here. I thought you might fall into the lifestyle of our parents."

She glanced at Sawyer, who frowned as he brought another muffin to his plate. Maybe this was his normal face? No need for her to be afraid. He was her kid brother, after all.

"I mean, I was just worried about you," she explained quickly.

He nodded. "I was all over the place and came back to Ohio because my buddy told me that there was good money in driving a truck during harvest season. That's when I met Meadow."

His voice softened and for the first time since his return, Piper observed an emotion other than anger. "Your girlfriend?"

"Big, hazel eyes and hair that bounced when she walked." He smiled at the recollection. "It was hard to concentrate on my work. She drove a beet truck too."

"Oh Sawyer, I'm so glad you've experienced love. Are you two getting married?" Piper giggled. "Not that I'm expecting that, but if you are, I'd like to make your cake, and—"

Sawyer held up his hand. "Let me finish. You should know by now, things never work out right for a Moonlight." His face made an abrupt return to its previous, angry state. "Meadow and me had a thing. We met at a hotel every Wednesday, so her uncle—our boss—wouldn't find out. He thought of his employees as dirt under his feet."

Once again, Piper was reminded that Obie Lumquest and his family were the second best thing to happen to her since coming to Piney Falls. The first was Lanie and Cos. She was lucky they accepted her without question, always treating her with the respect they showed everyone.

"One night she came to meet me and confessed that she was getting married," Sawyer continued.

"You must've been devastated."

He nodded. "I was. I couldn't imagine my life without her at that point. I asked if I had been an easy distraction, or if it was a game she played with people she thought were less than her." Sawyer moved his legs under the table. "And that's when she said she was pregnant and no one could know it was my child. That's why she was marrying this dude. She didn't love him, she just couldn't have *my* baby."

"Oh, bud. That's awful. How could she do that to you?" Piper adjusted herself on the least-sturdy chair in her kitchen. Now his visit made perfect sense. He needed comfort from the only family he had left.

"I found out the next day that I wasn't the only guy she was meeting at this hotel. She had a Monday, Tuesday, Thursday...you get the picture. Meadow had herself a real good con, taking money and other stuff from all of us. I don't know when she found time to meet with her fiancé." Sawyer chuckled, though it was more of a sinister sound than something jolly.

"You must've been furious."

He sat up straight and turned to glare at her. After a moment, he turned back to his coffee and the remaining muffin.

"I was pretty angry. I went to the bar and got drunk. A couple of my buddies had to help me back to my room. The next day, I woke up to someone shaking my shoulders. It was some cop, telling me I was being arrested for attempted murder. Of Meadow."

"Oh."

Piper stared at the floor, afraid to show any emotion that might upset him.

"Yeah, 'oh,'" he scoffed. "I didn't do anything, but I had no memory of the night before. By then, I didn't have two nickels to rub together. I hadn't gotten my first check from Meadow's uncle, so there was nothing to offer a good lawyer. The public defender didn't care if I spent the rest of my life in prison. I would have too, if it weren't for my cellmate." He paused. "You want me to keep going?"

"I...yes."

"I can't tell you his name, because he's a really private guy, so I'll call him, 'Boyd.'"

A laugh escaped Piper's mouth. "I'm sorry. That sounded like a spy movie."

Sawyer stood and put his plate in the sink.

"Finish your story. I didn't mean to upset you."

When he remained silent, she persisted, "Sawyer, what really happened to Meadow? Did someone kill her? What about your child?"

"She was found in an alley in bad shape. I'm guessing it was one of the other guys she'd cheated. Far as I knew, she was recovered and back to her busy schedule while I was rotting in a cell. There was no baby, by the way. Should have figured."

He rubbed the back of his neck where the tattooed numbers, 3,3,4, 8,4,9 were visible above the collar of his shirt.

That was something else she wanted to ask him about.

"Boyd had lots of resources, so he got me sprung with one of his expensive lawyers. My first day of freedom, I went to my favorite diner for the omelet of the day. I was drinking my coffee and reading the paper when I read about it."

"Read about what?"

"Her death. Someone killed her the day I got out. I'm sure whoever it was wanted to make it look like it was me. Even though all charges were dropped against me, I didn't want to give the cops a chance to pin something else on old Sawyer, so I hightailed it out of there. Don't know where I'll go next, but it's been a long time since I've seen my sister. Hoping you don't mind if I stick around and get to know you."

He uttered it with the same amount of passion as if he were making a grocery list. Obie would tell her this was a textbook case of someone offering to be a victim. He would pat each shoulder and then shake his finger in her face. "You know better, Piper. Lots of people in this world are just out to take what they can from us."

But Sawyer was her brother. Her only sibling. How could she say no?

"Of course. I could use help with all of these orders. I'm lucky if I finish by eight o-clock every night."

Her phone buzzed. "It's my dad. I mean, Cosmo. I should take it."

Sawyer turned away from her and crossed his arms, staring out the kitchen window where the cattle were staring back with equal concern.

"Did I miss a step? Are the kids not sending texts anymore?"

"I got your text. Sawyer and me were having breakfast and we lost track of time. What's up?"

"My new driver is MIA. On the first day! I called his house and his roommate said he left home two hours ago. Whatever's going on with Rusty Mellow, the conference center in Blackberry Cove needs their croissants. I was wondering if your brother would be available."

He certainly had the driver's licenses for the job.

"I'm sure he will." She stared at the screen door, where the shiny new delivery van sat untouched.

"Okay, great! Load up the van and send him on his way!" Cosmo replied cheerily. "I'll give them a call and tell the convention center to expect a delivery within the hour!"

She turned around to find Sawyer deep in thought. "Bud? I need your help."

"Don't you remember me better than that? You know the kitchen is the most foreign room in the house to me." He chuckled. Her shoulders dropped at the sound of his laughter. She hadn't realized they were almost touching her ears.

"You don't have to bake. I can do that. But we have a delivery in Blackberry Cove that needs to go out ASAP and our driver is missing. Would you mind? I'll be happy to pay you."

She walked over to a wooden, spatula-shaped hook holder and grabbed a set of keys, handing them to Sawyer. "I'll have another order ready for the Fallen Branch Convention Center this afternoon. If you're willing, I've got plenty of work for you."

The more she thought about it, the better it sounded. She'd keep him busy and he wouldn't have time to think about this horrid woman or the life he missed because of her.

"My boyfriend Obie's coming over for dinner tonight. You'll get to meet him."

"My big sister has a boyfriend? I never thought I'd see the day," he joked.

"And Sawyer, there's one more thing. I don't want you to be uncomfortable, but Lanie and Cosmo are my family now. They're the reason I'm running this business on my own in this farmhouse."

She could feel the tension in the room rising again, so she did the only thing their relationship handled well: diversion.

"Pack up, Mister! I've got orders to fill!"

He saluted her with a gleam in his eye. "Yes, ma'am."

Chapter Seven
Lanie

Vem just dropped a bombshell, as she is prone to do, and I couldn't move her away from Cedar's door fast enough.

Taking her arm, I guide her downstairs, into the living room. "Please join us for dinner tonight, Cedar!" I call. "It will make Cos so happy!"

When we're standing by the couch, far out of Cedar's earshot, I spin November around to face me. "Okay, missy. Spill it. What do you know about Cedar's boyfriend? How do you know he's dead?"

November places her hands on her hips defiantly. "I'm sensing some distrust here, Lanie. After all we've been through, do you think I'm making this up?"

Deep breaths.

"Vem, please just tell me where you saw this alleged body."

"It was in a ravine outside of town. At least I thought it was him and I'm pretty sure it was a ravine. Though it could have been a painting." She touches her chin and cocks her head to the side. Her deep thinking position. "You never know with my visions."

There is much to be said about patience, especially when dealing with my best friend. "Let's start at the beginning."

"Lanie, upon further review, I know it was Sterling Truth that I saw. And I can assure you," she pauses for dramatic effect, "he's dead. As. A. Doornail."

"You're going to have to be more specific, Vem."

She brings her fingers to her temples and begins mumbling. "Brfladgrut..."

One of her latest areas of study is mind melding. She thinks if she utters nonsense I'll become attuned to her brain.

"Let's do this later," I say, touching her arm lightly to bring her back to the present. "For now, I need you —and your actual words—to tell me where you saw his body?"

"He was at the bottom of a cliff and Lanie, he was as flat as a pancake."

"Where? We need to call Boysie right now!"

Vem shakes her head. "I can't tell you that until I sleep again."

Anger wells up inside me. "Are you telling me

that you had a dream about Sterling Truth? And that you're basing the idea that he is dead on that dream?"

Vem sniffs my shoulder and I bat her away.

"Lanie, I sense distrust. You remember last month, I took a class on honing your dreams for the purposes of daily life? I'm really good at it."

This conversation is going nowhere and I'm out of patience. "Go take a power nap. Tomorrow afternoon we'll search for Sterling. If he's really dead," realizing my faux pas, quickly I change course. "Because we KNOW he's dead, he's not going anywhere. Come over at one." Smiling, I rub her firm bicep. "There hasn't been a mystery in Piney Falls yet that this team can't solve."

She nods, reassured by my trust in her.

"Make sure you draw a map in this dream, so we'll know exactly where to go," I add.

The next morning, I can hear her Mellow Moans for Seniors class practicing their low growls. It's the perfect time to slip out unseen.

Once I pull into the parking lot of the Fallen Branch Inn and Spa, my shoulders ease down into their normal position. I feel like a teen who snuck out their bedroom window for a tryst with another teen. Glancing in the mirror to double check that all my makeup ended up in the right spot, I see a man wearing a burgundy suit jacket moving at lightning speed. "Andy! Wait!"

The hotel manager is always in a hurry, even if

it's just to get inside his car. He's not so much a walker as a scurrier.

Andy pauses when he hears the sound of my voice and waves before opening his car door.

One of my steadfast rules is that Lanie Anders-Hill does not run. Moving at a brisk pace, my briskest, I catch him just as he starts his engine.

"We need to talk!" I yell through his window.

"Good to see you today, Mrs. Anders-Hill!"

Andy is always the most cheerful person in the room. On the days when I'm feeling my worst, Andy has a smile and a funny story.

"I'd like to buy you a cup of coffee and ask a few questions, if you wouldn't mind."

"Actually, I'm just on my way out. Root canal."

"Oh gosh. That sounds miserable!"

Andy smiles and shakes his head. "Nah. I've had them before. One afternoon of ice cream and funny talking and I'm back to my old chipper self."

"Well, I'll be brief. I was just wondering if you remember seeing this guy?"

I show him the photo of Sterling Truth that was on his company website. If he brought up the subject of Piney Falls to Cedar, Sterling must've spent some time here.

"Not lacking in the looks department, is he?" Andy quips. "Yeah, I think I do remember him. Here three nights, I believe. He booked the best suite we have."

"The Passionate Pine? That runs for nine-hundred-dollars a night!" I'm flabbergasted, though I shouldn't be. He is a wealthy man. I remember taking the tour before the grand opening. This suite includes a spiral staircase leading up to a large master bedroom. There are six full rooms on the main floor with a nice patio table that looks out over the ocean.

"Is there anything else you can tell me about Mr. Truth?"

Andy cocks his head to the side and gives me his trademark half-smile. "Are you investigating another case? I'm always in awe of your endless sleuthing abilities."

Avoiding an opportunity to blush, I nod. "Thanks. I'm not really on a case, at least not formally."

"Well, let's see. I was training a new staff member that day, so my attention wasn't directed at our client. Very slow learner, that one." He sighs, and for one tiny second, frowns. "Mr. Truth was very preoccupied. The front desk manager, I believe it was Wendell that day, had to ask three times for his credit card. They were all over each other."

I'm starting to feel very angry. Angry and protective of my sister-in-law. She doesn't deserve to be treated like this. "They?"

"Yes. He was here with a very attractive woman.

Red hair, I believe. That's not appropriate for me to mention, is it?"

My anger rises inside me as a picture of this cheater and his comely redhead, lounging in the soft white robes provided for guests in the suites, fills my mind. "Was he kind to the staff?"

In the seminar, *Don't Step on the Ants—We're All Ants* I attended in Detroit, I learned that you can tell a lot about a person by the way they treat maids, busboys, etc. I was so tired that night, I fell asleep in the bar.

"Oh yes! The maid was thrilled that he tipped her with a one-hundred dollar bill when they left."

"Which maid worked those days?"

"Carmella. She's the one who told me about the tip. You can ask her if you want. She's working now."

"I will, thanks Andy."

As I turn to walk inside, I remember one more thing. "Did they happen to say why they were in town?"

Andy scrunches up his face, making me think of a little kid who is getting ready to throw a tantrum. "If I'm not mistaken, it was to buy some land. Don't know if that ever happened, but we wouldn't mind that infusion of cash in our city coffers, would we?"

Yes, as a matter of fact, we would.

"Thanks!" I wave and enter the lobby. Wendell, the nervous lobby manager, looks over his glasses at me. "Lanie! What a surprise! I didn't know you were working today!"

I kiss him on either cheek, something he always insists upon. "Just tying up some loose ends. I saw Andy in the parking lot and he thought you might be able to help me."

"Oh?"

"Yes, there was a very attractive couple—"

"I know exactly who you're talking about. If I wasn't mistaken, that Greek God was flirting with me."

Wendell sticks his tongue in the side of his cheek, as he does when he knows something the rest of us don't.

"Okay Wendell. If I know you, and I'm fairly certain I do, you observed more than his good looks."

Wendell's face remains stoic and I wonder for a moment if I've read him wrong.

"You're right, Lanie," he says, breaking the heaviness in the air. "I can't keep anything from you!"

He takes one of his keys and opens up a drawer under the counter. With a twinkle in his eye, he hands me a small magnifying glass, the handle covered in crystals and something greasy.

"Am I supposed to know what this is?" I ask, unsure if it's something that should be handled by anyone other than Wendell and a hazmat team.

"Lanie, girlfriend, haven't you seen these before? It's a Gemfinder. They're very popular on the dating circuit. When you find someone you think is a 'gem,' you give them this little darling to let them know. Usually they're cheap, plastic and any jewels are fake." Wendell places his hands on his hips and his chest juts out. "I've already had this one appraised."

"Without any other conversation?" I can't help but be incredulous. "It looks expensive!"

"Are you trying to say I'm not worth it?" he asks, the hurt oozing through his words.

"That's not what I meant. You're worth it, Wendell. My question was more about his giving something this valuable to a complete stranger. Was there a reason he gave you? Like—"

"Like he wants to hook up with a hotel desk clerk?" He sniffs. "There's an entire Piney Falls underground, Lanie. You'd be surprised."

When I don't respond, he continues, "Sterling saw me admiring it and wanted me to have it. His company makes them. He promised we'd be seeing more of him because he purchased some land."

"What?" My voice shoots up two octaves, causing the other people in the lobby to stop what they're doing and stare at the hysterical woman.

"All I meant was that I heard he was here to look, not to buy. Do you know what property he bought?"

Wendell leans forward on the counter and laces his fingers together. "How badly do you want to know?"

I sigh with displeasure. He can be such a pistol.

"Badly enough that I'll go to Andy and report that you're taking expensive gifts from guests if you don't spill it."

"Geez, Lanie. I was just kidding." Wendell stands tall again, brushing invisible crumbs from his Fallen Branch-issue burgundy suit jacket. "He told me that he purchased the old popcorn factory building on Cheezler Drive."

"I didn't know we had a popcorn factory!"

"It was originally a cannery, and when that closed, some rich dude turned it into a popcorn factory. That guy left, and it just sat empty for probably thirty years. That's according to my mother, anyway."

"Could you give me directions?"

"Sure."

"I'm checking out for the day. I've got a terrible headache!" We both turn when we hear Carmella's voice.

"Would it be okay if I ask you a couple of questions first?"

She glances wistfully at Wendell and then at me. I can tell Carmella would rather just leave.

"November Bean makes the best headache remedy. You don't want to know what's in it, but suffice to say several insects and a tree branch lost their lives in sacrifice for human pain."

I reach into my large purse and pull out a clear bag filled with dark, brown bits. The twigs are visible, but everything else is nondescript. "Wendell, could you get a cup of hot water and some lemon?"

He nods and disappears for a moment as I turn back to Carmella. "I promise you, in ten minutes' time, you'll be back to your old self."

When Wendell returns, I pour a small amount of Vem's headache cure in the cup and stir it around. I squeeze the lemon in and mix more. After it's sufficiently mixed, I hand it to Carmella. "Down the hatch, as they say!"

She eyes the cup suspiciously and sniffs. "You want me to drink this?"

"I want you to trust me."

Carmella brings the cup to her lips, hesitating momentarily before drinking it. "Oh, that's nasty!" she says, her eyes watering as she coughs.

"Wendell, set a ten-minute timer." An impish grin overtakes my face. "Now, while you're giving Vem's potion time to work its magic, could I ask you a few questions?"

"I guess so," Carmella replies, still distrusting of me. "You'll call an ambulance if this does something horrible to me, right?"

I nod.

"Last month, there were two people here you might remember. One was —"

"A Greek God," Wendell chimes in. "He was far too pretty for the likes of Piney Falls."

I roll my eyes at Wendell and continue. "He was

here with a woman who was equally attractive. She was tall, with red hair. Does any of this ring a bell?"

Carmella leans against the counter. I can't tell if she's about to be sick or just thinking. If she's going to have a negative reaction to Vem's headache cure, I have no idea how to help her. We may have to call in a poison specialist from Portland, and that could take hours.

"I remember them. The man always asked about my family. 'Hope your children are well,' he would say every morning. Normally, people don't care about the maids. They pretend like we're invisible unless they're out of something, and then it's just a matter of demanding this or that and they want it now."

"I'm sorry, Carmella. You work very hard and should be recognized for that." I glance over at Wendell.

"Two minutes and ten seconds," he replies, as if reading my mind.

"Can you think of anything else about these two that stood out to you?"

"Well, I overheard them arguing on their last day. They were getting ready to check out and they'd left their door open and slid a suitcase into the hall. The woman was saying things like, 'you promised this wouldn't happen!' I couldn't make out his response, but it sounded like an apology voice. You're married too, Lanie. You know what I'm talking about."

"Indeed I do."

Every time Cos knows he's at fault, he has a low, mournful mumble. One time we argued on a hike and I mistook his apology for a bear in the woods.

"I was cleaning the next room over, so I had to go back to my cart to dump the trash. I didn't mean to stare at them. I guess my mind drifted but my eyes stared right into their room."

"What happened next?"

"The woman started screaming at me. 'Its was none of your damn business and you'd better not tell anyone, or we'll make sure you regret it!' I was shaky for the rest of my shift."

"Do you know what she could have been talking about?"

Carmella shakes her head. "After they left, I found a one-hundred dollar bill on the bed. I took that as an apology from him."

"Time!" Wendell calls out.

Carmella feels her forehead and then the back of her head. "I'll be! It's gone! This is amazing!"

"See? I told you!" I'm one part proud of Vem and one part relieved Carmella is still breathing.

"Miss November asked me to join a Moaning for Muscle Aches class on Saturday. I'll be sure and thank her!"

"Oh, one more question. Did you find anything odd in the room after they left?"

"Not that I remember."

My phone has been buzzing in my pocket ever since I gave Carmella the headache remedy. Unable to stand the incessant feeling any longer, I retrieve my phone. Vem. That woman has uncanny timing.

I wave goodbye to Carmella and Wendell before calling her back. "Vem, good news! I shared your headache remedy with Carmella from the Fallen Branch Hotel, and—"

"There is no time for accolades now, Lanie. Though I will insist you remember them later."

"What's going on?"

"It's Cedar. I went over to your place to check on her and she was nowhere to be found."

"Oh, she probably went to work with Cos."

"No, I was watching your place with binoculars before my Squinty Eyes Moaning class this morning. There was a red-shafted flicker on your bedroom balcony. Really a beaut. Oh, and you should shut the shades while your husband is doing his workouts. Either that, or he needs to wear clothes when he's lifting weights."

I'm not fazed. "Vem, get on with it!"

"Standing in your driveway, where Cedar's car was parked, I found a pool of water. It was red, Lanie."

That could mean a million things. Cedar probably drove on a muddy country road.

"Red means blood, Lanie," Vem continues, reading my mind.

"We can deal with that later. I'm going to take a trip out to the old popcorn factory on Cheezler Drive."

"No, you aren't."

Vem is using her pouty voice, the one that is high-pitched and reminds me of a goat in heat.

"What *am* I doing, then?"

"You asked me to make a map of the area where our Mr. Truth is

laying—"

"Dead as a doornail, I remember," I interrupt. "And did you?"

"Do dung beetles bury their balls of dung to snack on later?"

"What?"

"Yes, Lanie. I know right where he is. Come home now and I'll take you there."

Chapter Eight
Piper

"Sweetie, you know I'll always support you, but from what you've told me, he's got some serious issues."

Piper called her mother to tell her about the conversation she'd had with Sawyer. Lanie expressed concerned about Sawyer's stint in prison, but she admitted prisoners weren't necessarily bad people. "Your father also served time in prison, and he's the most moral, upstanding man I've ever known."

Piper experienced a soft-blanket feeling of security every time her parents spoke highly of each other.

"As far as Sawyer goes, I guess we have to take a wait-and-see attitude. That being said, rely on your gut. If you don't feel safe, ask him to leave."

"Yeah." She was secretly hoping that Lanie would offer to keep her safe. Like she was a little kid.

"Boysie called to say he saw Sawyer driving our new delivery van."

Secrets were hard to keep in Piney Falls.

"I know, Mom. That was the other thing I wanted to tell you. He's not the same sweet little boy I knew, I'll admit that. But once we got to talking—I mean really talking—he was the same kid I grew up with. I'm sure it will be fine."

"You have a good head on your shoulders, hon. I trust your judgement."

All day, as she baked scones, breads and cookies, she replayed Sawyer's first moments in her home over and over.

He was holding two black duffel bags. As if reading her mind, he blurted out, "All I have my name. This is it, sis."

"Follow me."

The one concession she made to her better judgement was to house him in the guest bedroom farthest from hers. It had its own bathroom, so he wouldn't need to leave the room once she said good night. She was also relieved Truman had recently replaced the lock on her bedroom door.

Piper led her brother up the steps and down the hallway. "This room was just finished. You'll be the first person to sleep on that bed!"

"And where will you sleep?"

She swallowed hard. "I'll be at the end of the hall, in the opposite direction. I like my decompression time at night, so once I'm in my room, that's it for my social time."

"Yeah. I have a problem with people too."

Sawyer never went to a public school. He never learned the proper way to address others, or how to make polite conversation. She'd had friends off-and-on during their many moves, but Sawyer remained under his mother's watchful eye.

Piper felt better as she was rolling out the last batch of biscuits. There wasn't anything wrong with him at all. It was her perception that was out of whack.

She felt hands on either side of her hips and in one motion, turned and thwapped them away with her rolling pin.

"Ouch!" Sawyer stuck one finger in his mouth. "Geez, if that's the way people in this place say hello, I'd better buy some protective gear."

"Sorry. I'm just not used to visitors while I'm working. How was your first day of deliveries?"

Sawyer sat down on her stool and took a cooled biscuit from the counter while she rolled out dough. He downed it in one bite.

"Good. No problem finding places with the GPS, and I finished early."

Piper glanced at her watch. Five p.m. "You must've gotten lost. The last delivery for you was two hours ago."

His face darkened.

"So you want me to account for every second now? I didn't realize I was still in the can. Should I start calling you the warden?"

"No. Forget it. You are entitled to do whatever you want after you're done with deliveries."

She put all of her anger into the rolling pin, rolling the biscuit dough almost flat to the counter.

"All of this is yours? Pretty nice. These people must really like you."

Why did everything he said, no matter how innocent, make her feel defensive?

"Yeah, you're right about that. I've put quite a lot into this place too. We had to completely remodel everything upstairs and down. I'm happy with the way it turned out.

He pushed the stool away and stood, stretching his arms out wide and almost hitting her in the face. "I need a minute to get the feeling back in my legs." Next, he placed his large palms on the floor and began to move his hips side-to-side. When he finished, he snapped his body upright. "How much do you think a place like this would go for?"

"What?"

"If you were gonna sell it, how much do you think you could get for it? I mean, with all the remodel stuff you did."

"I'm not selling, Sawyer. Whatever money you lost, I'm sorry for that. I've had to work hard for everything I have. I'm not saying—"

"Yoo-hoo!"

November Bean ushered herself in the back door. Today's fashion statement was a lavender jumpsuit, matching headband and glasses frames. She'd also found a pair of lavender tennis shoes.

"Pied Piper, how the heck are you?" She punched Piper's arm playfully. In recent months, November had taken to calling her by that annoying nickname. After protesting numerous times, Piper gave up and just accepted this would be her lot for the foreseeable future.

"Good, November. Great, in fact."

"I heard you've got a gorgeous giraffe of a man sharing your abode?"

November moved next to Sawyer, sniffing his upper torso so close that he took a step back and crossed his arms in front of his body defensively.

"I don't do well with contact," he warned, easing his arms down once he realized she was a friend of Piper's.

"November, this is my brother, Sawyer. You might remember him." She gestured to Sawyer. "You already know we were raised by wolves, so it's no surprise he isn't good with introductions." Instinctively, she tensed. Her brother wouldn't appreciate her joking about their upbringing.

"No, I think I would have total recall of a Handsome Hunker like him." November stepped in close again. This time, he moved away but didn't brace for a fight.

Piper desperately wanted to put an end to—whatever this was. "Did you get tomorrow's delivery schedule yet? It's on the printer."

He scratched his curly head and looked at the floor. "Think so. Cosmo says he wants to talk to me tomorrow, so I'll need to leave earlier than usual."

Piper pivoted back to November. "What brings you out to the country?"

Though there was a counter and tables for customers, Cosmic Bakes was mostly a commercial bakery, with the original and main location on Main Street being the place Piney Fallians went for coffee.

"Oh, I was out for a drive. This month is See Something Sassy. Every day, I must find myself somewhere new. That becomes a real challenge when you've lived somewhere this long. I hadn't been out here to see your place so I said to myself, 'Bean, you should take a sassy drive out to visit Piper!'

Sawyer stared at her with his mouth slightly agape.

"November has a unique way of looking at the world, Sawyer," Piper explained.

He shrugged.

"I don't have anything fresh today, but there are some day-old scones in the case." She pointed to the counter, where a tray of Poseidon Pumpkin sat.

"Oh boy. I'm kind of restricting my sugar intake right now." November placed her hands on her hips and walked over to view the case. "I'll only be able to take three of these off your hands."

Piper wiped her hands on her apron and began boxing up the order. The floor creaked as Sawyer stepped into what used to be the living room of the old farmhouse.

"I'm going to go up to my room and stretch my back. I'll be down in time for dinner with your boyfriend."

They listened to his footsteps as he climbed the stairs. When he'd reached the top and they heard him walking around, November tugged on Piper's forearm, pulling her frame up against the pastry case.

"Ow! Why are you doing that?"

"Your mom sent me out here," November whispered. "She thinks you might be in trouble."

She was equal parts angry and amused that Lanie would think she needed help. They'd only spoken a few hours ago. "You can tell her I'm fine. Nothing is going to happen."

"Don't be so cavalier, missy. You don't know what happened in Tellum yesterday."

"What happened in Tellum, November?" she asked, hoping November understood her sarcasm, though it was highly unlikely.

"A murder. Yesterday. They think it was a drifter. The poor guy was just minding his own business, selling fish sticks at his little stand. Someone came and..." November made a slicing motion across her throat. At least she'd let loose of Piper, who'd been standing on her tip toes so she wouldn't choke.

"That's awful! Do they know why?" She put the scones in a bag and handed them to November.

"Robbery. And maybe anger. He was stabbed twenty-four times. That's a rage killing, you know."

"Sure. What does that have to do with me?"

November leaned over the counter and whispered, "The description of the suspect. Over six feet tall, dark, curly hair, very thin."

Piper's face felt hot. "There are lots of people in the world who look like that."

November tapped the top of Piper's head three times. "Use. Your. Noggin. This brother of yours is here to bring nothing but trouble!"

They heard Sawyer's heavy boots clunking down the steps as he descended the stairs.

"Everything okay, Bud?"

"Peachy."

Piper gave November her most serious look. "Tell my folks I'm fine. And then tell Boysie I'm fine. And Obie is coming for dinner, so I'll tell *him* myself."

"I'm not going to lie to them. Lanie is my best friend in the entire world and she has to know the truth. Someone needs to come out here every day and..." she cupped her hands around her mouth before whispering, "make sure you're still alive!"

Piper blinked rapidly as she plastered a big smile on her face. "Thanks for stopping, November! I've got to get back to work now."

She purposely avoided texting Obie before he came for dinner. He knew about the mysterious stranger and that his father came to save her when she didn't actually need saving. But he knew nothing of Sawyer's time in prison.

When he stepped in the door, after tapping the doorframe three times and touching his shoulders, he took Piper in his arms and kissed her passionately.

The sound of a throat clearing paused their embrace.

Obie looked up, shocked, when he realized they weren't alone.

"Oh, um..."

"Should I be fighting this guy for my sister's honor?" Sawyer asked jokingly. He stuck out a long hand. "Sawyer Moonlight."

Obie glanced at Piper warily before taking Sawyer's hand. "Obie Lumquest."

"Oh, sorry, I forgot to tell you. Sawyer, Obie has something called Obsessive Compulsive Disorder. He doesn't like to be touched most—"

"I know what that is, sis. Don't you remember us doing a report on psychiatric disorders? Mom wanted to prove to us that our lives were perfectly normal."

"Oh, right."

"Sawyer, Piper tells me you spent time in Ohio driving a truck."

Obie removed his coat and took off his shoes. Piper held her breath, waiting to see what Sawyer's response would be when he realized Obie was a police officer like his father.

When Sawyer appeared unfazed by Obie's uniform, she released her breath with relief.

"I have some bread I just pulled out of the oven and some soup. Shall we eat?"

Both men followed her into the commercial kitchen, where she had a small table set up next to the window. It was adorned with cheerful wild-flowers and three blue-and-white checkered placemats.

After they sat, Sawyer stared at Obie, either with wonder or disgust. Piper wasn't sure which one of his expressions was actually a happy one yet.

"I guess you two wanted the element of surprise," Sawyer teased. "And since my sister is dating a cop, I'm guessing the surprise is what he'll have to say to an ex-con over soup."

There was one thing Obie Lumquest wasn't, and

that was easily triggered. His police training kept him calm at all times.

"I'm sha...sha...sure you had a hard time of it," Obie replied evenly, spooning pieces of brightly colored vegetables into his mouth.

"That doesn't even scratch the surface, my friend."

Sawyer sat his elbows on the table, which, in this intimate setting, meant he was practically in Obie's bowl.

"Unlike most people, my sister and me didn't get a normal family to teach us the basics. That's how most people end up in the big house. They never had a mommy or daddy to teach them right from wrong. The guards have to act like their parents. It's pathetic, really."

Piper couldn't tell if he was trying to bait Obie or if he truly believed what he was saying. She frowned.

"Sawyer, the reason you were in prison had nothing to do with our parents."

He didn't bother replying, but slurped soup into his mouth as if he'd never eaten it before. His spoon made a splash every time it hit the bowl and as he ate, the soup splattered all over the table and the other two.

Piper glanced at her boyfriend apologetically. His mouth formed a kiss.

"You have any dessert?" Sawyer asked. "I've become addicted to sugar."

"I have some lemon cake in the fridge." She started to get up.

"No, let me." Sawyer jumped up, hitting his knee on the small table and causing all remaining liquids to spill. "I'll get a rag and clean that up too."

Obie rose from his chair as well, unable to sit with a mess of soup nearby. As soon as Sawyer's curly head was buried in the refrigerator, Obie leaned over Piper's shoulder and whispered, "We need to talk."

"I know," Piper replied. There was no easy way to remove themselves without it seeming obvious.

As Sawyer took plates out of the open cupboard, his phone rang. The ringtone a loud, screeching voice that yelled, "All Cops Are Losers!" blared menacingly.

Oblivious to the awkward situation, Sawyer looked at his phone screen. "I gotta take this. I'll be back in a minute."

Chapter Nine
Lanie

"Take me there now!" I order. There's no sense in being short with her; Vem is who she is. But I'm out of patience for today. She insisted on taking me to the location of Cedar's ex-boyfriend, Sterling. His body, to be precise.

We jump in my car and she directs me on the twisting road that leads from Piney Falls to Tellum. When I've reached cruising speed, she yells, "STOP. RIGHT. HERE!"

It's a good thing my brakes are brand new because I'm burning rubber now. We skid to a stop just short of a county road sign that reads "Abysmal Lane."

"Here? You're sure?"

"Positive, Lanie."

We turn down the road, which, it turns out, is a beach access road. It's not well marked nor is it well used. We bump along until we've reached the end, out on a cliff overlooking the Pacific Ocean.

"Now what?" I ask.

"Well, I can assure you that you won't see any dead bodies with that attitude."

I clear my throat, planning to regroup and try again. "November Thursday Bean. You are the most delightful person I've ever had the pleasure to know. Would you please guide me to the spot where you saw Sterling Truth?"

She sticks her chin out defiantly and for a moment, I wonder if she's really going to help me. It wouldn't be out of the question for her to refuse and force us to repeat this again tomorrow.

"Do you remember the time last summer when we were on the hunt for Boysie's stolen police cruiser?"

"Maybe," she replies tersely.

"Well, you told me you saw it sitting in a driveway on Raspberry Drive. I said—"

"You said, 'no one would be that dumb, Vem.'"

I don't like the way she's mimicking me, nor do I like that fact that her authoritative voice sounds dead on.

"That's right. But when we got there, you were absolutely right. Zeb was planning to repaint it and sell it in Portland. And I apologized and had Piper make you a cake. So, I'm telling you now, that I believe you." I pat her leg reassuringly. "Let's go find us a dead body!"

"I suppose."

She jumps out of the car and runs around to the driver's side door, swinging it open. "Hurry up, Lanie! If we get a rough tide, that thing'll be gone before we get a chance to turn it in!"

I get out and follow her to the edge of the cliff. There is a stiff breeze today, one the locals call a Salmon Strutter. The local lore is that the salmon stand and walk on shore when the wind reaches twenty miles per hour. I'm thankful that Piper convinced me to leave my hair long enough to put in a ponytail because today it really needs it.

"Over here!" November is perched treacherously close to the edge of the cliff, one foot stepping on a branch growing out of a rock.

"Careful, Vem! That body doesn't need company!"

I stick my head out as far as I can comfortably stick it. "I don't see anything. It's just rocks and—"

My eyes zoom in on a brightly colored object. The more I look, the more I realize it's someone's coat. Next to it is a mass of red hair. "Oh my goodness. It's not Sterling. It's his girlfriend."

Without even looking at her, I know what Vem's thinking. "Don't do it, girlfriend," I warn.

"Someone is going to have to see who it is," she replies as she brings her foot back to safety before finding another, just-as-dangerous path. She steps cautiously through the weeds and sand, making her way to the bottom.

I pull out my phone and call Boysie. No answer. Reluctantly, I call Obie. He will ask more awkward questions than his father. *Why are you here, Lanie? It's not wise.*

Time is of the essence though. Vem is right; the tide could wash all of this evidence away.

"Obie? I tried calling your dad, but he didn't pick up. November and I think we may have found a body."

"Not 'may' sister friend, 'did.'"

I make a shushing gesture with my hand and turn my back on Vem.

"I can come now. Send me your location."

After I hang up, I wonder if we should let Cedar know. Since she didn't know Sterling was alive (at some point) and in Piney Falls, it's probably for the best that we keep it a secret for now.

I pull out my phone again, this time feeling confident about the call. "Cos? I'm with November. We think we may have found a body."

"What? I'll be right there. Don't call Boysie until I've had a chance to survey the situation."

I hate the sound of hurt in his voice. He can't possibly believe Cedar is behind this, can he?

I close my eyes as my best friend makes her way down a pathway that's not really there.

Turning my back to her, I listen for the expected thud when she hits the bottom. At least help is on the way.

In a matter of minutes, Obie's cruiser pulls up. He joins me with a pair of binoculars. "Point me to the body," he says matter-of-factly.

"It's at the bottom of this cliff. November has very unwisely decided to climb down and check it out for herself. If she's nothing but broken bones, please warn me before I turn around."

Obie nods and walks over to the edge.

"Oh, hi, Obie! Sent the backup team today?"

I'm both relieved and annoyed to hear the echo of Vem's voice.

"It's probably not a good idea to disturb a crime scene!" he calls.

"Oh, it's not a crime scene. It's just a coat and a wig. Had me fooled!"

Obie taps me on the shoulder.

"I heard," I snap. "Why do I always fall for her crazy ideas?"

He shrugs. "Because sometimes they aren't so crazy." Obie pats his shoulders three times before continuing. "My dad's out today. He had a doctor's appointment in Portland, but let me see if he'll answer his cell. He may want more evidence collected."

He returns to his cruiser and sits down, and not a minute later, Cosmo's motorcycle lurches to a stop beside Obie's car. He doesn't bother taking off his helmet. "Where, Lanie?" he asks.

I walk him to the edge of the cliff and point to the evidence Vem is unwisely trying to carry. She's maneuvering her own pathway, ironically just like her own life. "Down there, Obie. It's a wig and a coat. No body attached."

We gaze at each other with fear and love.

"It could come from anywhere," I say first. "Some kid thought it would be funny to drop his mom's stuff over the side of the cliff."

"Yeah," he replies with uncertainty.

November has inexplicably made her way up the cliff carrying the wig and coat. She rushes over to us like a child with show-and-tell.

"It hasn't been down there long, Lanie. Barely even dirty."

Cos squeezes my shoulder and instinctively, I know to distract Vem.

"Could you take that over and give it to Obie? I need to give Cos a grocery list for dinner."

"I thought you were having leftover—"

"GO!" I snap. I'll apologize for that one later.

When she's out of earshot, Cos places both hands on my shoulders. It must be serious.

"What is it, Cos? There wasn't a body. That's good news, right?"

"I saw those very items in the back seat of Cedar's car."

"Are you sure?"

He puts his arm around my shoulder and squeezes it. "Positive. This is going to be tough."

I pat his arm and whisper, "I know, hon."

Obie walks back over to us, notepad in hand. "Ms. Bean tells me you came out here because of a dream?"

I shrug uncomfortably. "Something like that."

"It's a very out-of-the-way location, and oddly specific."

I point to November, who is seated on a rock, moaning her moan for the dearly departed. I don't even question anymore how or why I know that.

Obie nods, understanding fully as he writes in his notepad. I'm thankful that he is just as intuitive as his father. "My dad suggested calling the coast guard. They can lower guys into otherwise unreachable locations and collect evidence. I called and reported that they could be here within the hour."

"Cos," I say after Obie is gone. "We have to face the chance that your sister isn't telling us everything."

"Yeah. I kinda figured we'd get to that point."

My eyes widen and immediately I regret it. The scenic beach takes up residence in them. "I'm so surprised to hear you say that. Your sister is the kindest, most generous person I've ever known."

"She is. And maybe that's how she got in over her head and didn't know how to eject."

"What should we do now?"

He puts his hands in his pockets and rocks back and forth on the balls of his feet. "We'll buy some nice Sassy Lasses Marveline Merlot, get her rip-roaring drunk and question her until we get the truth."

I burst out laughing. There is nothing more life-affirming than Cosmo Hill at his best.

I've almost forgotten about November in all the excitement. I can see her gesturing broadly as poor Obie nods his head. If I were a nicer person, I would go over and make her stop.

"Lanie Anders-Hill. You're practically devilish today."

I can't wait for time alone with Cos. Back at home, we hurry through dinner and thankfully, Cedar excuses herself to do some reading.

Finally, we have some time alone. I bring Cosmo a tea and we cuddle in bed under our giant, sea foam-green comforter.

"Cos, we don't have any more proof your sister is a murderer than we did this morning. A coat and a wig don't mean anything, and they certainly don't point to Sterling Truth."

He removes his arm from my shoulder and sits up, causing me great anxiety. The last thing I want to do is alienate my husband.

"I know my sister. She didn't kill anyone."

"I sense a but..."

"But, she was certain about this, and if she didn't

kill him, then someone went to a lot of trouble staging her room, and now, throwing things off the cliff. Perhaps his redheaded girlfriend did him in?"

After returning his arm to its rightful place around my shoulder once more, I reach into my pocket and pull out the business card Piper found during our family dinner. "This was on the floor after Cedar left the room."

He squints, unwilling to put his reading glasses on. "What does that say?"

I harrumph with mock-irritation by his laziness. "It's the number of a criminal defense attorney, Cos. She's looking into ways to defend herself."

"Still doesn't prove anything," he replies.

"It doesn't, you're right. But if your sister came here, needing our help, we should do everything we can to provide it."

Cosmo stands and places his coffee cup on the table. He returns and begins pacing back and forth with his hands in his pockets. I wait patiently until he has worn the carpet flat.

"Now you've got me thinking, Lanie," he says. "Cedar is covering for someone else. That's why she's got this attorney's card. She wants to see how she can best help them, because that's who my sister truly is. It would explain why she's spent more time away from us or in her bedroom than being our guest. She's here to figure out the best way to help this murderer."

There is absolutely no way I'll get through to

him. I've always admired his bullheadedness, but tonight, I am experiencing it from an outsider's perspective and I'm quickly gaining empathy for others in his business world.

"Here's my thought," I say, considering my words carefully. "She's hurting. We know that for sure. It's not up to us to decide her innocence or guilt. As her family, we're just here to support her."

He nods his head in agreement.

"And in the meantime, I plan on using all of my resources to get to the bottom of it."

There is a sudden thumping coming from the living room. It only takes a few more thumps to realize it's not the living room, but the front door. Cos and I exchange worried glances. "I'll check it out," he says, grabbing the baseball bat we keep beside the bed.

"Be careful!" I whisper.

I feel like such a coward, hiding in my bed while he faces potential danger. I'm about to put on my robe to join him when Cosmo appears, his face tense.

"As if we haven't had enough of her—"

"Lanie! I need to talk to you ASAP!" November pushes past him and grabs my hand.

Though she appears at inopportune times, November Bean never arrives on our doorstep late at night. She has a series of moans, facial masks (five, to be exact) and chants that have to be done before her head hits the pillow.

I follow her to the living room, touching Cosmo's arm as we pass. "I'm sure she'll be brief."

Wrapping my arms around my waist, I ask, "What's this about, Vem? We were just getting ready for bed!"

"I was in the middle of my mud-and-mint mask when I glanced out the window. You know how I have to check your place every night, or I can't sleep?"

Now that I have a good look at her, I can tell her face is covered in something brown with a slight green tint. "Yes, you've mentioned that. Once a week, if I'm not mistaken."

"Tonight, when I looked out the window, I noticed Cedar's seatbelt was caught in her car door."

"Oh, that's nice of you. I'll run out and—"

"Lanie, I did it myself."

"Thank you, Vem. You didn't have to come and tell me though. A text would work just fine."

"Sister friend," she calls, her voice breaking. "I shoved the belt inside and closed the door. When I stood up..." She holds the opposite hand from me in the air. It's covered in blood.

Chapter Ten
Piper

"They're really cool. You don't have to be nervous," Piper assured her brother as she slipped her key into Lanie and Cosmo's front door.

She readily agreed when Lanie invited them over. "Cos says he's doing a great job. Let's reward that!"

Immediately the scent of a rich, spicy pot roast with oranges and fresh bread swirled around them, teasing their empty stomachs.

It was Lanie's new signature company dish, Piper remembered. After years of a lasagna-only company dish, Piper offered to teach her mother some new recipes. This was the winter dish that Lanie was so proud of. "It's more about spending time with my daughter than the actual food," Lanie remarked at the time.

Piper's heart skipped a beat, thinking about how hard Lanie and Cosmo worked to make her feel loved.

She hung up her coat on the hook and took Sawyer's, causing something to fall on the floor. As she bent down to retrieve it, he did as well, causing them to clunk heads.

They both stood, Sawyer slipping the mystery object into his pants pocket.

"Two heads together make the best soup!" they said in unison.

"That doesn't make a lick of sense."

They turned to find Cosmo standing behind them, hands in his jeans pockets as he rocked back and forth on his heels. Piper knew immediately he was uncomfortable by this stance.

"You're looking good, Da..." she caught herself again before she called him "Dad" in front of her brother. Sawyer still didn't know about her adoption. Soon, she told herself.

"I'd kiss you on the cheek, but I've got a little cold coming on. Tomorrow, I'm going to wear a mask to work, just to be safe." Cosmo turned to Sawyer and stuck out his hand. "Our new delivery man is a handsome devil! We met briefly the last time you were in town. You must've been taking some good vitamins between then and now. Grown at least a foot!"

Sawyer shook his hand and smiled. "My dad

wasn't very tall, and my mom...I guess you knew them."

"You've already seen him. I don't think he's grown since this morning, Cos," Lanie called from the kitchen.

"Yes, boss!" he replied playfully. "Come on in and sit down at the table. Lanie's got dinner ready. Can I pour you both some wine?"

Cosmo walked over to the hutch he'd made from a downed tree last year. He took out four wine glasses and set them on the table.

"Sassy Lasses just came out with a new blend. It's a Syrah and merlot blend called, "Serious Sass." Can I pour you both a glass? My wife sings its praises. Supposedly won a fancy-pants award."

"That would be great," Piper answered enthusiastically. "Sawyer? What about you?"

He shook his head. "I don't drink. That's the easiest way for someone to control your mind, by taking mind-altering substances. I like to stay on top of things."

"Can I get you some water then?" Cosmo asked.

Sawyer eyed him suspiciously. "Do you have any that's still in the bottle?"

"Course we do. Have a seat and I'll go get some."

When Cosmo disappeared into the kitchen, Piper whispered, "You can trust them. They're wonderful people!"

Sawyer snickered. "Didn't they both want our

mother to leave town? Didn't their actions cause her death?"

Piper ignored his comment and counted the plates. "Who isn't joining us this evening?"

"Cedar's got a date!" Cosmo called from the kitchen.

Lanie appeared, carrying a terrine of stew. "She never said anything about a date. She wanted to meet up with old friends. That just leaves more for us!" Lanie set the heavy dish on the table and whispered, "I've got Cos doing the heavy lifting." She winked at Piper. "He'll be back soon with the bread and your water."

Once her hands were free, she kissed Piper on the head. "How are you, hon? Is this big order getting the best of you?"

Sawyer snickered once more, perhaps at Lanie's familiarity, though Piper couldn't be sure. It irritated her that he could be so rude when they'd done absolutely nothing to deserve it.

"I'm getting there. One more batch of chocolate chip cookies in the morning."

Lanie sat down opposite them and rested her chin in her palm. "What do you think of our active ocean, Sawyer? It's got its own story to tell. Nothing like the calm California surf you're used to, I'd imagine."

Piper tensed, knowing her brother would challenge Lanie.

"There's nothing wrong with our ocean. I prefer it to this, I think." He gestured toward their big picture window, which looked out over Piney Cove. There were two commercial vessels in the distance and puffy, pink clouds reflecting a beautiful sunset. It was a photo in real life.

Cosmo returned and sat down beside Lanie after depositing his goods on the table. "I've been looking forward to this all day." He pecking his wife on the cheek and then smiled at her with adoration.

"Practically melts in my mouth!" Cosmo commented as he ate hungrily.

Sawyer abruptly dropped his fork and blurted, "Why do you trust my sister with your business?"

Piper gawked at him with horror. "Sawyer! Why would you say that?"

"Because you've always been a flake. I can remember Mom getting upset when you'd start a project and then it would sit around until we moved. 'Piper doesn't have an ounce of motivation in her entire body,' she'd say."

Piper felt her cheeks become hot. "No one ever said that to my face. I was trying to learn who I was, and—"

Lanie reached over and placed her hand on Piper's arm. "You don't need to explain yourself, hon."

Piper frowned at her brother. It felt like she'd been ambushed.

"The only Piper I know is the one who has proved herself, time and time again as a hard, dedicated worker with a heart of pure gold," Lanie reassured her. "That's the person I know and love."

There were four loud bangs outside and they all jumped up.

Cosmo beat everyone to the door, using one hand to hold it open and raising the other as if ready to strike. "Ah, geez!" He snorted, when he realized what, or who, it was.

"Cosmo Hill, is that how we treat our neighbors? I don't think so."

November Bean, dressed head to toe in a ruby red jumpsuit, head band and glasses frames, was standing on their lawn with a remote control in one hand and a drone in the other.

"What are you doing out here?"

"I heard about a murderer being on the loose and I didn't want to go to bed before I knew you were safe." November leaned around Cosmo, viewing Piper and Sawyer.

"Was I not invited? Lanie, why wouldn't you invite me to a family dinner? I'm family too!" she asked with hurt in her voice.

"It was last minute, Vem. Piper wanted to bring her brother over to show him our home, that's all. You're welcome to come in and—"

November Bean stormed up the steps, practically bowling over the top of Cosmo. Even though he was a strong man, he was no match for her super-human strength. She shoved Sawyer and Piper out of the way and dropped her coat on the couch.

They all stared at this human wonder while she retrieved her own bowl from the cupboard, slid an extra chair up to the table, and commenced dishing up her own stew.

"So much for leftovers," Cosmo grumbled. "Help yourself, Bean."

"Thank you, Cosmo," she mumbled between bites of bread.

"Sawyer, you've met November Bean, our neighbor?"

"Yeah. She came out the other day to make sure I hadn't done something horrible to my sister."

"He's an ex-con, just like you Cosmo Hill," November interjected, slurping her stew.

"Really?" Cosmo raised a brow. "I don't recall Piper mentioning that."

"Yeah, we do have that in common. I was released early, thanks to the work of a great lawyer. She was hired by my cellmate. I guess money talks, right?"

The table was silent, except for the sounds of November's knife screeching on the plate as she cut her meat into small, un-Vem-like bites.

"Lucky, don't you think?"

"What's that?" Cosmo asked.

"Oh, that two murderers like us can get a second

chance, all because of one little twist of fate." Sawyer spoke with an iciness to his voice that made chills run up and down Piper's spine.

"I served every single day of my sentence, kid. The only reason I got out was because I jumped through every hoop. No fancy lawyers or shortcuts for me."

Lanie jumped up. Piper noticed her plate was untouched. "I've got two great desserts in the kitchen. Piper, would you help me?"

Piper wasn't sure she was comfortable leaving Sawyer alone with Cosmo. For whatever reason, Sawyer didn't like him. She didn't budge from her seat.

"Piper?" Lanie insisted. "I really do need your help."

Piper stood reluctantly and followed her mother into the kitchen. When they were both far enough away from the dinner table, Lanie leaned up against the counter and crossed her arms. "Spill it, daughter. It's clear he's much more wound up than you led me to believe. What's going on?"

"He hasn't had the time to immerse himself in normal life like I have, that's all." Piper replied, feeling less and less like defending her brother. She couldn't bring herself to meet her mother's gaze. "Sawyer needs everyone's patience, just like I got when I was learning how to be normal."

"The only reason I ask is because I love you. Vem

says when she visited that Sawyer wasn't at all welcoming. That's why I invited you both for dinner tonight, so I could see for myself."

Lanie opened her arms wide and Piper fell into her comforting chest. "If you trust him, then so do I, hon," Lanie whispered soothingly in her daughter's ear.

These were the feelings, the touches Piper enjoyed the most in her new life. Her mother loved her wholly and without reservation. An unexpected sound interrupted their solitude. It was the sound of joy.

They returned to the dining area, Piper carrying a decorative glass plate holding a four-layer chocolate cake. Lanie trailed behind, carrying dessert plates and forks. Cosmo and Sawyer were laughing and talking like old friends.

Piper glanced at her father for explanation.

"Sawyer was just telling me stories about life in the Ohio State Pen. I guess it's the same everywhere."

"They eat stuff that tastes like glue," November reported. She pivoted toward Lanie. "And everyone acts like my creations are distasteful."

"I think your brother is going to stick around for a while, Piper." Cosmo's voice was uncharacteristically cheery. "His visit came at the perfect time. With Rusty Mellow in the wind, your Dear-Old-Dad needed a new driver."

Sawyer's expression changed in an instant, to the

dark, serious face Piper had come to recognize. "What do you mean by that? Why did you say you were her dad?"

Cosmo glanced quickly at Piper for clarification. She shook her head and frowned.

"Never mind. I—"

"Cosmo and Lanie adopted our little Pied Piper." Vem leaned over and squeezed Piper's cheeks. Piper slapped her hands away, irritated by the unwelcome touch.

"It was a big surprise at their wedding," Vem continued, unaware of the drama she was causing. "Of course, I knew about it ahead of time. They'd been planning it for weeks. Piper practically lived here anyway—"

Sawyer jumped up and shoved his chair away from the table so hard, it caused his plate to drop to the floor, shattering into small chunks of bright-blue ceramics.

As everyone watched in shock, Sawyer stomped over to the door. "I'm going out for a smoke," he called. "Don't want to interrupt your family time!" The door slammed so hard, the glasses on the table rattled.

"Well! I'm just going to say it," November began. "That kid has no accounting for taste. If he was gonna break something, the salad bowl should be the first casualty. I've been telling you that for years, Lanie. Blue isn't a salad color."

"November, why did you have to blurt that out?" Piper shouted. "Didn't you think about how that might hurt him? Sawyer was locked away in prison for a crime he didn't commit, and I was here, living the easy life. Now he has to learn about my new family from someone besides me. You're so... so...thoughtless!"

For once, November was speechless.

"Hon, I don't think it was anything November said." Lanie attempted to grab her daughter's arm and offer comfort, but Piper pulled them both into her lap.

Piper jumped up and stomped her way to the front door, repeating her brother's performance with a slam that once again rattled the glasses.

Sawyer was sitting on the front stoop, a cigarette in one hand and his phone in the other. Maybe she hadn't been paying attention, but this was the first time she'd seen him smoke.

"I'm sorry. This has to be hard for you. We got close when I started working at the bakery, and they asked if I'd like to be a member of their family. That's all. It's just a change on paper. You're still just as much my brother as they are my parents."

He sprinkled his ashes in a flower pot containing rosemary and basil. "I get it. They want their happy little family and you never had one." Sawyer took a long drag. "I'm a part of your old life, not your shiny new one."

"Please stop saying that!" she begged. "You're my brother forev—" Piper's pocket buzzed. Out of habit, she pulled it out to make sure it wasn't an order. Instead, she saw the words, "Honey Buns" in the caller ID.

"It's just Obie. I can call him back later. You're more important to me."

Sawyer glared at her. "Why? We barely know each other. Our mom wouldn't allow us to develop like normal siblings, so instead we grew up as strangers. You don't know me at all."

"Then why are you here, Sawyer? If you don't want to be in my life?"

Her phone buzzed again. She sighed loudly. "It's Obie. He only does this when it's important."

"You'd better take it, sis. After our dinner last night, he's probably worried that you're alone with a big, bad ex-con. I'm going to take a leak in the woods." Sawyer stood and walked off.

She was just as offended that he wouldn't use the bathroom as she was that he sprinkled his ashes in her mother's potted herbs.

"Obie? This isn't really a good time. We're at my folks house and November came over and ruined everything."

"I'm sorry to hear that. I've been trying to get ahold of you because there's something you should know."

"What?"

"Dad received a call this evening. Someone found a body."

"Well, that's not all that uncommon here," she joked, but then thought better of it. "I already heard. Some guy in Tellum."

"It was Rusty Mellow. Your new delivery driver."

"What? Do they know what happened?"

"Not yet, but there is one thing—"

"Does that mean you'll be working extra hours?" Piper couldn't help it; after their awkward dinner the previous night, it would be easier if he wasn't around while Sawyer was in town.

"It does. It also means I need to question your brother."

She glanced up at her brother, who was meandering down a path.

"He matches the suspect's description."

Chapter Eleven
Piper

Although she was positive Sawyer could never kill anyone, Obie had placed a seed of doubt in her mind. "You've got street sa-sa-smarts, Piper. Don't let your devotion to your brother blind you to what's going on."

If she was easily swayed by the men she cared about, then what did that say about her relationship with Obie?

Immediately she brushed off the idea, but as they drove home that evening in silence, it was almost as though she could feel the evil oozing from him. Twice she dared catch a glimpse of Sawyer. Both times, his brow was furrowed and he appeared lost in thought.

"Sawyer, I'm sorry that I—"

"You don't have to—"

They both spoke at once, giggling when they did.

"Ladies first."

"I'm sorry. I should have told you about my adoption, but you've been through so much and I didn't want to cause you any more pain."

If she was being honest with herself, it was also because she didn't want to share this part of her life with him. It was hers alone and Piper didn't want to share.

When they arrived at the farm, she jumped out of the car quickly.

"Wait!" Sawyer called. "Before you go to bed, I've got something for you."

"Okay! I'll meet you in the kitchen!" she called, running up the steps and continuing until she reached her bedroom.

As they were leaving Lanie and Cosmo's house after the family-dinner-gone-wrong, Cosmo had pulled her aside and pressed something into her hand. She felt the smooth pearl handle of the knife he'd given her. Truman bought it for Cosmo on his last birthday, telling her father, "Remember that it is the actions, and not the commission. George Washington understood the need to be decisive!" Truman waved the knife around as he spoke, causing everyone in the room to keep their distance.

"Living out there all by yourself, you should have some protection," Cosmo continued quietly. "Never know when someone might have evil on their mind."

She knew it wasn't a random someone he was

referring to. Piper thought it odd that, after Cosmo and Sawyer seemed to hit it off, he would still be wary of her brother.

"And honey? I spent long enough behind bars to know when someone still has the gasoline in them. Your brother is just waiting for the match."

After she put her pajamas on, she decided on some tea to calm her nerves. November gave her a new one for sleep that she called, "Night in Your Noggin."

Reaching the bottom step, she was surprised to see that Sawyer had helped himself to a beer and was sprawled out on the floor of her kitchen. He was using a fifty-pound bag of flour as a pillow.

"Sawyer, wouldn't you be more comfortable in your own room? I could bring you another pillow."

"Nah. When I was in the joint, the food was so terrible that I'd spend my nights awake with stomach pains. They don't care if you were awake the entire night, you still have to get up at dawn."

He eyed her as though he expected a response, but Piper smiled and said nothing.

"That's when a guy told me that he laid on the floor of his cell every night after eating that slop. It really did help."

"I don't know whether I should be offended that you didn't like Lanie's food, or happy that your digestive system doesn't have to endure that anymore."

"There's something I've been meaning to give you. A gift for letting me stay with you."

Nice pivot, brother.

"I'm going to have some tea. Would you like some? It might settle your stomach."

She placed the kettle on the stove and stood on her tip toes, reaching the mugs. The next time Truman was in the mood to create something, she would ask him to make more shelves on her level.

"Sure. Whatever you're having is fine."

After the kettle whistled, Piper poured two mugs and set them on the table. She pulled out a chair and sat down, taking care to step around his long body to get there.

"Food was great. It was more than I'm used to eating, is all." He stared at her ceiling. "Did you know that some mobsters put messages in the ceilings of their homes? It's in case they're killed, so the family knows where the money is. There is a guy who specializes in that kind of ceiling work. I shared a cell with him for about two months."

"Sawyer, you said you had something for me?"

"Huh? Oh yeah. I was driving up the coast to see you and I found something in this little town called Tellum." He stood in one quick motion and disappeared momentarily into her living room. When he returned, he was carrying a large box, wrapped in brown paper.

"Open it, sis."

Tentatively she tore the bag open. "What is this?"

"It's a radar detector. So you know when the cops are around. My buddy sells them, so I get a good discount."

She swallowed hard. "Thanks. But I don't think Obie would like it if I had one of these in my car. He might see it as a middle finger to his profession." She giggled uncomfortably.

Sawyer swatted the back of his chair, causing it to tumble across the floor. "You're a complete stranger to me, Piper, whatever-your-last-name-is. Nothing like the girl I grew up with. She had guts and didn't care what other people thought."

"I worried more about what they thought than you knew, bud. I wanted desperately to fit in some-where. This isn't about me, though. Something about you has been off since you arrived. What's going on? I mean, really going on?"

Sawyer rubbed the back of his neck and stared at the floor. "I don't know how to tell you this, Piper, but that boyfriend of yours is a real idiot. I get it, you're in a small town and your options are limited, but he's gotta go."

"He's not!" she protested. "Obie is kind and smart and probably better than anyone you met in Ohio. If you'll spend some time getting to know him, you'll understand."

Though she knew exactly what he was doing—

deflecting the topic away from himself—Piper still found it difficult to hold her temper.

"I don't need to get to know him to smell a young cop trying to prove himself!" Sawyer yelled. "He's out to get me. He's already turned you against me, and it won't be long until this entire town does the same!"

With that, he stormed up to his room, stomping so hard on each step that Piper worried they would split.

"I'm going to bed," she uttered through gritted teeth. It didn't matter. No one was listening. She climbed the steps gingerly, listening to each groan of the boards as she went.

Chapter Twelve
Lanie

Cosmic Cakes and Antiquery is practically buzzing. The news that yet another body was found, this time on Dreary Days Beach, didn't take long to reach every living soul in Piney Falls.

"I heard it was the serial killer who escaped from prison last month," one of the regular gossipers spouts with authority. "They're gonna need to analyze his prints. Dollars to donuts, he's got more victims out there."

I don't bother correcting him. The serial killer was caught within hours of his escape. At another table, a group of women who are crocheting have determined the body in question belongs to a child who disappeared from Tellum a decade ago. At least this theory holds a little water.

Cos asked me to help out this afternoon while Doris went to get her teeth fixed. "Got me a new fancy set of chompers a-coming today, Lanie," she announces proudly as I lower an apron over my head.

"You'll have to get your hair done and have your picture taken!"

Doris makes a clicking sound and points at me. "That I will, girl, that I will."

As I'm busily taking orders, there is one person who is noticeably absent. Urica Jollopy, the owner of Urica's Fine Arts, hasn't made her entrance. Next to Gladys, she's the biggest gossip in town. She wouldn't miss a chance to tell everyone what she does (or doesn't) know about the crime.

"Cos, is everything okay with Urica?" I ask when there is a lull in the customers. "I'd expect her to be front and center today."

His apron is covered in a combination of flour, blue frosting and grease from cleaning an oven. He rubs his neck while he thinks. "She hasn't been in for a couple of days. How do you want to handle it?"

I know exactly what he means. Do I want to ask Gladys, Urica's best friend, or do I want to handle this on my own and avoid a potential city-wide alert, issued by Gladys?

"I'll go over to her place when things slow down this afternoon." I turn around as I hear the next wave of customers entering.

What I can't remove from my head is the image of that red wig and coat, the same ones Cos saw in the back seat of his sister's rental car. I tried encouraging Vem to invite her for coffee. Cedar and Vem used to be close, growing up in the cult, but ever since Cedar moved away, the two of them drifted apart.

"It's normal, Vem," I explained. "When you lived in California, you didn't keep in close contact with anyone in Piney Falls, did you?"

"Lanie, my magnetic personality must be shared with all who encounter it. If I don't share the gifts I've been given, then what's the point of having them?"

"What does that mean, exactly?"

"That I kept a list of people I liked and contacted them every month. On a rotating schedule, of course."

"Of course."

I still haven't told Cos. He wouldn't be able to handle it.

"Lanie? Did you hear me?"

Boysie is standing in front of me looking concerned.

"Boysie! So sorry. I've got some things on my mind."

"Yes, that's obvious." He peels a ten-dollar bill off a roll of cash and leaves it on the counter. I pour his usual coffee and find the Boysenberry Blast-Off scone I hid in the back for him.

"Once this crowd calms down, I'd like to ask you something," I say, cursing the words as they come out of my mouth. It's a betrayal of my family to tell him about a potential crime committed by my sister-in-law.

Luckily, there are no more customers coming in, so I take the opportunity to sit beside him. Cos waves and returns to work cleaning the kitchen. He doesn't suspect anything. *Good.*

"I thought there was something weighing you down today, Lanie," Boysie says as he shoves the last of the scone in his mouth and licks his fingers. "Boysenberry Blast-Off is my new favorite. My compliments to Piper. She's always coming up with something that hits it out of the park."

"She's so talented," I agree. "We're continually grateful to have her in our lives."

"That's not what you wanted to talk about though," he says, wiping his fingers. "Is it, Lanie?"

I've never had a problem speaking, but today, the words stick in my throat. "Boysie, I...um...What if I were to give you a scenario and you were to tell me what might happen?"

He frowns until he understands exactly what I'm suggesting. "Okay. We'll pretend this is all just a story you came up with while you watched your husband wash the dishes." He winks at me, giving me the go-ahead to begin.

"A friend confessed to a murder."

"Wait a minute," he places his hand on my arm. "I thought this was going to be a fun little pretend situation, like a murder mystery dinner."

"Okay," I say, deciding in that moment it would be best to call this a different crime. "A friend starts a house on fire."

"I don't know that it's much better," Boysie grumbles, "but go ahead."

"A friend commits arson," I repeat, "and they confess. You know they are a good person, someone who wouldn't commit arson unless it was absolutely necessary. And the truth is, there is a very good chance there was no arson in the first place."

Boysie knits his brows together. "Now you've got me confused. When is arson necessary?"

My patience is starting to wear thin. "Boysie, it's not the crime that's important, it's what happens in the aftermath. The person is a mess. They don't want to talk about it, but others in this person's life want to get to the bottom of the crime. They've seen the ash on their friend's hands and they know the friend isn't making this up."

Boysie, normally ready with a story or joke, is uncharacteristically quiet.

"This is a tough one, Lanie. You know me, I like to give everyone a fair shake. Are you talking about the body that was found yesterday? If so, you need to tell me everything. This isn't a game."

I'm upset that he isn't understanding me. Lanie Anders-Hill is an expert at painting herself into a corner.

"Boysie, there's nothing I have to share with you right now," I say quietly. I stand and touch his shoulder. "You'll be the first person I tell when the time is right."

He tilts his head slightly. "Sure thing."

My phone buzzes and I'm grateful for the distraction. "Vem? What's going on?"

"Lanie, I'm beside myself. After I found the blood in Cedar's car, I did a cleansing ritual. Today, I continued that process by smearing goat dung and pine needles all over my body. I stood in the woods for over an hour, howling."

"And?"

"And I'm still clouded over. Like surveillance camera number three, after the great pigeon migration. It was the one pointed at your bedroom."

"You could try a good moan. You've got several that might work."

"No, for once this won't go away with a moan." Her voice is uncharacteristically sorrowful. So un-Vem-like.

"Sweetie, let's talk about this when I get home, okay? I'll bring the leftover scones from today and you can eat them while you get it off your chest."

"Lanie, that coat we found the other day belongs to a dead woman."

"What? How would you—"

I stop myself. All of this moaning and excrement have really done their job.

"And there's more. When I went out to wave goodbye to everyone this morning, I had to peek inside Cedar's car. There are red hairs all over her back seat, exactly the same color as the wig I found."

I never mentioned Cos's revelation to her, with good reason. I didn't want her jumping to conclusions like she is right now. Moving as quickly as I can without causing suspicion, I find my way outside, away from listening ears. "Vem, let's keep this between us, okay? You remember when you had that little incident, and you begged me to keep my lips zipped?"

She's quiet.

"Oh, you're talking about the pizza."

I wasn't.

"Yes, the pizza."

"Well, I took those four large pizzas because that pizza guy has a thing for me. I thought he was flirting."

"Vem, he's a teenager," I say with disgust. "And those were meant for the high school basketball team's party. Let's focus on Cedar. I know this isn't all you found, so spit it out."

"I went through the trash. Her plane ticket was there, dated a week ago. I didn't open the trunk, though. I've been dying to try out my new toy, BreakingandEntering Two Hundred."

"I've told you that's probably illegal," I scold. "Though, I'll admit, your gadgets have come in handy. Wait—did you say Cedar's plane ticket was dated a week ago? Are you positive? She just got here three days ago!"

"I took a picture. I'll send it to you now." Vem sighs. "Lanie, there's something else you should be aware of."

Hearing her voice today is bringing more anxiety to me than Cedar and Boysie combined. "What else could possibly go wrong?"

"It's about Piper. Her brother is up to no good."

My stomach tightens. "I know. I've been trying to figure out how to handle that. Dinner was a complete disaster. Just as Cedar is to Cosmo, Sawyer means the world to Piper. When it comes to him, she doesn't think clearly."

I'm glad I'm standing outside. Cosmo has taken a real liking to Sawyer. He sees himself, an over-whelmed parolee trying to find his way in the world, in Sawyer. He's placed trust, too much trust, in Piper's brother.

"Do you have one of your listening devices we could—" I stop myself again. *No, Lanie. This is inappropriate.* It goes far beyond normal parental concern. "Forget it. I was just thinking out loud."

"I'll be over as soon as you get home, Lanie," Vem replies. "With all the leftover scones."

"Where's Cedar now?"

"She's walking up to Piney Falls. I asked if she wanted company, but she insisted on going alone. To think, or something."

"And?"

"And I followed her, but somehow I lost her. She's got the scent of deceit, Lanie."

"I've no doubt."

When I'm back inside, I purposely avoid Boysie's table and his gaze. He can spot a liar just as easily as Vem.

Cosmo is leaning against the counter, talking to Doris.

"Lanie, you missed the unveiling of the new Doris," he says gesturing toward Doris. She proudly opens her mouth and displays straight white teeth that could adorn the mouth of a super model.

"Like one of them fancy folks with a—what'd you call it, Cosmo?"

"A grill," he replies, amused by her excitement.

"Doris, you're positively glowing," I remark. In the space of one day, she's gone from a tired, older woman to a complete dazzler.

"The dentist sure gave me an earful. Everybody in town has an idea about what happened to Rusty."

I shuffle my feet uncomfortably, hoping it isn't noticeable.

"The coroner is his cousin, you know. Said Rusty was most likely killed by strangulation and the bullet in his head was sometime later. He's gonna send the whatnots off to a lab in Portland though, so we've gotta wait to be sure." She chuckles to herself.

"Was that all?"

Cosmo frowns and shakes his head. He hates it when I participate in local gossip.

"The coroner says it's possible the body was moved. Oh, and he mentioned to his brother that there was a handful of hair in his fingers. Brown wavy hairs. Poor Old Rusty fought hard."

"So sad," I say, gleeful. I can't help myself. "Brown hair is so common, though."

"No, I got that mixed up. There were two kinds of hair found in his hand: brown, like I told you, and the other was full of silver hair, just like Cosmo's, according to my dentist. You haven't been doing things you shouldn't, have you Cosmo?" she jokes.

Vem's words come screaming back to me, like the scene from a scary movie. *I found her plane ticket from a week ago, Lanie.*

Vem must've been mistaken. She still has glasses with last year's prescription because she likes the lime green frames. When I ask her, she'll tell me that she was wearing her old prescription frames and we'll have a good laugh.

"Lanie?"

"Sorry. My mind is elsewhere today. Cos, I'm

ready to go home now. Would you mind if I left a little early?"

He lifts one brow, as he does when I repeat one of Vem's chants. "Was it something I said?"

"No, my darling. I need to tie up some loose ends. I'll see you at home."

Chapter Thirteen
Lanie

"What was she doing here?"

I'm pacing back and forth in Vem's kitchen. It is the safest spot for us to talk. Cedar could walk in on us at any moment at home.

"I have some thoughts, Lanie," November says. "I was remembering the old Cedar from back in the Fallen Branch Cult Days. On the nights we were able to quit work early, she and I would play this little game."

I stare at her, fascinated that there are still parts of her world I know nothing about.

"We called it, 'run, dare, hide.' You dared the other person to do something, and their options were to run away, to do whatever it was, or to hide. That could mean hiding something we would normally share."

"Like a secret? Or those necklaces you wore?"

I remember she and Cos telling me about the individual medallions made for each of them.

"No, in our game, it meant hiding something important from the other person. We were in charge of laundry, so if I decided to hide a shirt, then Cedar would have to search until she found it. They were all counted out every day and if there weren't enough shirts, the laundry kids got into trouble." Vem stands on one foot, practicing her balance while she speaks. She's a great one for multi-tasking. "Cedar always chose hide. That was the highest risk option, but every single time she found whatever I hid."

I lean against her brand new white marble counter. "So what you're telling me is that Cedar came here early to...hide something?"

November jumps up in down in place. She shakes her hands, which I know by now means she's trying to release all of the disturbing energy I'm putting out in her kitchen.

I wait patiently until she's done.

"Lanie, what I'm telling you is that Cedar's brain is still the same noggin that it was when we were kids. If she came here early—"

"When," I correct her. "When she came here early..."

"You're creating a big old bee in my bonnet, sister friend!" Vem says in her sing-song voice. "Cedar was looking for something hidden. I just know it."

"Okay. Where would this hidden item be?"

"These new rental cars have a GPS on them, don't they?"

"Yes, but that's only to tell you where to go, not where you've been."

"We can figure out if she's used it to find some-place. As long as she's distracted, I can figure it out. Oh, and I'd need her keys."

"I can handle both. Meet me at my place in an hour."

When I reach the door, she calls, "Lanie? Can you make some of those pizza rolls for supper? I'm trying to watch my food intake this week and I want something light."

Cosmo is home when I arrive. He kisses me on the cheek and then stands back, looking me up and down.

"What?"

"Nothing. It's good to show gratitude every day. You are the one thing I'm the most grateful for. With Cedar and Piper coming in a close second."

I bring him into my arms and hold him tight. "It's never too late in the day to hear that. But I am a little suspicious as to why you're doing it now."

Cos bends down to remove his shoes. "Sawyer came back a little early from his deliveries, so I thought we could chat, you know, ex-con to ex-con."

"I'm sure he'd appreciate any words of wisdom you'd like to share." I move into the kitchen and open the freezer, searching for the pizza bites. I only keep them on hand for Vem. "Did you convince him to go in for questioning about the murder?"

"He's a good kid, Lanie. We've been wrong about him. He's a charming guy and he loves our Piper. It's not uncommon for guys like us to be suspicious of the cops. Sawyer'll change his mind eventually."

"You'll be a great mentor to him." I dump the bag on a baking sheet and set it on top of the stove. "Where's your sister?"

"She said she needed a nap. It seems late in the day for that, but the poor kid's on vacation."

I sigh with relief, turning my back quickly so he doesn't sense anything odd. I glance over to the chairs surrounding our kitchen table. Cedar's purse is there. Good.

"Not that I don't love everything you make," Cosmo begins.

"But you hate pizza bites. I know. These are for November. She'll be over as soon as she finishes practicing her Mood Lighting Moan. It's a new class she's working on."

"And what are we having?"

"The last time your sister was here, she couldn't stop raving about Cheese With Your Burger. The new owners have outdone themselves."

"I just took my shoes off!" my husband whines.

"You can drive in your socks, if that's helpful." I smile hopefully at him.

"Okay. I'll get us some burgers and fries. I suppose it gives Cedar more time to rest anyway."

He kisses my cheek before slipping back into his shoes. I wait to hear the sound of his truck leaving the driveway before I text Vem.

It's go time.

With shaky fingers, I open Cedar's purse. The keys are sitting in a pocket, so I grab them and toss them at Vem as she's walking up the driveway. "Hurry!" I hiss.

It's not like I haven't done anything sneaky before. In fact, it wouldn't be a normal week if I didn't have some sort of wacky plan in motion. It's the fact that Cedar is my sister-in-law and our relationship is built on trust. Also, she's Cosmo's sister.

I pace nervously around the kitchen until Vem walks through the front door. "Well?"

"I took pictures of all of the locations. She's been a busy little bee."

Vem takes her phone out to show me, but I push her hand away. "We can talk about this tomorrow. Give me the keys!"

Once they are returned to Cedar's bag, I feel much better. Vem sits down and tells me about her day while I heat up her pizza rolls. We laugh over a bottle of Sassy Lasses before Cosmo returns.

"I thought you got lost!" I call when I hear him entering our house.

He appears in the kitchen and sets two paper bags on the counter. "Lanie, you wouldn't believe what happened."

Now that he's in the light of the kitchen, I can see his face is ashen. "What is it?"

"I was waiting for my order at Cheese With Your Burger and Wilfred Nugget happened to be there waiting too."

"Oh. He's such a nice man!"

Two months ago he installed our new water heater. He offered to come back and help me plant flowers in the spring.

"Yeah. He told me he went on a strange call today. It was an old factory out on Cheezler Drive."

"Those places are haunted," Vem interjects.

"That's where Wendell said—" I stop myself before revealing that I've been searching for Sterling. Wendell was positive that Sterling was planning to purchase that property.

"November Bean, there isn't anything to haunt out there," Cos replies with his usual November-drives-me-nuts voice. "The buildings are so far apart, a ghost would need excellent fitness to move between them," Cosmo retorts. "And besides, this has nothing to do with a haunting."

"Go ahead, Cos," I urge. I can hear my stomach rumbling.

"Well, he tells me that when he got out there, he saw three guys in a car just tearing down the street. They almost took out his plumbing van on the way. It scared him so bad, he decided he'd call Boysie when he finished."

"That's too bad. Is that all?"

"No. Like I was saying, he went in to fix clogged pipes. Nobody was home, but they told him where the keys were, so he let himself in. He could smell something strange, but it never occurred to him that it was something illegal. When he finished, he left the keys on the counter like the owners asked him to do."

"Well, I'm glad it all worked out."

I can't take it anymore, so I open the bag and grab the burger on top.

"No, Lanie. I wasn't done. He was walking down the steps when he happened to look down at the basement window. There was blood splattered on it from the inside."

"See! I told you! Ghosts!" Vem asserts. The oven timer is beeping, Vem's cue to remove her pizza rolls. "Lanie, I'm glad you listened to me. One bag is plenty when I'm eating light."

"That's creepy, Cos," I say between bites. "Did he go back inside?"

Cosmo looks at me with disbelief. "Would you? He's not crazy, dear. Wilfred decided he'd call Boysie when he got back to town. With the three young men who left so quickly, he didn't want to take a chance they'd return."

"No, that was wise of him," I say as I shovel French fries in my mouth. I'm feeling a little like a ravenous November and it's not a good look for me.

"Here's the kicker. Wilfred returned to the location with Boysie. The window was wiped clean. Not only that, Boysie determined that the house wasn't occupied. It's been for sale for several months now, but because of the plumbing issue, no one has been interested."

November opens her mouth to speak and Cosmo jumps up. "Before you say another word, I want to remind you that I just told you this isn't a ghost story."

"What isn't a ghost story?"

Cedar is standing in the doorway, looking every bit the dazzling woman we've come to expect. She's wearing a white sweater with a purple and turquoise triangle pattern all over the front. Her black leggings are baggy.

"Extra sleep does wonders for the soul," she says as she kisses her brother's forehead and then mine. "Is that Cheese With Your Burger I'm smelling?" She opens a bag and pulls out another burger. "I didn't mean to interrupt. What were you saying about ghosts?"

"The whole point of this story, ladies," Cosmo says with frustration, "is that there weren't, in fact, ghosts. It's some kind of illegal activity. Boysie is checking into it and I'm sure we'll learn more the next time he comes in for coffee."

"Where did all of this take place?" Cedar asks while licking ketchup off her finger. "This is just what I needed tonight. But also not what I needed. I'm going to need new clothes after spending time with you guys."

"It's out on Cheezler Drive," I reply. "Apparently it's a factory that's been empty for some time."

Cedar's mouth drops open. "And what was found there?" she asks quietly.

"Nothing, sis," Cosmo says. "A plumber thought he saw blood but it turned out to be nothing at all."

"Oh, good." She continues eating, but the mood of the room has definitely changed.

"I thought I'd go to a moan class tomorrow, if that's all right with you?" Cedar asks.

Vem's face lights up and she jumps up from the table, bringing the last two pizza rolls with her. "I have three tomorrow! Which one? All of them? You'll be so impressed by my studio. Oh, and the pre-and-post moan music is attendees' choice. Though I didn't approve of last week's Italian rap music. Did you know those pretty words are cursing?"

"Whichever one you think would be best," Cedar replies without much interest.

I wonder if she isn't just saying this to change the course of the conversation. It's very creepy thinking of Cedar as a criminal. I don't want to think of that, in fact. But the blood on her seat belt is too odd. She would have said something if she weren't trying to hide.

"Cedar, what else might you have planned for tomorrow?"

She looks surprised. "I don't know. Are you thinking about a little sisterly outing?"

"Yes. But first, I want to stop by the hospital. I try and donate blood when I can."

Cosmo stares at me curiously. "That's, um... nice of you?"

"I keep forgetting to tell you about the community blood drive. If Cedar's a good sport, maybe she can donate too?"

My phone rings and I'm happy to see it's Boysie calling. I feel like we left things in an awkward place earlier. "Boysie? What's the good word?"

"Lanie, Mother wanted me to call." His voice is somber.

"You're scaring me, Boysie. Is Gladys all right?"

"It's not Gladys. It's Urica. She was found unconscious this afternoon."

A million scenarios flicker through my mind. None of them good. "I was going to stop by today after work and I completely forgot."

"Wouldn't have made any difference. A passerby found her beside the highway. Looks like someone tried to strange her."

Chapter Fourteen
Piper

S he and Obie would sometimes exchange cheesy texts, each trying to out-groan the other. A loud thud outside upset her for a moment, but the cattle often made strange noises at night.

When he didn't respond, her first thought was that she had upset him in some way. It was leftover insecurity from her fractious childhood, and nothing to do with sweet Obie.

As minutes turned into hours, her mind began playing tricks on her.

Normally, she was fine living alone, enjoying the solitude. But ever since Sawyer arrived, she was jumpy and nervous all the time. When construction was going on, Truman told her it reminded him of President Grant's porch. "He lived in New York after his presidency. When I visited his home, I pictured him rocking on his porch as he watched his grand-children play. You should feel lucky to have such a fine place to rest your bones."

She thought it was silly at first, but Piper found that after a long day of baking, there was nothing more relaxing than sitting on her porch with a glass of Sassy Lasses in her hand. She'd grown accus-tomed to the sounds and smells of the cattle grazing next door and the occasional car that whizzed by.

There was a strange *Thump. Thump. Thump.* emanating from the remodeled barn that served as both her garage and a storage area for equipment that didn't fit inside.

At first, she told herself it was a figment of her imagination. She opened her window and felt the cool ocean breeze on her face. Silence. As she turned to crawl into bed, she heard it again. *Thump. Thump. Thump.*

Without any thought for her safety, Piper grabbed the small knife Cosmo had given her and raced down the stairs. Once she was outside, the thumping grew louder.

"Stop being a baby, Piper Moonlight Hill!" she chided herself.

She pointed her phone light at the garage. The lights were definitely on. "I'm not scared of you!" she yelled, her hands shaking.

Continuing toward the garage, she flashed her phone light around her, just in case there was something unexpected. A high-pitched squeal from behind caught her off guard and she spun around, flashing her light on the row of trees next to her driveway. Two small eyes glowed in the dark. When they met hers, she realized it was a familiar friend. "I don't have any stale bread for you today, Rascal McTrash Paws." Though her parents had scolded her more than once for feeding a wild animal, she'd grown fond of this raccoon.

Thump. Thump. Thump.

The closer Piper got to the barn, the more her body began to shake. More than anything, she was irritated that she wasn't any braver.

Placing a hand on the door, she turned the knob and burst inside, shouting, "I'm not afraid of you! The police are on their way!"

From behind a large pallet, a familiar face appeared. Ignoring his rule to wait three minutes and ten seconds before the first contact, Piper jumped into Obie's arms. She squeezed his body tightly, and then held his face between her hands, kissing him hard.

"Piper Moonlight Hill, you never fail to surprise me," he whispered.

She smelled the familiar smell of red licorice on his breath. It was his favorite snack, outside of the baked goods she made for him. Despite Obie's aversion to anything sticky, he ate the stuff by the tub full, especially when he was working a challenging case.

"Obie, I'm so glad to see you. I was..." her voice trailed off. She didn't want to admit to him that she was scared. "When you didn't respond to my last text, I thought you might be angry with me, but I'm so glad you showed up instead!"

"I wish I could say that's the reason for my visit. On the way back from Tellum, I got a flat tire. Luckily, it wasn't far from here. You don't mind if I stay the night and fix it in the morning, do you?"

Piper smiled, grateful that fate had brought him to her doorstep tonight. "There's always room at Piper's B and B."

She took his hand and guided him up the porch steps and inside. Relief gushed over her like a high-tide wave.

"What were you doing to cause so much racket?"

"I got the ladder we used to clean windows last month because I wanted to climb up to your window. At least I tried." He touched his head. "Our decision to turn that rickety old thing into firewood is a good one. And I've got a head start on taking it apart."

As soon as the light was on, Piper noticed blood coming from his head.

"You're hurt!"

"The hazards of being the romantic type, you know."

"Why don't you take a shower and I'll make us some tea?"

Obie nodded and kissed her once more before climbing the steps. There was something so much more soothing about his movements as opposed to Sawyer's.

When she'd made his tea—jasmine because it was Tuesday—she checked to make sure the door was locked before heading up the stairs herself.

Obie was drying his hair in her dresser mirror. She suppressed a giggle at the sight of him. The brave policeman who never blinked in the face of danger was wearing his green, footed pajamas, for Tuesdays, of course. Obie also sported a small wound on his forehead.

She set the mugs down on either side of the bed and waited patiently.

"You know there is a task force now, set up between the Piney Falls, Blackberry Cove and Tellum departments, right?"

She nodded.

"You've probably already heard—they found Urica today."

"What? Nobody told me! Is she..."

"No, not dead. Just unconscious. I have to go back to the hospital first thing tomorrow to check on her condition."

"That's good. Do you have any idea what happened to her?"

Obie reached over and picked up his mug, blowing four times before taking a drink. "We're going to retrace her steps tomorrow. Right now, Dad believes someone came into the gallery and kidnapped her. We found carpet fibers in Urica's hair, just like we did with Rusty Mellow. Some kind of grey industrial carpet, from what we can tell."

Though she'd only met Rusty Mellow once during the interview process, he seemed like a very nice man. Piper brought her own tea to her lips—peach mango.

"I'm worried, Pips. Whoever is hurting people isn't messing around."

They drank the rest of their tea in silence before slipping under the covers.

He kissed her tenderly before gently tucking a stray hair behind her ear. "The last time we spoke, you were mad at me."

"Time for Fingertip Confessions." Piper pulled the covers over their heads.

Lying face-to-face, they gazed deep in each other's eyes and pressed fingertips to each other. There was no escaping the truth when they were in such an intimate position.

"Sawyer's not going to come in voluntarily," she began. "He doesn't trust the police after all he's been through. If you don't want to be with me anymore, I get it. You knew I had a lot of baggage from my past, but you didn't agree to my brother being a part of that baggage."

Obie looked at her with surprise. "Why would I do that?" He pulled one hand away and instantly, she retrieved it.

"Piper Moonlight Hill, you're my everything. Whatever happens, I'll never quit loving you, never."

"Obie Lumquest, everyone in my life has been worried about me," Piper began. "I guess I shouldn't be upset. It's what I always wanted. It just hurts because it's my brother, and no one knows him like I do. Your turn."

She forced the tears forming in her eyes away. There was no withdrawing a hand to wipe away emotion. An agreed-upon rule.

"You've got a heart big enough for everyone, Pips. Your brother is probably a great guy, and it's unlikely he would hurt his only family. Everyone has a right to—"

She tried to pull away but he was too quick. Obie grabbed her hand. "You know the rules, Pip, we have to listen till the end."

She nodded and he eased his grip.

"Tell me about Sawyer. Make me understand him," Obie insisted.

She began with stories of their childhood. "I once convinced him to eat an entire jar of peanut butter. I told Sawyer it would stick to the gum he swallowed and get it out of his system." Piper smiled. "He's always wanted to make people happy."

After five more stories, Obie's eyes fluttered and he yawned. "More Fingertip Confessions than usual, and I've got a long day ahead of me tomorrow."

When the sunlight woke her, she rolled over, planning to burrow her nose in his neck, drinking in his scent, a mixture of high-quality soap and orange peels.

Instead, the other side of the bed was empty. She tiptoed downstairs, forgetting that her brother would already be out on deliveries. She started the coffee pot and jumped when she heard Obie clear his throat.

"There you are, babe! I was worried when you weren't in bed!"

He was already dressed in his uniform, the spare he kept in his trunk at all times. Obie was holding the radar detector Sawyer gave her.

"It's not what it looks like. Sawyer was being very thoughtful when he gave that to me. I explained that my boyfriend wouldn't appreciate my using one. I'll return it over the weekend."

Piper turned back around, pulling a clean Cosmic Bakes Takes You on a Ride mug from the dishwasher. As soon as she filled her mug and turned around, she was unsettled to find Obie standing in the same position.

"What?"

"Piper, your brother didn't buy this."

"How would you know that, Obie?" she asked, annoyed.

"Because we found the receipt in Rusty Mellow's apartment after his murder. He bought it the morning he was killed."

She studied his face, looking for signs of the loving man she'd fallen asleep with the night before. Instead, all she saw was a police officer who was grilling a suspect.

"I'm sure there are plenty—"

"The serial number on the box matches the receipt, Pips. I've got pictures of the receipt on my phone."

"I don't want to see it, Obie."

"There's something else I need to tell you."

"I've got to get ready for work," she insisted. "I don't have time for this."

Obie set the box down and grabbed her arm. "Please! Just give me five minutes."

She nodded and set her mug down. "Five minutes. Then I really need to get started."

He patted both of his shoulders and walked in a circle three times before he began. "I did some research on the Broken Branch movement. At first, they tried to do volunteer work, like playing bingo at the nursing home and opening a food bank for the hungry. But they had a change in leadership and they devolved into a bunch of thugs who robbed elderly people."

"If you're thinking my brother was involved, you're wrong. He left the group and traveled around the country. I'm sure that's why."

Obie nodded. "Well, after a robbery-gone-bad, when they killed three people, the Broken Branch ended up in the Ohio State Prison. That's when things get interesting."

Piper's eyes widened as she took in this information. Sawyer probably had no idea.

"They joined forces with Starfish Syndicate Crime Syndicate. It's a big operation, with branches in four states."

"Why are you telling me this?" She was growing tired of this story.

"Please, be patient, Pips. I promise, it will all make sense." Obie took a deep breath. "It's long been rumored that The Faceless control their own from prison, but the leader of the group remains unknown. Three years ago, this unknown thug ordered a hit on a woman who'd been involved with his brother on the outside. The woman pretended to be pregnant and bilked his brother out of lots of money."

The hairs on Piper's neck stood up.

"That's the murder your brother was in prison

for, Piper. I found it very strange that he was released so soon. So, I called the warden. He said the Starfish Syndicate, a mob composed mostly of ex-cons, have lots of money, which means good representation. They always know when someone joins, because pretty soon lawyers in expensive suits show up." Obie took a deep breath before continuing. "Three people were released after the judge commuted their sentence, your brother and two known members of Starfish Syndicate Crime Syndicate."

She was...what was she? Angry at Obie? Angry at Sawyer? Ashamed? Horrified?

"I had to be sa-sa-sure, Pips, before I talked to you. This morning, I confronted your brother. He didn't deny any of it."

"Wait—you spent the night so you could spy on my brother?"

She lurched forward, grabbing the box with the radar detector in it.

"I wanted to keep you safe, ba-ba-babe."

Obie, whose stuttering was evidence he was upset, opened his arms. Instead of the desired effect, his gesture upset her even more.

"Leave right now!" she cried. "I don't want to see you ever again, Obie Lumquest!"

His face displayed shock. He didn't move, perhaps unsure if he heard her right.

"I SAID LEAVE!" she screamed.

Obie moved slowly toward the kitchen door. "Think about what I said, Pips. I love you. That's the only reason I'm here."

"No it isn't! You're here because you can't ever quit being a cop! You hatched this plot to spy on my brother and used me to do it! I'm sure Sawyer was just as shocked as I was, and probably tried to tell you what you wanted to hear, just so you'll leave him alone. She paused to blow her nose. "I've wasted years of my life with a man I don't even know!" she sobbed.

Piper flopped down in the nearest chair. He reached for her shoulder and she brushed his hand away.

She listened as he walked outside and started his car. One part of her, the part that was weak, wanted to chase his car down the gravel drive and tell him she didn't mean it.

As she went about her day, she was grateful she had so many orders to fill. It kept her mind of the giant wound inside her. When Sawyer arrived, finished with his deliveries, she was relieved her tears were dried.

"Hey there!" she greeted him with all the fake enthusiasm she could muster. "How'd it go today?"

Sawyer scratched the back of his neck. "I got a call from a buddy of mine. I hate to bail on you, but he wants me to help him tomorrow. Would it be okay if you did the deliveries?"

She was equal parts angry and relieved. "Who is it?"

"Surprised your little brother has friends?" He chuckled. "A prison buddy. He told me if I was ever out this direction to look him up. I called when I arrived and he finally got back to me."

"Oh." He wasn't trying to make himself less mysterious. "What time do you think you might be back?"

Sawyer stared at her with blank, dark eyes. A shiver ran down her spine.

"Hard to say. I'm going to leave now. He's got a place and invited me to stay the night."

She couldn't shake the horrible, awful feeling that she was much safer without her brother around.

Chapter Fifteen
Lanie

"Lanie. Lanie. Lanie."

"What?"

Vem called in a state of high anxiety, which does nothing for mine. With the news of Urica's attack and Piper calling tearfully this morning to inform me she'd broken up with Obie, I'm already at my wit's end. It's not even nine a.m.

"I had another dream last night. I know FOR SURE where the body is!"

"Vem, they found the body already. Rusty was found in Tellum, remember?"

"You're not listening to me, sister friend."

Vem pauses to clear her throat. It's not a quick process. There's a tree bark mixture that needs to ferment before she can use it. While I get to experience her varied gurgles and grunts, Cedar joins me in the kitchen.

"I thought I should spend some time catching up on work today, Lanie," she says cheerily, kissing me on the cheek. "Until our girls' lunch."

"Enjoy some breakfast and we'll talk about it just as soon as November is done with her story."

Cedar nods and takes a plate full of miniature chocolate frosted cinnamon rolls, scrambled eggs and fresh berries to the table.

"Are you still alive and kicking?" I say into the phone.

"You're not as funny as you think, Lanie. While you were talking to Cedar, I came to a decision. A barter, so-to-speak."

I load my plate with breakfast, holding the phone to my ear with one shoulder. "What are we bartering? You take whatever you need from my house already."

"I'll turn off camera number three for a week if you'll go with me this morning. To find the body."

Her offer is tempting. Cosmo has purposely walked around naked near the window, just to infuriate her. "Okay, I'll go with you. But only for one hour. I've got other things to do today!"

"You come over in fifteen minutes!" she demands.

"Twenty!" I say into a dead phone.

Joining Cedar in the dining room, I'm pleased that she smiles when she sees me. Her face is relaxed, as is her posture. Glancing at her plate, I'm pleased to see that she's eaten almost everything on it.

"If I didn't know any better, I'd think that you were happy to be rid of me!" She laughs, her eyes full of the merriment I'm used to. Whatever has been torturing her beautiful soul is, at least for now, out of her mind.

"Not at all. I need to get some work done too. The Fallen Branch Resort is coming up on its busiest season and we're beginning a nation-wide campaign." I smile at her, hoping she'll recognize this major accomplishment.

"What would they do without you?" she asks, taking a delicate bite of a cinnamon roll. "Mm. These are fabulous!"

"Piper's creation."

Instantly, my brain switches to my daughter's world. I'm so sad for her and Obie. It feels like my own loss. Is this a normal emotion for a mother? "I'll invite her over again. She'll want to absorb all the auntie time she can while you're here."

"Yes, I'd like to take her shopping and whatever else she enjoys."

"She wouldn't say no to a pedicure," I remark. "It's almost like she and I were destined to become mother and daughter."

Cedar chuckles, causing me to stare at her. "I'd forgotten how much I love your laugh. Please do it every single day for the rest of your visit!"

"I'll try." Instantly, her face and her mind travel to somewhere else. Somewhere sad that has been chasing her ever since she arrived.

"Anyway, as I was saying, I need to go in to work, and—"

Don't over explain, Lanie. It's the surest way to raise suspicions.

"Are you all right, sis?"

Cedar leans over the table and touches me. I pull my hand back in shock—the last time we touched hands, perhaps it was during her Christmas visit, her hands were as soft as a baby's bottom. Today they are rough and worn."

"Did I do something wrong?"

"Oh, no hon. Your poor hands!"

Jumping up, I retrieve the lotion that's working miracles for me and hand it to her.

She reads the label and looks at me with skepticism. "Rub Me Wrong? Is this a joke?"

"This is November's new product. She's working on a whole line of skincare products. Despite what you might think—what I thought as well—it's the best lotion I've ever used," I insist. "Your hands will de-age two decades overnight."

She takes the lid off and smells it. "What is that? It smells like heaven!"

"This is the one she calls Basil in the Yard. Give it a try!"

While she's rubbing it on her arms, she remarks, "Do I want to know what's in here?"

"Probably not."

It's all natural, Lanie. Full of things I found on the forest floor.

Is there any kind of animal poop in there, Vem?

Lanie, you insult me. It's called "waste."

"Lanie? Did you hear me?"

"What? Oh, sorry. My mind tends to wander. What did you say?"

"I was asking if you wanted to meet at the bakery for lunch around one. Will that work?"

"Perfect, sis. I'll see you there. I should have most of my work done by then. Now, don't work too hard. You are on vacation this week," I caution. "Your brother will blow a gasket if he knows I let you open your laptop."

She gives me the thumbs up sign. As I walk out the back door, I'm alternately relieved and guilt-ridden that I've escaped so easily.

Vem is pacing in her garage when I arrive. Her magenta jumpsuit is a blur as she moves quickly in front of me. It doesn't come as a shock, she's very punctual and I did tell her we'd leave thirty minutes ago.

"Lanie Lovey Ander-shill, when you tell a person you're coming at a certain time, you need to show!" She taps her large-faced magenta watch for emphasis.

Ignoring her botched attempt at my name, I tilt my head to the side. "I'm so sorry, Vem. Cedar got up late. I couldn't just run out. She'd be suspicious."

Vem folds her hands across her chest, displaying admirable bulging biceps. She taps a magenta shoe on the cement in irritation.

"Vem, I could apologize all day, but then we'd miss this important window of opportunity. You're just as curious as I am about Cedar's comings-and-goings."

"We're going to find the body, Lanie."

"What if we do both? And then we'll meet Cedar for lunch."

"Hmph," she sniffs, unlocking her car door. Today, it appears we're taking the armor-plated SUV she bought at a government equipment auction. All of the windows are blacked out and it's got several self-defense mechanisms, including a button that will shoot a toxic plume out the exhaust. It gets six miles per gallon.

"Vem, are you sure this is a good idea? You're the only one in town with this type of vehicle. If we're somewhere we want to remain incognito, this beast isn't going to do it."

Her eyes flash in anger. "Lanie! Get...in...the...car!"

Unused to being on the receiving end of her temper, I lift myself up to the elevated seat and close the door, proud that my current physical fitness allows for these kind of gymnastic moves.

She starts the ridiculously loud engine and opens the garage door. As we're backing out, she says, "This way, Cedar will think you went to my place for a moan."

"You've got a point, Vem," I say, remembering that I told Cedar I would be leaving and my car is still in the garage.

"And number two," she continues as we make our way winding down the mountain we live on, "we have no idea what kind of nefarious activity your sister-in-law has been involved in. For all we know, she's going to lead us into a twisted den of violent crimes and thuggery."

This is usually the point where I bring Vem back to planet earth, explaining why her outlandish theories are wrong. But today, I have no response. The Cedar who showed up at our place three days ago is not the Cedar I know.

"I've taken the liberty of entering all of the locations from her GPS into mine. You might appreciate knowing that Cedar rented a very cheap car. When I was stealing her information, an ugly grey carpet practically leapt onto my head."

"Vem," I begin, suppressing a giggle, "your beautiful hair grabs onto anything nearby. Tree branches, leaves, frosting, you name it."

"True, true."

There is a very large display screen on her elaborate dashboard. I've had television sets with smaller screens. I see several pin drops around town and in the country. Vem touches the screen and a voice, her voice says, "Good morning, you sexy goddess. I'll take you to your first location now."

"I didn't realize this was a self-driving car!"

"I'm a woman of mystery, Lanie!"

Fascinated by this unexpected turn of events, I stare at the steering wheel as we hurl down the highway. "I keep expecting us to get in a horrible crash," I admit.

"I've got my other hand on the emergency brake," Vem admits.

We turn off on Gooseberry Lane and continue down a dirt road for another hour. I've never been here before and I wonder if the car will be able to get a GPS signal.

"Don't worry, Lanie. I've got a backup," Vem says, as if reading my mind. She pulls out a very complicated-looking device I can only assume is a GPS. In harmony with the car, it says, "turn right," and "stop in eight-hundred feet."

When we come to a halt, Vem and I look at each other.

"Not to discount your fancy devices, but are you sure we're in the right place?"

For once, Vem is speechless.

We both jump down to the ground and attempt

to shut the doors. They are so high it takes a windup and a grunt to push mine closed.

This spot is right smack in the middle of nowhere. There are large boulders and a smaller, fuzzier type of pine tree than the majestic dark evergreens near us. In the distance, we can hear the babbling of an energetic brook.

"Where are we, exactly?" I ask. "Why would Cedar come out here?"

"To commune with nature, Lanie. There are all sorts of critters who make this space their home."

November takes my hand and we walk together over the uneven terrain. When we reach the brook, a breathtaking view awaits us. To our left, a snow-covered Mount Hood rises over the tall trees. To our right, a two-level waterfall gushes.

I gasp. "Oh, Vem. This is gorgeous!"

"I'm in agreement, sister-friend." Her head snaps around so fast it's a wonder it's still attached. "Wait... wait just a doggone minute!"

"What is it?"

"I'll be gosh dingleberry darned. This is exactly what I saw in my dream! Bean, you're a genius!"

She takes off, practically sprinting over large boulders, forgetting her friend isn't as nimble.

Once I can join her, we walk closer to the brook, which we can now clearly tell is more of a raging river. There is a half-cut log with a railing attached by way of a bridge. Vem trots up to it and glances back at me. She's positively giddy.

"I'm not sure about this!" I call over the sound of the water.

"What? Are you afraid? I'll help you across!" She holds out a hand.

My mind flashes back to a time we found a hidden trail last summer. It became a treacherous climb against a cliff that gave me nightmares for weeks. "I'll help you, Lanie," November assured me.

When we got to the slipperiest part, where I lost my footing twice, Vem was nowhere to be found. I screamed for her, but from a distance I heard, "Take shallow breaths, Lanie! I'm watching two caterpillars mate!"

"Maybe you should go and I'll wait here," I say, hoping she won't argue.

"Okay," she replies, shrugging.

I watch her make her way across the half-log with confidence I'll never possess. If I'm not mistaken, she skips towards the end. When she's out of sight, I find the flattest boulder on which to rest my weary bones.

Pulling out my phone, I'm dismayed to find I don't have any service. "Guess I'll have to appreciate nature," I grumble.

If I brought Cos out here, I'd feel much more confident about crossing the rushing water. He'd offer to carry me across and for a minute, I'd consider the offer.

As I chuckle to myself, I see something in the water. Some small fish swim angrily around it, wiggling their bodies in irritation.

Bringing myself closer to the water, I study the object. It's definitely a phone. I recognize it from the television ads that seem to play every hour. The Hearit 25 is the size of my tablet. Cos and I often joke about someone trying to fit it in their pockets.

The other thing I know about this phone is that it costs $5,000. Whoever lost this phone is no doubt trying to find it. Why it wasn't obvious it was dropped here is a mystery for another day. Searching around me, I find a sturdy stick just long enough and drag it inches at a time until it's close enough for me to pick up.

One of the selling points of this phone is that you can take it in the bathtub or shower with you and it will still function. In fact, in the ads a famous man is taking a bath and he dives underwater to read his phone.

After shaking the water from it as well as I can, I search for a way to turn it on. There are three buttons and none of them appear to turn the stupid thing on. When I give up in frustration and place the phone in my pocket, I hear a muffled voice.

It repeats, so I pull the phone out. "Good morning! Do you want me to turn on?" A woman's buttery-smooth voice asks.

"Yes, turn on."

As it's loading, I can see Vem coming back across the log. She's waving some tiny object in the air. I can't watch as she crosses the stream with one hand, using the other to show off her treasure. Probably a rock that has a meaning I've never heard of.

"What did you find?"

She jumps off the log, making me a twinge jealous of her abilities.

"This."

She opens her palm to reveal two bullets.

"You dreamt about bullets? That's amazing, Vem! That you found them out here is, well, unbelievable."

Vem chortles. "You're taunting me, Lanie. I dreamt about a dead body, and I found it. These were beside a red-haired woman."

Chapter Sixteen
Piper

As she was making her second-to-last delivery of fruit-filled rolls, Piper rounded the corner of Peacock and 5th to find a car blocking the road.

"Move it, move it!" she shouted, beating the steering wheel in annoyance. It was bad enough that Sawyer had taken the day off, but now it seemed every street was had an obstruction of some kind. Road work, kids playing—the forces were working against her, and she needed to get a jump start on tomorrow's baking.

An older model gold sedan with no license plates was parked in the middle of the street at an angle that didn't allow other cars to pass.

She tried waiting for it to move, occupying her time by checking her messages. *Nothing from Obie.*

What was she expecting? She'd been very clear with him.

Piper laid on her horn and yelled through her windshield, "Can you move this boat? I don't have all day!"

Two men emerged from the car, each tucking something into the waistbands of their pants. Sensing danger, she hit the automatic dial for Obie and put it on speaker.

"I could be in real danger, Obie! Please tell whoever is following me to get here now!"

As the two men walked closer, she realized one of them was Sawyer. The other man was muscular and wore a scowl on his face. The closer they got, the more she realized he was sporting a numbered tattoo on his neck, just like her brother.

She rolled down her window a slit, emboldened by the fact that she knew help was on the way.

"What's going on, Sawyer? I need to get down this street to make my last delivery!"

Sawyer leaned against the car, placing an arm on top of her door. Now she was trapped. He could force her to stay in her car. Maybe he was going to light it on fire. She's seen that in movies.

His companion moved to her passenger side, bending down and looking inside. Piper would have found him attractive in any other setting. She felt as though he was staring right through her, causing her to shiver.

"Fancy meeting you here, Sis."

"Yeah, I thought you were going to be out of town? If I'd known—"

Before she'd finished a thought, Sawyer glanced over the top of her car and in a muffled voice mentioned something about it being his sister and something else Piper couldn't make out.

"I need to get through this street, Sawyer. I have to make a delivery. If I don't get it there on time, he'll be really upset." She was hoping she could appeal to his softer side, if he still had one. "You know I'm still trying to prove myself as a business woman," she added.

"We're kinda in the middle of something, sis. I can take your delivery for you. Car problems, you know. Mom and Dad used to run out of gas at the damnedest places!"

This wasn't at all what she was expecting. "Really? I mean, if you need gas, I could get some for you! I've got a credit account at the Pump Stump. They'll be happy to let you charge whatever you need."

He tapped the top of the car with one hand, perhaps as a signal to his friend, before leaning in her window. "Always the helper. Piper Moonlight, lover of all."

Her cheeks burned. She couldn't tell if he was being sarcastic, or if he really believed she was the helpful type. "It's Moonlight Hill now," she corrected him. "Well? Do you want my gas card?" *I'll cancel it tomorrow.*

"Nah. Just give me your order and I'll deliver it."

They had reached an impasse. The very last thing to do, she'd learned from November's self-defense class, was to push someone who had a hair trigger.

"Okay. The address is on the box." She reached over to the passenger seat and handed him the box. "Don't let Mr. Craig tell you I've shorted him. Last month, when he had a similar gathering of church friends, he tricked me into an extra two-dozen cookies."

Sawyer chuckled and shook his head. "See you back at home, Sis."

He motioned to his friend and both of them walked down the street.

As soon as they were out of sight, she heard tires screeching behind her. Looking in the mirror, she saw a Piney Falls Police vehicle.

The deputy, someone she didn't recognize, jumped out of the car and rushed up to her. "We got your call, Ms. Hill. Who is bothering you?"

"It was all a big misunderstanding. My brother and his friend were acting weird. I apologize for making you come."

He glanced over at the car still parking sideways in the street.

"I'll run the serial number and see what pops up."

Chapter Seventeen
Piper

The dead woman, whose name was Harmony Gregory, died in the same manner as Rusty Mellow: gunshot and strangulation. But everyone in Piney Falls knew what that meant: they'd acquired their very own serial killer. The whole town was abuzz.

Because there were so many violent endings in Piney Falls, single murders didn't even cause a ripple in the town. The locals made light of it, making hats and shirts that read, "Piney Falls: You'll come for the scenery and stay for the ending."

Lanie refused to include this in any of her marketing materials though, finding it totally distasteful. Piper was proud of her mother for attempting to bring some decorum back to their little community.

The local paper decided to capitalize on their newfound notoriety by creating a Name The Serial Killer contest. The winner would receive a plaque with their name on it, a year's supply of Cheese With Your Burger coupons, and a free sunset cruise on the Flanagan Fair Weather, dinner extra.

The town was divided evenly, with half finding the contest repulsive while the other half had "name the killer" parties at their homes and coffee houses.

Piper volunteered to fill in for Doris while she attended a gathering in the park for the victims, followed by a community barbecue. Piper had an ulterior motive: she was able to avoid her brother.

"I have to work in town for a couple of days, Sawyer. Since we're all caught up on orders here, you should do some sightseeing."

Sawyer's eyes narrowed in what she now recognized was his show of distrust. "Why? Are you afraid of me?"

"No, that's not..." her voice trailed off as she swallowed hard. "You're welcome to come to the bakery in town with me. I just thought you might get bored after your deliveries."

His expression softened. "Oh. Gotcha. But you don't have to worry about me. Remember that friend I told you about?"

She thought back to the afternoon she was trying to finish deliveries and they were blocking the street.

The whole situation was never really explained to her. "Yeah, Tom, wasn't it?"

"Sis, you're still so bad with names." Sawyer chided her. "It's Brad. He's got a cabin outside of town and he invited me to come stay. As long as you wouldn't mind, I'd like to drive out there after I'm done today."

She struggled to keep a straight face. *Would she mind?* She would be eternally grateful to Brad!

"Go enjoy yourself, Bro."

Sawyer bent down and kissed her on the cheek. Piper jumped instinctively with his touch.

As the day wore on, she realized she felt so much lighter. Along with the realization that Sawyer was the source of her stress and her neck pain.

"Pips, did you hear anything I said?"

She looked up, realizing she'd been off in another world. It was a relief to come back to this one and Obie's loving face. "Hi, babe! Aren't you a sight for sore eyes!"

Immediately she regretted her words. "I mean, it's good to see you, officer."

Red faced, she glanced at the officer accompanying Obie. He was about Obie's age but his uniform was dark green.

"This is Officer Billings. He's assisting us, on loan from Blackberry Cove."

The muscular, chestnut-haired man thrust his

hand out. "Pips, is it? Why haven't I come for coffee before today?"

"It's actually Piper."

She stole a glance at Obie, who was tapping his fingers on the counter in five thump increments. It was his "I'm going to stay calm" tap.

"All day, people have been showing up at the station using any excuse they can to try and extract information about these cases. I've never seen anything like it," Officer Billings confided, as though they were now friends.

"Dad's ready to lock the place up," Obie added. "He's actually checked into orange cones to set in front of the building. You know how my dad is, though. All talk."

Piper poured Obie's favorite coffee and set one sugar packet, two stir sticks and one napkin on the counter, just the way he liked. "What can I get for you, Officer Billings?"

He grinned so wide she saw every single one of his molars. "Whatever you poured for my friend, here."

She followed him to a clean table, where Piper used a fresh-from-the-cleaner rag to wipe it down again before they were seated.

Obie dusted off a chair with his handkerchief and patted his shoulders twice before seating himself. "Piper's mother found the female." His voice was matter-of-fact.

"Technically, it was November Bean who found her. My mom waited on the other side of the bridge for the police. Did they figure out who it was?"

Obie glanced around. It was farcical to think the rest of the place didn't already have this information. "Her name was Harmony Gregory. From the Gregory Winery family."

He paused.

"Is that name supposed to mean something to me?"

"They invented Sparklegeez, the carbonated wine in the can!"

"Ohh." She'd never heard of them or their strange wine. "Was she kidnapped or something?"

Obie shook his head. "We don't think so, but we're still trying to piece things together. Her family said she was on a trip with her boyfriend, a Sterling Truth."

Officer Billings smiled again. "We haven't found Mr. Truth yet. You know boyfriends, they're always trouble." He winked at Piper and she turned her head away quickly.

Though there was plenty to keep her busy, she scanned her mind to find a reason to stay by their table. "What's this about our police department being used as a tourist stop?" she asked.

"You wouldn't believe some of them, Pips. Mrs. Ogilvine lost her purse two months ago, and oh, by the way, what did we know about the serial killer?"

Piper put her hand up to her mouth as she giggled. "What else?"

"Let's see...The Snells—Jonas and Barbara, not the juniors—stopped by to see if we'd ever found the owner of the dog that wandered into their yard."

"That seems legit!"

Obie leaned forward. "I looked up their initial report." Obie placed his palm in the air. "It was five years ago."

"Let me guess," Piper rolled her eyes, "they were also interested in the serial killer?"

"Ya-ya-you got it." Obie sipped his coffee and stared at the people milling around the antique side of the shop.

Their familiar banter left her sad. "I should get back to work." She didn't make any attempt to move.

Obie's hand bounced excitedly on the table. "After all of our problems, I never thought I'd say this, but it's really great to work a case with him. He's got so much experience, it's like learning from a master."

Just this morning, Boysie was in for coffee bragging about his son. "The boy's really a chip off the old block, Piper."

"Your dad feels the same way about you, Obie."

Obie shook his head. "Ya-ya-you don't have to butter me up, Pips. I already love you. It's not like my dad to say something like that."

She swallowed hard.

"Oh, are you two a thing?" Officer Billings scratched his head. "Never would have figured."

"We're not," Piper said tersely. "Tell me what you and Boysie decided about the case."

Chapter Eighteen
Lanie

I set my alarm for early morning. I don't know why I bother, because it's not like this night produced much sleep anyway. Keeping secrets from my husband, no matter how small, makes for a very sleepless and cranky Lanie.

Sneaking out to the kitchen to start the coffee, I can see the light on in Vem's moan studio. She's always raving about her Moaning for Mornings class. "They know how to moan out their nighttime garbage, Lanie!"

I have an idea, possibly a really bad one. "Hello! And welcome to the Piney Falls Blood Bank Hotline. Are you ready to bleed? This month our volunteer coordinator is...Ureeeka Jollopy."

I giggle at the mispronunciation, but the thought of her still unconscious in the hospital is sobering.

Instead, someone else answers the phone. "Gladys?" I whisper. "It's Lanie."

"I gathered," she says, unwilling to match my soft tone. "What's got you up this early, toots? I thought you were more of a 'sleep till lunch' kind of gal."

It stings a little, hearing her say that. "I've gone with Cos lots of mornings to open the bakery." I retort. "We leave here by five a.m."

The other entirely-too-sneaky thing I did this morning was shut off his alarm. I texted Doris that I thought he deserved extra sleep. She agreed. I'll only be able to get away with this once, so I need to make it count.

"What time do you open?" I whisper. "The blood bank, I mean."

"You dragged yourself out of bed to ask me that?" Gladys's voice rises at the end.

"I can't explain it all now, but it's important. I'm bringing Cedar in today to donate."

There is silence on the other end of the line and I can only guess what Gladys is thinking. She's only this quiet when she's working up a good story in her head.

"So, just to be clear: you set your alarm, hopped out of bed and called me. You're so anxious for Cedar to give blood that you wanted to make sure you two were the first in line. Did I get that right? And does that make sense, when I say it out loud?"

"I get it, Gladys. This doesn't sound rational."

"It doesn't, toots. You've never taken part in our blood drives before. Not that I don't appreciate your doing it now. Is this something I'll have to testify about in court later on?"

I take a deep breath. "Nobody will come after you, I promise. Now, please tell me what time Cedar and I should be there?"

"Let me look at the schedule for today. Hold on."

"Lanie? What are you doing up at this hour? Did you get confused and think you were needed at the bakery today?"

I can hear the panic in Cosmo's voice. "It's okay, hon. Doris is taking care of everything. She wanted me to let you sleep in."

There's only a hint of guilt in my voice. Putting all of this on Doris's shoulders is low.

"Okay, let's see. I can squeeze you ladies in at ten. You're in luck, we have two nail technicians here today. They'll be able to give you pedicures while you're donating, if you'd like."

"I would like, Gladys! I'm sure Cedar won't argue either. We'll see you at ten. And thank you, for —everything."

I hang up and turn around to find my husband slamming his bowl on the counter. He dumps half the box of Go Bonkers for Bran cereal in the small bowl and sloshes milk over the top.

"You're angry," I say, stating the painfully obvious.

He takes a large bite and chews while he speaks. "Lanie, you never get up this early unless you're coming in with me. When I think about you getting up and sneaking out, I—" He stops mid-chew. "Wait a minute. You're up to something!"

"You're barely awake, Cos. You're not thinking clearly." I busy myself finding my own bowl and empty what's left of the cereal box in it.

"You were on the phone with a fellow conspirator," he begins.

My shoulders tense. My husband catches on quick when he sets his mind to it.

"And you were talking about bringing Cedar with you."

The room is silent, with the exception of his loud chewing. Normally it doesn't bother me, but today, it sounds like a large truck driving on gravel right through my living room.

"It's not what you—"

Cosmo drops his spoon and takes me in his arms. "Reason number five-thousand-and-two why I love you, Mrs. Anders-Hill. You're planning a surprise lunch for my sister and inviting all of her friends."

Oh dear.

I hug him tight as this impromptu story dances through my head. "You're always able to read my mind, Cos. Please don't say anything to Cedar. It will ruin everything."

"What are you keeping from Cedar?"

She appears in the kitchen, looking like her old self. Cedar is wearing a lime green cowl-neck sweater and black jeans, accentuating both her slim build and the slightly olive color of her skin. She's already applied makeup and there isn't a silver hair out of place.

"You'll just have to wait and see!" I reply happily. There is something fun about a surprise luncheon. "There's coffee ready to go, and I can make you some eggs if you like."

She shakes her head. "Just coffee, thanks."

"I'm going to leave you alone with your brother while I attend to some things." I wink at Cos and he winks back. My poor husband is proud of the secret we're sharing that's not a real secret at all. "While you're eating together, please remind your brother that he's allowed to sleep in once in a while."

Cedar cocks her head to the side, examining her brother's face. "Cos? Are you working too hard again?"

I leave the room quickly, relieved I can make my escape without it looking suspicious.

After texting Boysie about the blood sample, using the words "suspect, someone you don't know," instead of Cedar's name, I call Gladys back.

"Now Lanie, you didn't miss me already?" she teases.

"I need to plan a lunch for Cedar. It's too late to have Piper bring food and she's busy with her brother anyway. Could you call Chez Pine and order lunch for five?"

"To be delivered to the blood bank? That sounds...weird."

"No, let's have it delivered to the welcome center. She worked there for so long, I know she'd be thrilled to see the changes since she left."

"Who else am I inviting to this shindig?"

I want to reach through the phone and hug her. "Thank you so much for asking. I guess you could call anyone from the Fallen Branch Cult that she spent time with. Tell Chez Pine I'll come and pay for everything this afternoon."

"One of these days, you're gonna come into my art studio and tell me everything. Right?"

"Right."

Hanging up, I feel relieved, as well as very tired. This body isn't used to keeping these hours. At least I've covered every lie I've told this morning.

The front door slams shut and I rush out to see what's going on.

"Cos left. He's got too many orders to leave it all to Doris today."

"Well, see if I give him the gift of extra sleep again!" I reply in mock hurt. "We've got a full day anyway."

"Oh?" She sets her cup down and stares at me hopefully.

"There's a big blood drive going on, so I told

Gladys we would be happy to donate. I know that's not pleasant, but it's much needed."

"Oh." Cedar's face looks like I popped her favorite balloon.

"That's not the surprise though. When we're finished donating, we'll be going somewhere special for lunch."

She nods and looks away.

"Did I say something wrong?"

"No, sis. I'm sorry." Tears wash over her cheeks. "These past six months have been so stressful. There are things besides...well, it's just been hard." She pauses, her eyes darting back and forth. "Sterling did a number on my head, I guess."

Swallowing hard, I try not to think about the red-haired woman I watched them take out of the scenic area in a body bag. Though it was partially zipped, some of her curls cascaded off the side of the stretcher.

"I'm so sorry, Cedar."

"I was so naïve; I hate myself for playing right into his hands."

I pull out a chair and sit down next to her. "Tell me more."

Cedar, though in tears, is displaying an emotion I'm not familiar with. Is it disgust? Anger? Whatever it is, it's making me very uncomfortable.

"You actually don't have to tell me anything if you don't want."

"We talked about moving in together," she says quickly. "Sterling wanted to introduce me to his family first, though." Her words and her face don't match. If I'm not mistaken, she really didn't want to move in with Sterling at all.

"I told him I would eventually. I wanted to take things slow, cautious."

She sniffs and I hand her a tissue. "There were little signs here and there that I chose to ignore. Nightly calls at the same time every evening, for one. It didn't matter if we were in the middle of dinner, or another activity. He always stepped out of earshot to speak on the phone."

I frown. "That is odd."

"One night, we were in the middle of a romantic dinner. He got up and left as we ordered dessert. I decided this time, I would follow him."

"What did you see?"

"He was outside the restaurant, on his phone. The closer I got, the more I could hear him yelling into the phone. Something about keeping up appearances, and he wouldn't do it much longer. His voice was...evil." Her voice wavers. "And you know what happened in the motel."

"I've been meaning to talk to you about that, Cedar. Vem and I did some research. We haven't found anything at all to indicate Sterling Truth is dead."

I'm expecting her to throw her arms around me

and hug it out. Instead, she's got another surprise up her sleeve.

"That's how things work with the uber rich, Lanie," she explains matter-of-factly. "They decide when and where to announce a death. I'm sure it will come out in all of the papers, just as I'm being arrested."

I don't want to disagree, but we spent hours scouring the internet, even enlisting Gladys's help. There isn't a death certificate, a comment from friends on social media—nothing. Sterling Truth is most certainly not dead.

We should get going," I say, standing and taking her coffee cup. "Sterling was —is— a real jerk."

"The jerkiest."

When we arrive at the blood bank, Gladys is ready for us. We sit down and begin our blood with-drawal as the two nail technicians start working on our feet.

"A pedicure while your blood is being drawn is a great idea, Gladys!" Cedar says enthusiastically.

"Thought of it myself," she crows. "I wasn't sure we should do something fun while Urica is down for the count, though."

"Is there any update on her condition?"

Gladys shakes her head. "Still out like a light. I hope there's still somebody at home in there."

After luxurious pedicures and not-so-luxurious

blood draws, we eat our cookies and drink orange juice while Gladys labels our bags.

"It was my understanding that you give us a blood type after we're done?"

Both Gladys and Cedar stare at me.

"You plannin' on needing extra, toots?" Gladys asks.

"No. Of course not. It's...just a good thing to know."

"Somebody will call you. Probably next week. We're all volunteers you know."

Hiding my frustration, I turn to Cedar. "We've got another surprise for you when this is done, sis."

A quick glance at Gladys tells me she's handled everything.

"When are we going to be planning a wedding for you?" Gladys asks out of the blue.

"What?"

I'm trying to get her attention, banging on my armrest with my free arm. Gladys isn't getting the message.

"Oh, you're such a pretty gal, Cedar. Every guy within a hundred miles of Piney Falls wanted to date you. Can't imagine things are much different in San Diego."

Cedar stares at me helplessly with tears forming in her eyes again.

"She's taking a hiatus from dating, Gladys," I explain. "Aren't we lucky to have her here with us?"

"We sure are. I can tell you who isn't lucky though: that gal they found out in the middle of nowhere." Gladys stares at me. "Did you tell her, Lanie?"

"Tell me what?"

"That redheaded gal they found. Poor thing. Boysie's ruling it a homicide."

Chapter Nineteen
Piper

"Maybe I'm overreacting."

"I don't believe you are."

Lanie brought her coffee to her lips for the second time. Piper observed an interesting fact about her mother: when Lanie was upset, she sipped her coffee in a rhythm of one, two, down. Sip, sip, down.

Piper hesitated before telling her parents about the incident with Sawyer and his friend.

"You don't have to—"

"Worry? Of course I do. I wouldn't be worth the title of your mother if I didn't."

Sip. Sip. Down.

"What should I do? Throw him out? He's my brother. He doesn't have anyone in his life who cares about him like I do. I'm his only person."

Sip. Sip. Down.

"What if we invited him to stay with us? After Olivene's death, he was there for two weeks. He seemed very comfortable."

"I don't think he would do well with Dad. I know they're buddies now, but Sawyer's mood turns on a dime. I don't want things to become ugly with his boss."

"What's this about ugliness?" Cosmo kissed his wife on the cheek and touched Piper's shoulder before sitting down. "All I see is raving beauty before me."

Sip. Sip. Down.

"Cos, I was suggesting that Sawyer could stay with us for the rest of his visit. He can be a little moody and it's disrupting Piper's workflow. You know she's got so many orders to get out right now."

"I'm not concerned," she began, offering a weak protest. "Yes, I guess I am. Any time I try talking to him about his life and what's got him so upset, he looks at me like I'm the dumbest person in the world. That leads to him stomping up the stairs and a slam of the door."

"He sounds a bit childish," Lanie remarked.

"When I got out of prison, I lived in a halfway house for about a year. The guys with the biggest chips on their shoulders were the ones who earned their early release by promising to repay the debt once they got out. Could be as small as money placed in his prison account for extras, or as big as attorney fees, or...well, let's just leave it at that."

"Really? That doesn't sound like Sawyer."

Lanie turned to look at Cosmo and frowned. Piper had recently taken to calling it her, "worried mama" face.

"That sounds a bit dramatic, Cos," she replied.

Cosmo crossed his legs and rubbed his chin. "I'm not sure there's anything you can do. Contacting Boysie would just put Sawyer in danger, if my suspicions are correct. Never know who is watching. You're going to have to let this one play out, kid. And invite the boy to stay with us. We've got plenty of space."

Piper leaned forward far enough that she could squeeze both of their hands. "Thanks, Mom and Dad. I don't know what I'd do without you."

Boysie entered the bakery and pulled up a chair next to their group.

"What? Are you on a diet again? That didn't go so well last time," Cosmo chided him.

"Wish I was. My appetite's gone for today."

He glanced at Piper with the concern of a grandparent.

"What?" she asked. No sooner than the word was out of her mouth, she realized he must know. "What did Obie say? That's really private, just between he and I."

"You haven't done a thing, Piper." He patted her

leg and looked straight into her lavender eyes. "My boy is working a case this afternoon. I asked him not to contact his girlfriend until today's business is completed. He doesn't need distractions."

Boysie doesn't know. Good.

"Does this have anything to do with the death of Harmony Gregory, Boysie?" Lanie asked.

"Not sure just yet. Unfortunately, all we found on her was an ID—a fake one at that. It wasn't until I ran her prints on the computer that I knew her real name."

"Why were her prints in the system?" Piper asked. She'd been with Obie long enough to know that getting fingerprinted was a big deal.

"She was arrested for suspicion of selling Glitz. I called the station in California this morning and was told Ms. Gregory had a high-priced attorney who got her out of there quick. A follow-up court date was this week, but she was a no-show."

Boysie tapped his fingers together in front of him. "Now, as if that weren't enough for our tiny police department to deal with, we've got a missing person."

"It's starting to feel like we're being targeted," Cosmo observed.

"That's a horrid thought, Cos!" Lanie squeezed her husband's hand just the same.

"He missed his dentist appointment today and a fundraiser he was putting on for the volunteer fire department. His neighbors called us in when they saw trash piled up outside his place. The weird thing is that his car was parked sideways on his street for an entire afternoon. Then it disappeared."

Piper felt a shiver go down her spine. "You're talking about Denver Craig."

"How'd you know?"

"I was supposed to make a delivery there earlier in the week."

Boysie pulled out a small pad with the lettering, "PFPD" across the top, then took a pen from his breast pocket. "What time was this?"

She already felt like she was betraying her brother. What came next would make it even worse.

"I got there and the street was blocked," she began. She'd just finished telling Lanie this story and now that it was being told within the context of an investigation, it wasn't going to make Lanie any less nervous.

Sip. Sip. Down.

"My brother and his friend were blocking the street. He told me there was an accident."

Boysie frowned and pulled out his phone, scrolling through his messages. "Don't see an accident in town. Got several on Highway 101 though. Darn tourists are too busy gawking at the scenery, they don't pay attention when someone stops in front of them."

"I probably got it wrong. I was in a hurry to finish up for the day," she said quickly.

"Now, you're sure that was the address?" Boysie asked when she'd finished.

"Positive."

Cosmo eyed her with concern. "You gonna arrest him? My girl is worried, both for her safety and for the well-being of her brother."

She nodded toward Cosmo with gratitude.

"No, we're just having a friendly chat, Cosmo. I know how sensitive you are about those things. Can't say as I blame you. You'll be one of the first to know if an arrest is made."

Sip. Sip. down.

"Do you...do you think Piper is safe?" Lanie asked.

"I'd like to say yes, but you know this community, Lanie. We have lots of good folks and then, well, there's some real sinister types. Obie's had an off-duty watching Piper's place, so she's in good hands for now."

Boysie winked at Piper and stood, pushing his chair in. The police radio attached to a hook on his shoulder squawked.

He pushed the button and leaned his head to the side. "Go ahead Verna."

"You never told me there was a policeman watching your place!" Lanie said accusingly. "That does it. Your brother is moving in with us tonight!"

"It wasn't really important," she replied dismissively. She hoped Lanie wouldn't question her further. She wasn't prepared to share her unease with the situation.

"We've got a code 419 on Treebark Circle."

All three of them gasped at the same time. Not dramatically, but definitely in unison. They knew exactly what that meant.

"Another dead body?" Lanie gasped.

Boysie shook his head, as if to say, "don't talk while Verna's listening or she'll know I'm telling police business to people who shouldn't know it."

"Copy that, Verna. I'm headed there now." Boysie crossed his arms over his chest and tipped his chin down. "Now, I want all three of you to listen to me. Most of all Lanie."

Lanie frowned.

"I didn't want you to hear that address, but now that you did, I don't want a one of you to follow me." Boysie placed an index finger in the air as a warning. "This is police business. Have no doubt, we're gonna catch this guy. Understood?"

He glanced from Cosmo to Lanie to Piper.

"You've got our word, Boysie," Cosmo replied solemnly.

They all watched as he walked out the door, the jingle of the bell betraying the seriousness of the situation.

"How long do we wait?" Cosmo asked.

Lanie thrust her arms around him. "That's one of many reasons why I married you, Cosmo Hill."

"You guys are going out there?" Piper asked, mortified by their snoopiness. "Shouldn't we wait? If Obie's there, he'll be so mad at me."

"We'll call you, kid." Cosmo disappeared into his office and returned shortly after with his coat and keys.

"Isn't Boysie going to be upset?"

"Yes," they answered in unison.

Piper felt as though she and Lanie had changed bodies. She was a nervous wreck, barely able to keep her mind on her work. For the rest of the day, she vacillated between concern for her own safety and worry for her brother's.

Finally, her phone rang.

"Lanie? What's going on? Do they think it was Sawyer?" she blurted.

She hadn't bothered to check the caller ID.

"Why would they think it was me?"

Piper thought quickly. "I was under the impression that you were in on my surprise party."

"Huh?"

"Yeah...today I overheard some of the regulars

talking about it. Lanie and Cosmo are planning to surprise me with a party celebrating the grand opening of Cosmic Bakes."

Sawyer cleared his throat. "Hasn't that been open for a while now?"

"It has, but we've never done anything really big to make the public aware of what we're doing out there."

There was, in fact, a big party, complete with balloons and four sheet cakes she'd made for the occasion. Obie, Lanie and Cosmo had posed with her in front of her house, holding a plaque commemorating the day. She reached for a notepad and scribbled, "take photo of party off wall."

"When is this party happening? I have lots going on."

He sounded irritated that someone would believe she was deserving of such a fete.

"Next...on Sunday. At two."

Nice save, Piper.

"Okay."

She wasn't sure if that meant he was resigned to attending, or if he was going to make sure he had something to do. Either way, she'd gotten herself out of the situation. For now.

"I'm heading out to my friend's place again. All of the deliveries are done."

"Have fun!" she replied cheerily.

This entire day, the pendulum swung swiftly

from one side of her emotions to the other. She was scared of him, worried about him, and now, grateful for him. If she stood back and looked at it, nothing would make sense.

Glancing at the clock, Piper made the decision to close early. She'd finished her orders in record time, and with Sawyer gone, she could relax and collect her thoughts. As she was sweeping, she heard the bell over the door jingle.

"Sorry, we closed early today," she called absently.

"I'm ha-ha-here to tell you something."

She set her broom down and rushed to the front of the store, where Obie stood with his hands on his hips. She desperately wanted to kiss him, but there was an invisible barrier between them. One she put there.

"What's going on?" she asked, placing one hand on her hip.

"I've been out at a crime scene. No need to pretend like you don't know. Your parents were there too. Your mom was insistent that she see the body, but I finally convinced her it wasn't going to happen."

"Why?"

"Because Denver Craig looked like he put up a fight, Pips." Obie pulled out a chair and sat down, resting his elbows on his knees. "I've seen murder scenes before. But this one really got to me."

She reached for his shoulder to rub it. He always

felt better after one of her signature rubs. At the last second, she remembered they had broken up. "I'm sorry."

"Thanks."

Piper tried to find a way to ask him without seeming heartless for all that he'd experienced that day. "Do you have any idea what happened?"

"He was strangled and shot. Denver placed a call to a burner phone in the hour before he was killed. Tomorrow, I'll follow up on that. I'm just—spent for today."

"Oh no! Obie, I'm so sorry."

He must've remembered their last encounter, as he stood abruptly. "I shouldn't have come."

"No! It's okay!" Piper protested as he walked to the door.

Obie paused with his hand on the knob. "Talk to that brother of yours. If he doesn't come in voluntarily, I'll be picking him up tomorrow. He has some explaining to do."

Chapter Twenty
Lanie

"This is getting too dangerous."

We drive around the block six times before we actually stop.

"He's going to be so mad at us," I say, biting a fingernail.

There has been no word of the dead body for days, other than the identity of the deceased: Denver Craig.

Every morning, I text Cosmo, hoping that some of his regulars have at least spread some rumors. I'll take any crumb.

After finding Harmony Gregory's body, Vem and I couldn't help ourselves—we're knee-deep in this mystery. The information blackout is affecting my best friend too. Vem has a "knowledge headache" that won't go away until we confront Boysie.

"Boysie Lumquest should know by now, we're

the glue that holds this town together, Lanie," Vem reassures me. "He'd be nuts to turn us away. Besides, his mother-in-law would get an earful from you, which means he wouldn't have a moment's peace."

"That's true."

I don't feel so bad walking into the police-station-slash-library building.

"Always a pleasure to see you gals," Boysie says, unplussed by our flustered appearances. "Have a seat. I'm bringing lunch over to Mom soon, so you caught me at a good time."

Vem elbows me sharply in the ribs.

"Ouch!" After giving her my best stern look, I turn to Boysie. "Since we found the deceased female, and now you've found at least two others by my count, we were wondering if—"

"If you could help?"

There are few parking spaces on the street where the police station and library building stands. Because we are a small community, both organizations joined forces to reside in the same building. The Aisley County Jail is on the second floor of the library building. When the city only had enough money for one state-of-the-art building, it was determined most city and county offices could co-exist in one space. Locals often joke about the librarians being trained in self-defense for a possible jail break. The elevator to the second floor is only accessed from the outside, keeping all patrons safe from possible criminal activity.

"I wonder what's going on? Is there a sudden run on library books?"

Instead of parking in front of the building, I find a space three blocks away. It's not like anything is a long hike in Piney Falls, though.

Just as Vem's reaching for the door to the police station, Vem's phone sings, "November Bean, you West Coast Queen."

She looks down and clucks her tongue. "I've got to take this. I'll meet you inside."

"Who is this you keep meeting in secret? A new boyfriend?"

She turns away from me to take the call. I drum my fingers on the table, hoping the sound is bothering her.

When I enter the police station, Boysie is in a heated discussion with Truman.

"You have to understand, you're reaching the edge of my jurisdiction, Truman," Boysie says apologetically.

Truman's face is bright red and there is sweat dripping off his chin. He removes a bright blue handkerchief from the pocket of his overalls and wipes his face. I've never seen him like this, not even when he and Cosmo are in the middle of an arduous project.

"'Eternal vigilance is the price of liberty.' That

little ditty comes from Thomas Jefferson himself, Boysie."

"I understand you loud and clear, really I do."

I detect a helplessness in Boysie's voice that isn't normally there.

Stepping in between them, I decide this is my cue to intervene. "What's going on, boys?"

They turn simultaneously to look at me. I can't tell if either one is pleased to see me.

"Hello, Lanie. So nice to see you today!" Truman removes his cap, displaying a bald dome framed by thick, grey hair.

"I'm surprised you're here, Truman. What brings you into town? I hope you've stopped to see Cos. He'd be so disappointed if you didn't."

It's obvious he hadn't thought of that. "Plannin' to visit him when I'm done here." He turns to face Boysie again. "Mr. Lumquist here isn't one bit concerned about the trespassers on my property. Six of my presidents are lying there..." His voice quivers. "Flat on the ground."

Truman has a small shrine to every single president on his front lawn. He maintains them year-round, including keeping the lightbulbs inside each likeness on at night.

"I've been trying to explain to Mr. Coolidge, for the past thirty minutes, that I've got my hands full with all the local murders to investigate." He glances at me pleadingly. "I'll be happy to make a trip out to Truman's place as soon as things settle down."

I take Truman by the arm and guide him over to the benches where people are able to wait for their loved ones. We sit together and I catch Boysie out of the corner of my eye, rushing back to his office.

"Tell me what happened, Truman. Start from the beginning, please. I got in on the very end of this story."

I've bought Boysie a few minutes that will both serve him and put me in his good graces when I ask for a favor.

"It was the night before last. We'd just finished dinner, Grover and I, when I heard tires squealing. We rushed outside, and Grover took off down the road, chasing after the no-good-nick who damaged my property."

"I'd imagine they were long gone, given the sound of squealing tires."

Truman nods. "The more I surveyed my property, I came to realize the intruders ventured farther than my yard. They were in the field behind my house too."

I squirm uncomfortably. "And how did you come to that conclusion?"

"Oh, there are tire tracks all over that field. I found empty water bottles too. Can't be bothered to pick up their trash," he grumbles. "If Boysie doesn't make it out soon, the rain will wash away all the evidence."

Taking one of his gnarled hands in mine, I lean forward. "Cos will be out to take pictures of whatever you need. Go over to the bakery right now and tell him I said it was fine if he's late for dinner."

Truman stands. His face is much more relaxed than it was when I first arrived. He kisses me lightly on the cheek and says, "You're a true treasure, Lanie Anders-Hill."

Pivoting away from him, I make my way back to Boysie's office. Just as I reach the door, Vem appears.

"Who has been calling you so insistently?"

She shakes her head. "It's private."

This isn't the November Bean I know. Though we've tended to overshare with each other, she is entitled to her privacy.

Boysie is busily filling out paperwork when we enter, so I knock lightly on the door frame so as not to startle him.

"Lanie! Can't thank you enough for that. He's a stubborn old coot." He takes his pen and points to one of two torn leather chairs. "Have a seat."

"Thanks. You're busy, so I'll get right to the point. I'd like to know what you found out about Cedar's blood."

He yanks up his pants before standing to close the door. "I should have known it's been too quiet. I'll tell you what I know, but then you have to promise me that you'll stay out of the way. We've got three different precincts involved now, and if they think we've resorted to using community volunteers, we'll never be able to attend a state conference with a straight face again."

In the seminar, *Hold Your Temper, Hold Your Success*, the speaker, Clem Bender, said that you can't do any harm with silence, but you can end your career with a misinterpreted sentence. He came back to my hotel room after the carblover's buffet and we both fell asleep before anything happened. Though the seminar messages remain, I'm glad to be happily married now.

Boysie opens a drawer in his desk and pulls out a yellow rubber glove. In order to implement cost-cutting measures, Boysie's taken to using the dish-washing gloves his wife buys in bulk every time she goes to Blanfeld's, a big box store, when he's handling evidence.

Once it's on his hand, he picks up the phone to examine it. "One of them fancy phones." He chuckles. "Obie says he wants one for Christmas. This was found next to the most recent body. Hard to keep count."

It's been damaged, but I can tell it's the highest-priced model. The same model we found in the river the day we, or rather Vem, found Harmony Gregory.

"Once you open that, you'll see that it's got a

record of every location the phone has ever been. And you'll also see the contact list."

I bite my bottom lip, unsure if I should remind Boysie of the evidence we uncovered.

"Cat got your tongue, Lanie?"

"Boysie, my bestie here is overcome because she thinks her sister-in-law is a murderous traitor."

"I do not!" I retort, my cheeks burning. "Her name may be in the contact list. That's all I wanted to tell him, Vem."

Now his interest is piqued, and like a dog after a bone, he'll not let this topic go. "Cedar knew this lady? What was their relationship?"

"Oh, they—" Vem begins.

Quickly, I dig my heel into her shoe.

"Ow! Lanie! I've lectured you a million times about that! Foot pokes are to be used for Torture Moan Tuesday only."

"We don't know their exact relationship. Cedar mentioned when she came for vacation that this woman was missing. That's it."

"Missing from where?" Boysie is now using his irritated voice, the one he normally saves for unruly inmates in the county jail. "Lanie, I don't like where this is headed. Now just come out with it and tell me what's going on."

If I tell him everything, Cos will see at it as a betrayal. If I don't tell him everything and it turns out that Cedar is a killer, Cos will look at it as a betrayal.

Finding no happy ending, I decide it's best to clue him in. When I've told him all that I know, I realize my chest feels lighter.

"You think this Harmony gal was connected to Cedar?"

"We have no proof of that, Boysie," I reply quickly.

Vem smacks me on the arm. "Sure we do, Lanie! Harmony was the third person in this goopy love triangle. Cedar and her Hotel Hunk being the other two. Sheesh. Your memory isn't what it used to be."

All of the color in my body has risen to my face.

"And that's why you wanted me to run Cedar's blood through the system. It wasn't that cockamamie story you gave me about some secret genealogy site that reunited relatives of the old Fallen Branch Cult?"

There's no point in lying to him now.

Boysie's personal phone rings. "Yes, Mother. No mayo, got it. Your extra shoes are in the cruiser. Okay. See you soon!"

He hangs up and stares at us. "Why is it that you two ladies could find trouble opening canned corn?"

Feeling slightly offended, I say, "Boysie, there was no trouble to find. I'm being completely trans-parent about my sister-in-law. And we did find one item in the water, near where Harmony's body was found. Vem, give it to him," I urge.

Obediently, Vem opens her suitcase-sized purse

and pulls out a phone identical to the one sitting on his desk. "Pretty smashed up," Vem observes.

I don't want to give Boysie any time to reprimand us.

"And now, Vem and I have a lunch date before I attend her afternoon moaning class."

"Oh, Lanie! Really?"

Vem grabs my arm and squeezes it tightly. I've got that coming after stepping on her foot.

"I've been begging you for months now to try this class. I think you'll really enjoy it!"

"Yes, it's the yoga and moan one, right?"

"No, honey. That happens on Tuesdays. Tonight is the Moan for Gas Relief. It's been very popular."

Boysie is waiting for me to back out, I can tell without looking at him. I don't want to encourage more conversation between us. "Can't wait," I say in my most enthusiastic voice.

"I'll let you two know when I find something. Oh, and I didn't say anything to Mother. You can thank me later."

Just the fact that Boysie calls his mother-in-law "mother" is a good indicator that they are closer than he lets on. By the end of the week, Gladys will know more than I do about this case.

We head over to the bakery for lunch, where Cedar has already gotten us a table. Cos recently added seating on the side of the building, just for the warm and dry months. He was able to fashion a canopy over the top of the space that provides shade but also lets the ever-present wind blow through.

"I was beginning to think you forgot!" Cedar says, kissing me and then Vem on either cheek.

"Oh, you know our Lanie," Vem says matter-of-factly. "If she's not gabbing with someone, then she's on her phone. It's impossible to get a word in edgewise. When we hike, I'll have to hum to myself just to keep my mind from completely zoning out."

Overkill, Vem.

"I thought I recognized you ladies!"

Carlene, Gladys's daughter, appears with her arms full of boxes. She is the activities coordinator at Sassy Lasses Vineyard. She's begun to blossom under Marveline's tutelage.

Vem's phone rings and she hops up quickly, as she's done often as of late. "Who is calling you?" I ask. She has already disappeared into the restroom.

She's entitled to secrets, Lanie.

"We were just at the winery last week and we didn't see you! Cos thought maybe you were doing something else now." I take some boxes from her hands and set them on our table. "Carlene, you know Cedar, right?"

She squints before nodding. "You were a little one when I left the cult, but I do remember those beautiful eyes. How are you?"

"I'm doing very well. I live in San Diego, but I'm

home visiting my family right now." Cedar stares hard.

The way she says that makes me wonder if she's testing me. Does she trust me so little, that I would tell Carlene about Sterling?

"Come out and see us soon. Because there have been some bear sightings, our outdoor seating is closed so you'll need to make reservations."

"Do you need help with these? I could carry them to your car," I offer.

"Yes, that would be wonderful!"

After grabbing two of the five boxes, I follow Carlene to her cute little yellow car.

"I didn't want to say anything in front of everybody," she says as she sets the boxes on the passenger seat. "But we've got another problem. Marveline is beside herself."

Marveline is the owner of Sassy Lasses Vineyard and though she is incredibly knowledgeable when it comes to wines, she can be a bit prickly. "What's going on?"

She takes my two boxes and continues. "Well, last week we had reports of a prowler on the property. We had our security scour all the barns and they didn't find anyone. It wasn't until I went to clean up our new wedding hall that I found something."

Carlene stands up and places her hands on her hips.

"What did you find?"

"Some shoes, an expensive watch and food wrappers. It was like someone had a big party in our field."

"Did you tell Boysie?"

"That's the thing. Marveline doesn't want any more problems. You know in the past, we've had some bad luck on the property."

"Murders, you mean."

"Yes, murders. But she confessed to me that she was visited by three men. They asked her for the watch. When she said she didn't have it, they threatened her. She gave them everything I found. When they were gone, she called me down. I like to go to bed early and I didn't hear a thing. The poor woman was shaking like a leaf."

"That's terrifying! I really think you should tell your brother-in-law! Those boys need to be stopped!"

"I'd like to, but Marveline is adamant that we don't. She's afraid they'll come back."

"I promise you, I won't say anything, you have my word."

"Lanie, there is one more thing."

Carlene stares at her feet and I sense something very dark is about to come from her mouth. "What? The best way to release it is just to get it out."

"When I found all of these items, I also found a business card. It had Cosmo's name on it."

At first I'm at a loss for words. Then I'm angry. "You know, there are any number of reasons his business card might end up there. It could be that someone dropped it while they were taking a tour, or it just blew there from Truman's house. He gets a new card every time he comes into town. He thinks that's a good way to support the bakery."

I realize how foolish I sound. It's not like Cosmo is suspected of killing anyone. There's no need to defend him. "My point is, you have no reason to believe it's connected to Cos."

"Oh goodness, no, Lanie. It has nothing to do with him. I know you guys and would never think that. But it was found with the other items. It was bloody, so I know it was left at the same time as the other items. That's all I was saying."

She pulls out her car keys and walks around to the driver's side of her vehicle. "And now I've upset you. I'm so sorry!"

"No, Carlene, you didn't upset me. It just caught me—"

Before I can finish my sentence, she's jumped in her car, started the engine and taken off. After living off the grid for several decades, she can be easily upset. Even so, I'm feeling bad that I caused her pain.

When I return to the table, Cedar and Vem are perusing the new menu. "That took forever, sister friend!" Vem says. "Was she parked in Tellum?"

I give that my best artificial laugh. "What looks good?"

"I was just telling Cedar that my stomach is a

little wobbly. I think I'll have to go with something light."

Our waitress, a teenager Piper hired, comes over to the table. "Are you guys ready to order?" She asks with questionable enthusiasm.

"Yes, I'll have the French dip, three scones of the day and a large mocha."

Vem slaps her menu on the table. If only I had her metabolism.

"And you?" She points to me with her pen.

"I'll take the salad of the day."

I can't remember what it was, but I know it sounded appealing when Cos explained the menu for this week.

She shifts from one foot to the other. Without looking up, she says, "Guess you're last."

Cedar's phone rings and she retrieves it from her purse. It's the Hearex 25. An exact replica of the two found near dead bodies. Several kicks to Vem's foot prove fruitless to get her attention.

We hear a commotion from the street. There is screaming, loud voices and a lot of chatter.

I jump out of my seat and rush out the door. "What's going on?" I ask. No one seems to have the answer as they hurry past me.

"I'm going to follow the crowd!" I call to my lunch dates. Following the stream of people and excited voices, we head toward Dreary Days Beach. It's on the other side of the highway, but we have a walkway over the top so that we don't have to worry about traffic.

Finally, I reach the other side and I can see a crowd gathered.

Walking up to them, someone grabs my arm. "It's gruesome, Lanie," they warn. Shaking them off, I push my way to the front.

There, in front of me, is a dead body. I've seen them before, so it isn't anything new. But this one is very familiar. "Did anyone check the pockets for identification?" I ask. Immediately, all conversation stops.

"You're asking if we've touched a dead body? The answer would be no."

A smattering of laughter makes its way around the circle.

Reaching down, I stick my hand inside a pocket of his raincoat. Carefully, I saw back and forth until the object is out of his pocket. It's a driver's license, California-issued. Reading it, my heart races. "It's nothing. Just a coupon for a free car wash," I announce to the gathering crowd as I slip it into my own pocket.

"Was it worth it? Touching a dead man's things? What were you thinking, Lanie Anders-Hill?" A lady asks. If I didn't know better, I'd think it was Gladys. I stand and move to the back of the crowd slowly, so as not to cause suspicion. Once I'm on the walking bridge, I pause. Now I can examine the license closer. Age, 44. Height, 5'10. Weight, 200. He is a handsome man with dark eyes and wavy brown hair. His mouth is pulled up on one side, like he is amused by this process of navigating the DMV.

Moving back to the vital statistics, I read his name out loud:

"Sterling Truth."

Chapter Twenty-One
Lanie

My heart and head are in a bad place when I return to the bakery.

"What happened?" Vem and Cedar ask in unison.

"Oh, nothing. It's the remains of a dead whale. Washed up onshore completely untouched."

Though my lie will be easily uncovered, it's all I have the heart for now. I'm no longer interested in alerting Vem to the make and model of Cedar's phone either.

Then there is the matter of my husband.

He worships the ground Cedar walks on and if, for any reason, she was involved in a murder, it would crush him. I just hope I'll have the opportunity to speak with him before he hears about this through the town gossip chain.

"She's already shot someone, Lanie," I say out loud, causing both Vem and Cedar to stare at me.

"Um, why haven't you told me this before, Lanie?" Vem demands. As I'm trying to formulate a believable response, she continues. "Beulah's Plain as Pickles always tasted a little off to me. When I told you that, you insisted it was the grape leaves. Now, you're telling us that Beulah Morehouse uses dead bodies? To flavor her pickles?" Vem shakes her head. "I'll be limiting my next purchase to one jar, I can tell you for a fact."

"So sorry. I got lost in my own thoughts. Remembering the television program I watched last night. It was a murder mystery with lots of twists."

Cedar furrows her brow. "I don't remember watching anything. Maybe I'm the one who needs to worry!"

"Oh, I always watch television in bed, after Cos is asleep," I say quickly.

By the time I get home, I'm mentally exhausted. Vem, understanding me as she does, is completely quiet all the way. She does a little hum and a moan— I think this one is for peace—and then hops out of the car.

I wave to her and before my arm is down, she's rushed to my side, hugging me tight.

When our embrace is over, I watch her walk up her driveway and inside her home. She doesn't even ask if I'm coming to her moan session.

As I walk in the door, I smell something delicious cooking. "Cos?"

"No, sorry, Lanie. It's just me."

I'm relieved to hear Piper's voice, though I wish it was Cos. He needs to hear about Sterling.

"What are you doing here, hon? Don't you have a million more important things to do than make your parents dinner?"

I kiss the top of her head and lean over the pan to see what delight she's feverishly stirring. It looks like a stir fry of some kind, with green and red and yellow vegetables and thick, brown broth.

"I've been neglecting the two people I care about the most, ever since Sawyer arrived. I thought I should stop by and make sure they know I'm still alive."

Sweet girl. "I'm so lucky to have a daughter like you." I kick off my shoes and sit down. "Has Obie given you an update on our serial killer?"

Piper proceeds to relay the latest information on the investigation. Boysie was far less forthcoming.

"Carpet fibers? So the victims were likely kidnapped and taken to these areas to be killed?"

She nods. "That way any evidence is subject to the elements. Rain destroys quite a lot, but ugly grey carpet stays."

Without prior approval, my mind travels back to a conversation with Vem. We were following the directions found on Cedar's GPS when Vem blurted out, "you might appreciate knowing that Cedar rented a very cheap car. When I was stealing her information, an ugly grey carpet practically leapt onto my head."

As quickly as it entered, I discard those words.

Vem will have some way to process the crimes scenes that the police don't. Later, I'll call and ask her.

"Tell me about you and Obie. You must be pleased to have more time to yourself, now that Saw—"

"That'd better be my family in the kitchen! Otherwise, I might have to add some new members, because that smells wonderful!"

Cos and Sawyer appear from the garage. Sawyer doesn't smile when he sees his sister. In fact, if I'm correct, he's disappointed she's here.

"Hi Dad. Brought a strange dude with you, I see," Piper teases playfully.

"I hope you beautiful ladies don't mind. He's been here three days and we have yet to enjoy this handsome guy at our dinner table."

Despite my earlier concerns, the only evidence of Sawyer's presence is the occasional missing food from the refrigerator. I tried stocking the guest house for him, but I guess he must've found it not to his liking.

Cosmo squeezes Sawyer's shoulder. Sawyer jumps slightly at Cosmo's touch, something Cosmo has told me is common with people who've been in prison. A touch is usually the precursor to something bad.

"That's some high praise coming from Cosmo Hill." I hug and kiss my handsome husband before handing him the place mats. "He who brings the company, dresses the table."

Sawyer immediately sits down at the table. After Cosmo has set a place for each of us, he offers to get a beer for Sawyer from the garage. "Anybody else want one?"

"Me!" Piper raises her hand.

When Cos disappears into the garage, I turn to Sawyer. "How are you liking Piney Falls? You've certainly made a fan out of my husband."

Sawyer's face doesn't change. Not one scintilla. "It's fine." This is another characteristic of someone who's spent time in prison. Emotions are only there to show your weakness. Poor kid.

"Are you having any trouble getting around?"

His jaw tightens. "What do you mean?"

It's very odd that this would be the thing that upsets him. "I just wondered if all of those back roads and unmarked streets make it difficult to find your way around."

His jaw eases.

"I didn't mean anything else," I add, feeling like he wants to say something mean to me.

Cosmo re-appears carrying three bottles. He

hands one to Piper and then one to Sawyer. He taps Sawyer's bottle with his and says, "To a job well done."

Sawyer nods slightly and brings the bottle to his lips. Glancing from my husband's face to my daughter's I seem to be the only one in the room who is feeling the tension.

"I was just complimenting Sawyer on his ability to find those tricky streets. Whoever did the naming in this area must've been drunk."

Finally, a little chuckle.

"So drunk, in fact, that they got lost and died at Depression Rock."

Now he is stoic again. I've gone a step too far.

"Time to eat!"

As we load up our plates, I rack my brain for conversation ideas. "Wait! I completely forgot about Cedar! We shouldn't eat without her!"

"No need to worry. After you guys finished your lunch, she came back to the office. We had a good chat and she mentioned that she was going to visit some old Fallen Branch folks. They invited her for dinner somewhere out in the country. She asked me to send her regrets."

That was odd. She never mentioned a word to us today. Did it just slip her mind? Or was it something more sinister?

"Do you know who? I thought she was out of

contact with just about everyone," I say, trying to sound innocent.

Cosmo frowns. "No, and I didn't ask."

"Never mind. Would you pass me the rice, please?"

Piper obliges, giggling.

"Did I say something funny?"

"No, Mom. I'm just remembering when Sawyer and I ate with our parents as kids. Sawyer, do you remember the game we played?"

"Who can make the other one laugh? With our feet?" Sawyer's face is animated. He is a handsome young man when he allows his light to shine.

"We did this thing where we would tickle each other under the table, using our feet. The one who laughed first, had to do the other one's chores," Piper explained.

"Then when Mom and Dad caught on, we had to get really creative," Sawyer says. "We tapped out codes with our fingers on the table. One day when they were in town, we memorized morse code. All through those boring dinners we would tap out stupid things to each other."

"Stupid, insulting things," Piper says. "We were such goofballs."

"Yeah, I guess we were."

I detect a note of sadness in Sawyer's voice. Even though their family was a nightmare, it was the only family he knew.

"Guess I should tell you all what I told Sawyer today. Tomorrow's the day he moves!"

I interpret this as Cosmo's way of telling me he'll be moving into our main house. "The inn is kind of full right now, isn't it Cos?" I say, hoping he catches my hint. After my initial offer, I decided it wouldn't be a good idea to have him on property. Just in case.

"Oh, I guess I made a mistake. What I meant was, I've got that apartment over the bakery that's just sitting there, empty. Not that Piper isn't a great host, but, a guy needs his space."

"That's a wonderful idea!" Piper and I say in unison.

Cosmo stares at me with either admiration or confusion, I can't be sure which.

"You'll still come and pester me though, right bro?"

Sawyer nods. He trains his eyes on his plate.

The rest of the meal is consumed by the things our little family normally discusses: business, local chatter and November Bean.

When we finish, I stand first. "There is a gallon of Rocky Road in the freezer, provided Vem hasn't found it yet."

"I'm too full," Piper says, patting her tiny stomach.

"Me too," Cosmo echoes.

Sawyer doesn't say anything, so I assume he'd like to eat something else. I disappear into the kitchen for a minute, returning with a bowl, a spoon and the large ice cream container.

"I know young guys can eat more than us old folks, so I thought you'd probably like to dish it up yourself."

He jumps up from the table, towering over me. I'm so shocked by this sudden act of aggression that I let out a little scream.

"I didn't want anything!" he seethes.

"Hey, buddy. It's all right." Cosmo grabs his arm and holds on tight until Sawyer returns to the sitting position. He's handling this much more gently than I'd like. "She was just trying to help."

Glancing over at Piper, I can see she is just as uncomfortable as I am. It's a huge relief that he'll be leaving soon. He's got a temper that isn't safe to be around.

Chapter Twenty-Two
Piper

Piper hummed her favorite tune as she placed a pan of cinnamon rolls in the oven. A last-minute order for four-dozen came in just as she was about to drift off to sleep.

Piper, dear heart, we've had a rather sizable addition to the UFO conference. Ten more people showed up with no reservations. Will you be a love and amend our order for the morning?

Being relatively new to the community and the label of business owner, Piper never turned anyone down.

No problem, Wendell! :) I'll have them ready to go, along with your regular order tomorrow morning.

Staying extra busy served two purposes: she knew her father would be pleased by the ever-growing status of their second location and more importantly, she didn't have to think about Obie.

After their heated exchange, Piper refused to take his calls and ignored his texts. She knew she was being unreasonable, but for reasons she didn't under-stand, she couldn't admit she was wrong.

"You're as stubborn as a flock of pigeons in a bread truck accident, girl," she muttered to herself as she used the full weight of her small body to drag the long rolling pin over the dough covering her work-space. In an instant, she regretted her words.

When she was young, Olivene would utter them every time Piper dared question her mother or her motives.

Obie could have been more sensitive to her needs, she told herself. Though neither of them trusted Sawyer entirely, Obie knew about their shared history.

Wasn't he always the one telling her about his sensitivity training?

Yes, now that she thought it through, it was the right thing to do, taking a cooling off period to their relationship.

After the rolls were in the oven, Piper crept up the stairs quietly. Even though Sawyer was gone, she felt nervous. She paused when she got to the guestroom door before turning the knob.

The quilted blue comforter with the image of a scone in the center, (made by Urica Jollopy with love) was pulled up tightly underneath the pillows. There wasn't one wrinkle to be found. It was nothing like the Sawyer she'd known growing up; Piper was tasked with teaching him how to make his bed over and over. He always refused to learn.

She tiptoed in farther and pulled out one dresser drawer. Empty.

Feeling a sense of relief, she continued opening drawers until she got to the bottom. This one contained a small looking glass with some kind of fake stones on the handle. It wasn't the type of thing her brother would carry around, but it was harmless.

When Piper was satisfied the room was empty, she flopped down on the bed and stared at the ceiling. Why couldn't she just accept that her brother was still the Sawyer she knew?

After uttering a series of moans Vem taught her for relaxation, she got up from the bed. As she stood, Piper heard something clunk on the floor on the window side of the bed.

"Great," she muttered. "That's all I need. Broken springs on a practically new bed."

She lifted up the bed skirt to see the damage, but instead of a broken coil, something else caught her eye. It was a gun.

Chapter Twenty-Three
Lanie

"**I**'m renewing my objection to your driving this thing," I say as Vem and I are once more hurdling down the road, heading to the Sassy Lasses Winery in her tank-on-wheels.

"Oh, Lanie, my dear sweet Lanie. I don't know why you resist the luxury of my purchases."

November looks at me instead of the road, causing me to envision our deaths:

Lanie Anders-Hill, killed by the Veminator IV. Upon learning of the manner of his wife's death, Cosmo Hill rolled his eyes so hard, they stuck in the upward position. He is still hospitalized.

"Vem, I'd feel better if you'd watch the road. What would happen if an animal jumped out in front of us right now? Your car wouldn't know to stop." I move my fingers up and down the shoulder belt uncomfortably.

"Don't be silly! This has been tested over and over and over. It stops on a dime. Here, watch this."

She pushes a button and says, "child at five hundred feet."

We screech to a halt, lurching forward despite our seatbelts. Immediately I glance in the rearview mirror, hoping there isn't another vehicle careening into us, unaware of this experiment. "That's nice, but it doesn't help if the animal jumps out in front of us," I reiterate. "You still have to be prepared for the unknown."

Vem shrugs. Some days I'd like to be a guest in that brain of hers. The walls would be multi-colored and the sounds wouldn't be recognizable to the human ear. At least that's how Cos and I have always pictured it.

"Would it bother you if I put some music on, sister friend?"

This is always a trick question. If I say yes, she'll spend the next twenty minutes of our journey trying to convince me that her choice in music is much more enlightened than mine, and therefore it's the smart choice. If I say no, I'll be listening to what amounts to a dog whining in the back yard during a rain storm.

"Whatever you want to do, Vem.

November is dressed today in buttercup yellow,

from her headband to her glasses frames, jumpsuit, watch and sneakers. She pushes an inordinately long string of numbers into the flat screen. "There. You'll really appreciate this one. It speaks to the soul."

A woman's soprano voice begins singing with an acoustic guitar accompanying her. "Vem! This is lovely!"

"Don't act so surprised, Lanie," she replies with hurt in her voice. "Wait until we get to the good part."

She turns it up louder and the lovely voices turns into screeching, torturous tones that could mean a nearby cat is listening in agony. My ears don't know what to do with that sound either, so they just buzz. Quickly I bring my hands to either side of my head. "Turn it down, please!"

"You can't get the full effect of her soul cleansing ballad if you don't listen at high volumes!" Vem protests.

When I don't respond, she huffs before turning it down.

"We're almost there anyway," I say by way of apology. "Marveline swore she never saw Cedar here last night."

"A GPS doesn't lie, Lanie."

When Cedar arrived home, completely disheveled and upset, I texted Vem to check Cedar's GPS via her fancy machine and find out exactly where she'd been. The information she got was that Cedar stopped at a gas station before driving to the

Sassy Lasses Vineyard. She made no other stops on the way home.

"I know it doesn't, Vem." I sigh. This would be so much easier if it wasn't my sister-in-law. "After we found Harmony Gregory's body on what turned out to be the far reaches of Sassy Lasses property, I just couldn't connect that horror to my sweet sister-in-law.

We turn down Naybor Lane and drive up the long, gravel driveway, where Marveline and Carlene are seated on the porch of the formidable Naybor Manor. They both wave when they see us.

November opens her door and jumps down to the ground. "Hiya, ladies!" she says enthusiastically. Just like a child eager to see their grandparents, Vem skips to the end of the drive and bounds up the steps of Naybor Manor.

Without warning, she pulls Marveline in for an embrace. The poor woman has explained many times that she has an aversion to hugs, but once Vem sets her mind to something, there's very little that will change it.

My arrival involves much less fanfare. After gingerly making my way to solid ground, I consider one of Vem's appreciation moans before common sense gets the better of me.

Marveline smiles, perhaps because my presence means Vem has to release her. "Lanie! It's been too long! We've missed you!"

She gestures for us to sit at a round, white table covered in a blue-and-white checked tablecloth. After tucking her flowered kaftan around her, she sits next to Carlene.

"Tulips!" Vem says. At least two-dozen bright pink blooms decorate the center of the table. "I've been meaning to test a tulip-based salve. Do you have any that are almost dead?"

Carlene nods. "Sure thing. When they're done blooming, I'll save them for you."

I'm continually amazed at the change in Carlene Petrie since we first met. Tall, thin, with a weather-beaten face, she looked older than her mother, Gladys. Now, under the tutelage of Marveline, she's blossomed into a beautiful soul, inside and out.

"Carlene! You've cut your hair! It's so flattering!"

She touches her shoulder-length locks. "Do you like it? Marveline talked me into the highlights. I wasn't aware that women our age could wear them!"

She's prepared a light lunch for us, including finger sandwiches, fresh fruit and iced tea. "Sit down, girls. Let's catch up!" Marveline says in an uncharacteristically cheery voice.

As we eat, Vem and I catch her up on the investigation.

"As you can imagine, Carlene and I are still reeling from the news a body was found on the outskirts of my property."

Marveline takes a delicate bite of her sandwich,

wiping the corners of her mouth with a navy blue cloth napkin. "On the phone, you mentioned some kind of a gathering here last evening. I can assure you that no such gathering took place," Marveline insists between delicate bites. "But after lunch, we can all take a walk and see what we find."

Carlene disappears inside and re-appears momentarily with more tea and a plate of chocolate chip cookies. I can almost hear Vem's brain. I just hope there's some left for the rest of us when she's through.

"I've got another dozen in a bag for your trip home," Carlene says, as if reading my mind. It's nice to know that people understand the unbelievable metabolism of November Bean.

"Why do you think Cedar has harmed these people?" Marveline asks.

"We don't know. And we really don't know that Cedar did anything. Boysie doesn't have time to help us, since he's had three homicides and Urica's attack to deal with."

Marveline nods knowingly. "We'll do all that we can to help you, Lanie. You know I'm always in your corner."

When we're done eating, we all get up and head down to the series of large barns. There are four that have been remodeled to house weddings and large events. Marveline unlocks each one and we walk through the cavernous spaces, unsure of exactly what kind of smoking gun we're looking for. Though time spent on her property is never time wasted, it's discouraging, nonetheless.

Moving on to the field behind the barns, Vem goes bounding ahead of us. Tall grass is interspersed with red and purple wildflowers, truly a beautiful sight. When I've taken in all of the scenery, I close my eyes, willing my other senses to go to work.

The air is a lovely mixture of sea and fragrant flowers.

"Lanie! Lanie! Lanie!"

"What, Vem?" I snap. She's like a petulant child, only more persistent.

"I think I found something!"

My eyes pop open and I see her standing in the middle of the field, waving her hands above her head frantically.

Carlene is rushing toward her, but Vem and everyone else dear to me knows that Lanie Anders-Hill does not run.

The distance at which she has positioned herself is deceiving. She is not, in fact, in the middle of a field, but farther away. Vem's found a spot next to Spoonback Creek, the rushing brook that runs through the property.

"Is that the same body of water as—"

"The area where Ms. Gregory's body was found? Yes, we're downstream from that location. We've never utilized that space. It's rather nice to enjoy nature without interference, you know?"

Indeed I do. Cos and I have a cabin that sits in a hidden meadow. It's our place to rest and recover.

When we reach Vem, she's jumping up and down excitedly as Carlene is trying, unsuccessfully to calm her down. Unseen from a distance, the flowers and grass are lying flat on the ground.

"What did you find?"

Vem points down, where there is evidence of human visitors. Several discarded candy wrappers and an empty plastic cup litter the ground, as well as a pink sweater. "Whoever left this is a fool!" I remark. "This is adorable!"

Picking up the sweater, I examine the label and realize why I like it so much. It looks exactly like the one I bought for Cedar last Christmas. For her to casually drop it in this field is more upsetting to me than whatever she and her cohorts were doing here.

Bending down close the ground, I examine the footprints. Thankfully, a recent rain has made the ground muddy and footprints easy to spot. "There are very clearly three sets of prints. One is an expensive pair of hiking boots."

When I first moved to Piney Falls, I researched a good pair of boots for myself. I didn't want a lack of good footwear to be the reason I couldn't keep up with Vem. I should have known that it wasn't the footwear at all, it was my lack of muscle.

"I have some with the same exact tread. These retail for close to a thousand dollars," I remark. "Cedar asked to borrow them one time last year when we were going for a hike. She ended up finding them very uncomfortable."

Examining the prints further, I can see there is a sneaker print beside it. I pull out my phone and take close-up photos of all of them. When I'm able to blow them up on my home computer, I can better read the brand name. I sense Vem standing behind me as I study the picture.

"Stir-ah-m-oo? What is that Lanie?"

"It's Stramos. They're a big name brand. I don't know if they are as expensive as the boots, but they're definitely trendy."

"Ladies! You need to see this!"

Marveline, who trailed behind even me, has caught up to the group. She is standing to our left with an object in her hand. When we reach her, a small camping stool becomes visible. "As you can see," she says, pointing one long, cream-colored nail to the charred seat, "it's been used before."

"Let's think about this for a minute. A group of three people came out here in the night. They had a nice little snack, and then what? The pink sweater makes me wonder if they didn't have to leave in a hurry."

"I'm so sorry I told you ladies with such certainty that no one was here. This troubles me deeply."

Marveline places one hand on her hip and the other against her forehead. "We'll need to install more cameras, Carlene."

Carlene nods in agreement. "It wouldn't hurt to call in a specialist. There is a new security business in town. Unfortunately, we've seen a rise in thefts. The owner will come out and assess your property for risks."

Vem utters a noise of dissatisfaction. "Why would you pay a complete stranger, when I could provide you with the latest in property protection for free?"

While I would normally discourage Vem from offering her crazy gadgets to someone, she is masterful at the art of protection. Her devices, and her obsession with finding the best, are always top notch.

"Vem put cameras all over our property when we thought someone was trying to break into our garage."

"It turned out to be raccoons," she explains. "I did a moan for wieldy wildlife and they left," she snaps her fingers, "just like that."

Marveline and Carlene exchange uncertain glances.

"I'll ask Cos and Truman to inspect her work," I say before I give myself the chance to think about how this might offend Vem.

"Are you saying, bestie, that you don't trust me?

Or is it that you don't think a woman is qualified for such a project?"

"Neither, Vem. I just meant that after you've finished, they can double check to make sure there isn't a spot left vulnerable," I say quickly. "You remember, how, after you set up our security system, that you had Piper wave her hands in front of all of the cameras, just to make sure they reached to the edge of the property?"

Vem nods, placated for now.

"In any event, something untoward happened in our field," Marveline says. "I'll call Boysie and have him come out and investigate." She pivots her body around without moving her feet. "Are we sure this is the extent of it?"

"This is an odd spot for a pow-wow. They must've driven up to the field, somehow."

I walk farther as the rest of the women follow me like little ducklings. Now I can see tire tracks. Excitedly, I follow them as they cross a hill and end at a gravel road. When everyone else has caught up, I ask, "Marveline, did you know this was here?"

"If it was here when I purchased the property, I certainly don't remember being told about it."

"Curious." I turn to Vem. "You mentioned this morning that you needed a little extra cardio today."

"Yes? Are you finally going to join me in a jog?"

Ignoring this ridiculous suggestion, I ask, "Would

you mind following this road and seeing where it leads? We can keep in touch by phone."

Without missing a beat, Vem salutes me and takes off on a jog.

"Should we wait here?" Carlene asks.

"I need to see if we've missed any clues. There is also one added benefit."

"Of wearing November Bean out?" Carlene asks.

"You've got it."

We watch with admiration as she disappears from our view. I take this opportunity to look around at the beauty of Marveline's property. "You've got such a gem, here, Marveline."

"Thank you, Lanie. Some days I think it's too large for just the two of us, but days like today," she pauses to gaze up at the clear blue sky, "I can't imagine selling even one acre."

Gazing across the colorful field, something horrid occurs to me. Last night when I was sweeping the entryway, I swept up flowers the exact same color. I picked up a shoe, Cedar's, and found more stuck to the bottom.

"Lanie! Lanie! Lanie!"

I turn sharply to see Vem galloping through the field. She reminds me of a horse enjoying an open space for the first time. When she reaches us, she's out of breath and bends down, hands on knees.

"Take your time, Vem. We're in no hurry," I say, rubbing her back gently.

In a disgustingly short period of time, she stands, completely calm. "I found this," she gasps, holding up a small magnifying glass, the "Gemfinder" just like the one Wendell was gifted by Sterling Truth. "And also, these."

She hands me a hotel key card, one like they use at the Fallen Branch. In the other hand, she holds a navy blue jacket. The lining appears to have blood on it, just as Cedar's seatbelt did.

Vem stands and puts her hands on her hips. "The road leads to Truman Coolidge's place," she says. "And there are tire tracks leading to his driveway."

Chapter Twenty-Four
Piper

After finding a gun underneath Sawyer's bed, Piper imagined two paths for herself. First, she could call Obie, apologize for her childish behavior and hand over the evidence.

The second, more appealing option was to call her mother and ask what she'd do in Piper's shoes. It was an easy out for her; Piper knew Lanie would jump in and take control of the situation, removing the object and its troubles from her life entirely.

Her phone buzzed as she was pacing the kitchen, weighing what was in her best interest.

"Hi Dad. Hope you're feeling better. Mom mentioned food poisoning?"

"Yeah, something like that. Your mother convinced me to take up November Bean on her dinner invitation. It's better if we don't discuss what was on the table. For both of us."

She suppressed a giggle. Cosmo and November's ongoing feud was often a source of entertainment when they were all together.

"What's up?"

"Oh, I just wanted to let you know that Sawyer will be showing up bright and early to pick up the pastry order for Fallen Branch." He huffed in disapproval. "Every time I say that out loud, it makes me cringe. I wish the brains behind this operation would have come up with a new name."

"Okay. I'll have everything ready for him." She felt a lump forming in her throat. Was it because she didn't trust him, and went looking for trouble? Or was it because she truly loved and missed him?

That night, she tossed and turned. All sorts of scenarios played out in her mind about Sawyer coming, none of which were good. At least he would be driving the delivery van. Sawyer seemed to take pride in his job, so it was unlikely that he would do anything to jeopardize that.

She finally gave up and arose at four-thirty. Somehow, she would make things safe for herself. When her brother arrived, she would be ready.

At a quarter after six, the sound of crunching gravel alerted her to his arrival. Piper was dressed, wearing makeup, and ready for whatever came next.

"Hey! I've never seen you in makeup before! It's not a bad look!"

She blushed, unsure whether to feel offended or

pleased by his remark. "Your order is ready to go!" Piper motioned to the small room off the kitchen, a room she learned was called a "mud room."

The locals explained that it was a place for farmers to deposit their soiled clothing and footwear after a long day in the elements. When the entire place was remodeled for the commercial bakery and her living quarters, a large, walk-in cooler was added in the mud room. There were also two long tables on which items that didn't need refrigeration were placed.

"Okay, I'll load up in a minute. I need to use the bathroom first."

Instead of moving toward the main floor bathroom, Sawyer jumped up the stairs, two at a time. Piper had a very good idea why he felt it necessary to take those extra steps.

On his way back down, his feet were heavier. As soon as he was in view, Piper noticed his jovial expression was gone.

"Um, I left something here," he began.

"Oh, do you mean your gun?" Piper asked innocently. "I gave it to Obie."

"You did what?" Sawyer took a big step off the landing and a second one, placing him squarely in front of his sister. He towered at least a foot over her. "Why would you do something so stupid, Piper?"

"I have a cleaning service," she spouted, not her worst lie ever. "If they were to find that under your bed and connect it to you, I'm sure you would get into lots of trouble. Is it even registered?"

Sawyer's face looked like an angry storm cloud before it spewed hail and tornadoes. "No. There are things you don't understand."

They stood face-to-chest. They were at an impasse and for once, Piper wasn't giving in.

"Why don't you explain them to me, then?" she asked.

Sawyer stepped aside, breaking their stand-off. "I don't have time. I've got to make that big delivery, remember?"

She nodded with relief.

Though she had offered to help him load the vehicle in the past, today she sat down at the table, sipping her hot chocolate. When Sawyer finished, he walked back up to the kitchen and stood on the top step, not bothering to open the screen door.

"You understand that now I can't protect you, right?"

She didn't respond. How could she?

As he turned and walked toward the van, Piper had a change of heart. She opened the screen door and yelled, "Protect me from what?"

It was Sawyer's turn to ignore her.

Chapter Twenty-Five
Lanie

"It's your lucky day, Lanie!" Wendell says excitedly.

Since finding a hotel key card on the Sassy Lasses property, I hoped I'd returned it in time to track down its owner.

"Just call me Lottery Winner Lanie!"

He giggles as he exits the check-in desk, returning momentarily.

"And here ya go. The guest in question reserved the room for ten nights. The room and the key card were active until this morning, so you caught it in the nick-of-time."

"Oh. Did he just check out?"

"Let me see." Wendell's fingers fly furiously over the keys. "He never checked out. It says the maid cleaned the room two days ago and when she went in the next morning, the beds were still made. She reported all luggage removed."

"Hmm. That's quite a lengthy stay. It would require a credit card with lots of room for incidentals, wouldn't it?" I wink at Wendell, hoping he gets my drift.

"Yes, absolutely. Mr. Trigger Jarvis left a card on file, and I can get his last-known address for you."

Again his fingers move at record speed over the keys. "Here we are, Miss Lanie."

Wendell stares at me triumphantly. He needs a typing competition and a big trophy. "Trigger Jarvis, from Anaheim, California. Used a Metal Card Emerald. Ooh. Color me impressed."

"I've never heard of that. What kind of card is it?"

Wendell puts his elbows on the desk and rests his chin in his hands. "One that's only offered to people who've purchased big-ticket items. They have to have spent at least $100,000 in the past year in order to qualify." Wendell sighs. "So the answer to your question is, it's the kind of card that gets you a date with Wendell."

"Was there anyone here with him?"

He squints at the screen. Wendell is still young enough that he resists buying glasses, though he would most certainly find stylish frames. "Okay. Yes. He was here with another gentleman by the name of Jim Winterkorn. Two queen beds. They used room service for almost every meal." Wendell clucked his tongue. "That's so pricey. They must've charged it to a company account."

"Those men must've had a reason they didn't want to be seen." There is a lightness in the air when I realize Cedar wasn't checked in as a part of this crew. "Do you have the card?"

Wendell pauses and then points behind him. "Sent it to the printer, along with his address."

"You're a peach, Wendell!"

"So are you, Lanie-kins!" he says in a singsong voice as he disappears into the office. When he returns, he is carrying two sheets of paper and a handful of our new signature Fallen Branch Truffles. "I remembered that Cosmo loves these." Wendell dumps the contents of his hands on the counter in front of me.

"Cosmo loves these, but they don't necessarily love Cos," I muse. "I'm guessing they have about a million calories."

"Give or take." Wendell giggles. "You really bagged yourself a handsome one, Lanie. Did you find him wandering in the woods? I don't know why he wasn't snapped up sooner!"

It's my turn to giggle. "Cos was definitely a wanderer before we connected. No time for women or the nonsense that comes with them."

He'd used that line enough times that I was starting to wonder if it was really true.

I'm relieved that there is a whole new generation

of people in Piney Falls who have no idea my husband was once in prison for a crime he didn't commit.

"Let me know if you need anything else, doll. I sent the surveillance video to your email."

I wave goodbye to him as I make my way down the hall to the onsite restaurant. A young woman with a long, brunette ponytail and light blue eyes smiles when she sees me. She is wearing the restaurant uniform, a long black dress.

"Good morning, ma'am! Will you be dining with us today?"

The manager has done a wonderful job of training everyone. They are all welcoming. When he first arrived, I made a point of letting him know that we needed to provide extensive training so that everyone knew what kind of behavior was expected of them.

"Hi there," I leaned over the podium she was standing behind to look at her name tag. "Meea Chard. Oh, that's lovely!"

She blushes as she picks up a stiff page, the menu for Chez Pine.

"It's a family name. My aunt was allowed to name me, as per our tradition and she chose the name of my great-grandmother. My sister, Aurielle, was named after another aunt. If you'll follow me—"

"Oh, I'm not here to eat. I'm Lanie Anders-Hill, the marketing manager." Taking her hand, I can tell she exudes warmth and a touch of mystery. Vem is rubbing off on me. "I want to speak with whoever has been making deliveries to the rooms for the past week."

Instantly, the expression on her face changes. "I'm so sorry! What did they do wrong? We'll all be in trouble at the staff meeting if there has been an incident."

"No, that's not it at all!" I say reassuringly. "I just have some questions about a guest, is all." I can't help but notice, she has a big glob of makeup on her neck. I can't be sure if it is on purpose.

"Oh." Once again, Meea's face is serene. "If you're sure no one will be in trouble," she pauses, glancing at me for support.

"I promise. I plan on telling Andy that you were the utmost of friendly and helpful." Smiling as reassuringly as possible, I continue. "There was a customer last week who ordered room service for every meal. Do you happen to remember—"

"Trigger? How could I forget! He's so handsome. Every time I delivered his meals, he tipped me fifty dollars. Can you imagine having that kind of money?"

She is crushing hard on Trigger. Someone whose sudden appearance concerns me. "It sounds like the two of you hit it off! What did he tell you about himself? Did he happen to mention why he was in town?"

Meea looks up at the ceiling, tapping a pen on the podium. "Well, he was here to meet with someone. Maybe a relative? Of course, now that I'm saying that out loud, it doesn't make any sense. He hardly ever left his room."

"Meea, was there anyone else in the room with him?"

"Yeah. Trigger called him 'Ribeye,' but the staff was told to call him Mr. Winterkorn. He wasn't nearly as friendly, and he never tipped at all. When he came to the door, it was usually because he wanted to complain about something."

Furrowing my brow, I ask, "About what?"

"The sheets were too rough, the television doesn't have enough channels—you name it. I was sorry to see Trigger leave, but Mr. Winterkorn, not so much." Meea sighs.

"Meea, you've got a large glob of makeup on your neck that needs rubbing in. Would you like me to—"

Immediately, she slaps her hand over the spot. I've upset her.

"I'll bring my husband out here for dinner soon," I say quickly. "You're such a treasure. Have you lived in Piney Falls your whole life? It's strange I haven't seen you before."

"My sister, Aurielle, followed her boyfriend out here." She rolls her eyes. Even this act is darling. Meea has the most beautiful false eyelashes I've ever seen. They are brown instead of the usual black and curl up perfectly on the ends.

"She sent me pictures, and when I saw how beautiful it was, I didn't take much convincing."

"Where did you move from?"

The phone sitting on her podium buzzes. "I'm sorry, Lanie. I have to take this."

"No need to apologize. Thanks for the info!"

On impulse, I drive out to Cosmic Bakes, our farm location where Piper runs a large baking operation. We didn't leave things in a positive space the last time we saw her and I'd like to make sure she is doing all right.

As I pull into the gravel drive, I'm unhappy to see the delivery van parked behind Piper's car. That means Sawyer is here. I'll have to make the best of it.

Opening the squeaky screen door to the kitchen, the one I've suggested they replace numerous times, I call, "Piper! Sawyer? Is anyone here?"

I'm not usually one to stand on ceremony, but with Sawyer here, I don't want to startle him. *Why? Why don't I want to startle him?*

"Mom!" Piper comes rushing out of nowhere, covered in flour. Without fear of reprisal for the flour handprints that are surely on my back, she hugs me. "You should have told me you were coming! I would have made you lunch!"

"Thanks, hon. It was a last-minute decision. Just thought I'd check in and see how things are going."

She folds her arms across her chest. "You mean with Obie?"

Caught.

"Yes, I wanted to make sure you two were going to patch things up."

I pause for a moment, taking in her defensive posture. "Actually, I was thinking more about you. How are you doing?"

Piper's expression softens a bit as she glances at Sawyer, who entered the room quietly and is now standing behind his sister with his arms crossed. "I'm doing okay. We've been busy with orders and trying out new recipes. And Sawyer got home early from his deliveries to help."

I smile at Sawyer, who nods in greeting. "That's great to hear. I'm glad you two are working well together."

Piper nods, then adds, "Mom, about Obie--"

I hold up a hand to stop her. "Let's talk about that later, okay? Right now, I just want to catch up and see how things are going with the business."

Piper nods again, but I can tell she needs a listening ear. I make a mental note to check in with her again soon and make sure everything is okay.

"I need a smoke."

Sawyer abruptly pushes his way past his sister and outside, causing the mood of the room to lift considerably.

Piper looks away and knowing her as I do, there

are tears forming in her eyes. "Remember when my relationship with Finn was falling apart? You told me that I didn't have to stick around to make sure it worked out. 'You're still new to the dating scene, Piper. Take your time. The right one will come,' you said.'"

"Coming out of your mouth, I sound so wise," I joke.

"Yeah, well, I've been thinking, and maybe I need to keep looking. Obie and me aren't really a good fit."

"Oh, honey," I say, gently tugging on her arm. It doesn't take much encouragement for her to dissolve in my embrace, engulfed in full-on sobs.

"He...he... he thinks that Sawyer is a lowlife. And that by growing up with him, I'm a criminal too!"

"That doesn't sound like Obie at all!"

"That's what I thought too. Bu-bu-but I guess I never really knew him." Her sobbing is loud and she's barely able to take a breath.

"Let it all out, sweetheart," I soothe, kissing the top of her head. "You don't want to leave that kind of pain inside you."

We stand together so long that my legs are falling asleep when she finally pulls away.

"Do me one favor?" I ask, gently pushing strands of her dark hair from her eyes. "Talk to him one last time. Make sure you're ending things without any words left inside you. They'll eat you alive if you don't."

I can hear heavy footsteps from the front porch and before I have a chance to ask about him, Sawyer appears. His expression is surly and his renewed presence in the room drops the temperature by at least five degrees.

"Did I hear you talking about that loser, Obie?" he asks, touching Piper's shoulder protectively.

Instantly feeling protective of my daughter and her choice in boyfriends, I give Sawyer an icy stare.He doesn't seem to notice.n my mind, my eyes are staring so hard, they're creating discomfort for Sawyer.

"Lanie was just reminding me that I need to make sure I've said everything I need to."

It bothers me when she doesn't call me "Mom." It's like a step backward, though I can understand why she's sensitive to Sawyer and the fact that he was never taken in by a family. At least not one that wanted to make their relationship permanent.

"She's probably right. I'll feel better about it," Piper says with a sigh.

"Why? He's a jerk! If you want, I'll return his stuff. There's no reason you need to subject yourself to his abuse."

Sawyer is glaring back at me. Not just glaring, but attempting to bore a hole through my own chest. *Not gonna work, fella. I've stared down men with twice your grit.*

"I was just making a suggestion, is all. I should

probably get back to town. I've got a million things to do." As I walk toward the door, they follow close behind. I've never felt so unwelcome in my own bakery.

The Lanie who isn't satisfied leaving things as they are pauses and turns around, barely avoiding a collision. "I think Cosmo had some extra projects he wanted help with today. Would you mind, Sawyer?"

His face turns red and he sets his jaw. "Yeah. I guess."

I'll have to text Cos the moment I get in the car so he can come up with a project for Sawyer. I'm sure it won't be difficult.

"I can walk you out."

"Thanks for stopping by, Mot—er—Lanie!" Piper calls.

Chapter Twenty-Six
Piper

"The Bon Bon Butcher. Clobbering Claude. Walt the Whacker."

Piper shrugged with indifference. This was the fourth time today someone had asked for her opinion about names for the serial killer contest.

Piper was starting to wonder if the entire Oregon Coast was under attack. She'd made a quick trip into town to get more pastry boxes with their logo when she ran into Boysie. He was there for his morning coffee and scone, but wasn't afforded a moment's peace.

"I got word about one. Found near Blackberry Cove last night. Same method: suffocation and a gunshot wound to the head."

The strain on his face was obvious. "You haven't gotten much sleep," she observed.

"None. The wife is threatening to take me to the hospital and have them knock me out." Boysie leaned over the table and whispered, "You heard about the naming contest, I assume?"

Piper nodded. "It's ridiculous!"

"Totally distasteful. My deputy called the paper and asked them to cancel it, but they informed him that Sandy's Silt-Free Car Wash had already paid big bucks for sponsorship."

Piper's mouth dropped open. "I can't believe what I'm hearing."

"In addition to everything else in the prize package, the winner now gets two-thousand dollars and a year of free car washes."

"Can't beat that," Doris remarked on her way by. "I've already entered twice." She was balancing six dirty plates on both of her arms.

"I'm glad I ran into you, Piper. There is something I'd like to talk to you about, if you don't mind."

She DID mind.

In fact, Boysie was the last person she wanted to discuss her relationship issues with. Well, maybe Gladys Petrie came in first place.

"Sure. I do have orders to get out, though," Piper replied, knowing the conversation would happen at some point. Best to get it over with now.

"I'll be brief." Boysie cleared his throat. "Ever since he was little and we figured he was different from our other kids, I worried about Obie. Would he hold down a job? Would he find love? Kept me up nights, just wondering and worrying."

Piper swallowed hard.

"You know I'm not one to meddle in relationships," Boysie continued. "Especially not the ones involving my kids. I never thought he'd find anyone, to be honest. And when you two started dating, well, it all just fell into place."

Emotions of all sorts welled up inside her like a volcano ready to rupture. "You don't give your son enough credit! He's got a genius-level I.Q. and Obie has never blinked when a challenge stood in his way."

Boysie nodded. "That's all true. And the fact that you understand tells me that you do belong together. When myself and the missus separated and she went to stay with her sister, I acted like I was fine on my own. Well, I wasn't. Once your find your person, you have to hold on for the ride."

Piper sensed where he was going. "Boysie, I'm not—"

"Give the boy another chance. He's head-over-heels in love with you, Piper. Whatever caused your argument won't even matter a year from now."

She smiled weakly. Though his words made sense, Piper no longer trusted Obie. He'd gone behind her back and attempted to make her brother a villain. From what she'd observed in healthy relationships, that wasn't done.

"I hear what you're saying, Boysie," she began slowly. "But we've reached a point where we'll never agree. It's about—" she stopped herself before sharing too much. "Tell Obie I do love him," her voice wavered. "He'll always be a good friend."

Boysie, looking pleased with himself, placed his plate and empty coffee cup in the dirty dish bin. It was clear that someone, probably Gladys, put him up to this conversation. "Okay then. I've got to get back. This poor gal in Blackberry Cove had only lived there for six months. Aurielle Chard was her name. A young gal, about your age."

Piper nodded and picked up the empty boxes. "If you'll hold the door, I'll follow you out."

She fought to keep scenarios, each more horrific than the last, from playing in her head like a midnight showing of the latest hacker slasher movie as she drove home. And worst of all, her mind kept connecting them to Sawyer.

Piper was halfway home when something occurred to her. "I took Sawyer's gun. He didn't have a weapon to kill anyone! Ha!"

She waved cheerily to her cattle friends next door as she drove by. One looked up from her grass, chewing slowly as the car drove by.

As Piper pulled the boxes from her trunk, she happened to notice a car parked on the side of the road, just past her place. There were two occupants, both male.

Though they made no attempt to contact her, she felt a sense of unease. November's surveillance video would give her an idea of how long they'd been there.

Her phone buzzed as she was mounting the steps, so she set the boxes down to answer.

"Your brother has a warrant out for his arrest."

Piper frowned. "Who is this?"

"November Bean, of course!"

"Oh." Piper placed the phone in the crook of her neck and picked up her load before unlocking the door. "How would you know that?"

"Your mother has been concerned about you, little bird. She asked me to see what info I could find on Sawyer."

This same behavior incensed her so much that she cut off communication with Obie. Coming from her mother, she found it endearing.

"Okay, tell me what you've got. Please keep in mind that I have a tight schedule and I don't have time for much today."

November huffed. "I'm only calling because your mother insisted." She paused to clear her throat before continuing. "Deepest apologies. I didn't hydrate enough before the Moaning Marathon for Mid-Life Men."

"No worries." Piper set her load in the kitchen and sat down.

"As I was saying, your brother is a wanted man in

Ohio. He and two other men were involved in the murder of a gang member."

"Why would they think it's Sawyer? Dad told me how ex-cons are always the first people to come under suspicion when a crime's been committed. It doesn't mean they actually did anything wrong."

"Oh dear. You're not going to believe a word I say. I can smell your distrust through the phone."

"No, I want to hear it," Piper insisted, now that she'd been challenged. "You did all of this research and we can't let it go to waste."

"Okay, girlie, you asked for it. Sawyer and his alleged co-conspirator were in prison together at the same time as the dead man. There were threats made and when the deceased was paroled, he made the comment that he knew his days were numbered. If someone killed him, it would be your brother and his cellmate."

"But," Piper began. There was no use trying to defend her brother until she spoke with him. "Thank you for telling me. I'm sure it's all a big misunderstanding."

"Take some deep breaths, sweetie. And then think hard about what I've said."

"Oh, Ms. Bean, could you check your surveillance cameras? There's someone parked beside the road and maybe I'm being paranoid, but—"

"On it."

The phone made a clunking sound and Piper

presumed November dropped it. In a matter of seconds, she returned. "Yes, your visitors have been parked there for almost two hours. I've taken a picture of their license plate and will message the name of the owner of the vehicle to you soon. Should I also alert your impishly handsome boy toy?"

"No. He's...um...on assignment today. I'll handle things. But thank you."

"Mini sister-friend, can I share something?"

"Okay, sure."

"Love is like a rollercoaster ride. It's terrifying and thrilling, and sometimes you end up throwing up your cotton candy. But then you get back in line and do it all over again. Keep that in mind, okay, girlie?"

"You bet."

She shook her head as she hung up. Her father would get a kick out of that statement. Her stomach was growling and she realized the last meal she'd had was breakfast.

The phone buzzed once again while she was in the middle of a peanut butter, jelly and pickle sandwich.

"Hi again, sweetie, it's November Bean. I'm much happier when I talk rather than text. I know your generation feels differently though." She paused and cleared her throat. "The car belongs to someone named Aurielle Chard. Isn't that pretty?"

Piper felt her throat close as she choked hard on her sandwich. After several minutes of coughing while November yelled, "Raise your hands over your head!" Piper's coughing eased.

"I'm so sorry Ms. Bean. That woman was murdered in Blackberry Cove. It must be a mistake. Why would her car be—"

"What happened? Piper? Piper? Answer me!"

Chapter Twenty-Seven
Lanie

"Didn't expect to see you today, toots."

As I flop down in the chair, there is a sense of relief that flows over me. Despite the squeaky chair and even squeakier Gladys, I feel at home here in the public records building.

Gladys, up from her afternoon nap, is perky and ready for whatever I have to throw at her.

"I know, Gladys. There have been some troubling experiences lately, and I—"

"You talking about the murders? The naming contest? Or something more in the range of gossip? Cause I've got my ear to the ground on all three." She smiles slyly. "Good thing I have both a son and a grandson who keep me informed."

"None of the above. I need you to search the dark web for me and find out all you can about a Trigger Jarvis."

Her wrinkled face scrunches up so much it's hard to find her eyes. "Are you betting on the horses now, toots? If it's information on a race you're after, you'll be better off searching on your own."

"What?" It takes me a moment to put two-and-two together. "Oh, you thought Trigger was a horse." We both smile, though I'm not sure she understands yet. "Trigger is an actual human being. A man. I need everything you can find on him—date of birth, places he's lived, all of that good stuff."

Gladys taps an index finger on the desk. "Do I get clued in on why we're researching this particular, unfortunately named man, or are you going to make an old lady guess? Memory's not what it used to be. That could work in your favor."

There isn't a snowball's chance in the underworld that I'll get out of here without giving her something to nibble on, but I'm not ready to share everything yet. "He skipped out on the Fallen Branch Resort without paying. I'm helping them—well, you're helping them—by tracking him down." My ear-to-ear grin should be a dead giveaway that I'm lying, but Gladys isn't catching on.

"Why didn't you say so?" She leans forward and turns her computer on. "Did Boysie send you here? I know they're overwhelmed trying to solve all these murders at once. Gad's sake, the bodies are piling up faster'n this week's laundry. Wouldn't surprise me if they needed to call in another expert."

"Piney Falls, Vellum and Blackberry Cove have all decided to work together. They don't want to call in the big shots from Portland until they have a good idea of who they were dealing with. Should I wait, or—"

She glares at me through her thick glasses. "Toots, you know it takes Bessie a good ten minutes to warm up!" Gladys pats the large, elderly monitor. It's finicky and prone to odd quirks, much like Gladys herself.

"Cos and I have offered numerous times to replace Bessie with something a little faster," I say. "All you have to do is give us the green light and you'll be surfing the web like a twenty-year-old."

She shrugs. "I like the old girl. We've both seen better days, but somehow, we're still kicking. She's helped me with the naming contest. I'm going with the Pelican Predator."

I gasp. "You too? And Boysie approves?"

Gladys shakes her head. "Didn't tell him. I entered the contest under a pseudonym. Adore Caliente."

A giggle and snort escape me. "How did you come up with that one?"

She seems surprised by my reaction. "One of them stripper name generators. Showed up in my email, so I thought it was legitimate."

That's a conversation for another day.

Standing, I notice a new family picture on her

desk. With all of the Petrie kids, spouses and grand-kids, there are at least thirty people in the photo. "This must warm your heart, to have your entire family together," I muse as I pick up the photo to examine it closer. "I had lunch with Carlene recently. She's very happy to be a part of your family again."

"Yes indeed. Was kind of hoping your Piper would join the family someday."

And I was really hoping to get out of here without touching on that delicate subject. "You know how kids are. It takes time to settle down. Maybe they both need to experience the dating world a little more. You know, spread their wings?"

Gladys slaps her palms on the desk, causing me to jump.

"Are you trying to tell me that my Obie isn't good enough for the girl? Hogwash!"

"No, not at all." It's going to be difficult to extract myself from this awkward situation that I put myself in. "They've got to figure things out for themselves is all. There's nothing either one of us can do to fix it."

Turning quickly, I wave behind me. "Let me know when you've got everything I need."

"Will do!" she shouts.

Vem is waiting in my driveway when I pull up. To keep her body and mind in motion, she's doing squats with her hands pressed together in prayer pose. Her eyes are closed and she is uttering something, a moan of some type.

When I'm out of my car, I can clearly hear her newest moan, one that requires a staccato with one's tongue hitting the roof of the mouth over and over. It's not the easiest one, but she says it keeps night terrors away and prevents bad breath.

Torn between my curiosity over this new moan and relieving myself of my heavy bag, I opt to go inside. I'm barely in the door when I feel her behind me.

"Why did you abandon me, sister friend?"

"I just thought you needed privacy."

Flopping down on my favorite recliner, a whoosh of air bursts out of my mouth.

"Sister friend, I'm sensing major stress." Immediately, Vem pulls my shoes off and begins massaging my feet. She gives the best foot massages of anyone I know, but they have to be instigated by her. November Bean doesn't take requests.

"Now, tell me about your day," she insists as she uses both of her hands to pull upward on one of my weary feet.

I start by telling her I've gone to Gladys for information, which goes over like a lead balloon.

"You know how I like to help you, Lanie. But the fact that you went to Gladys first, well, that does sting."

"Vem, she has always helped me, long before you

purchased all of your fancy gadgets." This discussion is ruining my relaxation. I don't dare tell her or she might stop. "I like to save your hi-tech equipment for the really challenging stuff."

Vem mentioned when she first bought it that she could see in the bathroom of every house in America.

"Someone staying at the Fallen Branch has—" I pause and sit up, as much as I can with my feet under Vem's control. "Is Cedar here?" I whisper.

Vem shakes her head. "She had an errand to run. Even though I invited her over for a lunch of blended bark pasta and mushroom and worm sauce, Cedar wasn't interested. The girl must have an iron sense of self-control."

"Whew. I didn't want to risk her hearing this." Leaning my head back on the recliner, I close my eyes and resume the relaxation process. "There are two men who stayed at the Fallen Branch. They're both from California—at least one of them is— and didn't leave their room much at all."

"Are we thinking they need exorcised?"

"They're gone, Vem."

"Oh. Do you think they had something to do with the murders?"

"Perhaps. Gladys will be calling at some point to give me background info on one of them." Adjusting myself in the chair, I can feel my body beginning to relax. "Vem, if you ever tire of teaching moaning classes, you've got a real future in massage."

"Haven't you learned yet, Lanie?"

"What, hon?"

"There isn't anything November Bean can't do."

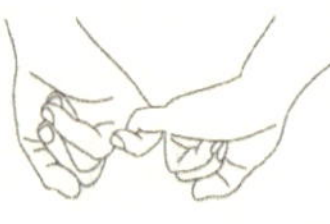

Vem decides I need a nap, so she holds my arm to guide me into my bedroom. The old, corporate Lanie would have found this type of behavior demeaning. Now I'm grateful that she cares about me so deeply.

My eyes close almost as soon as Vem tucks the covers under my chin. When they open again, I can smell something in the kitchen. Did I leave a burner on?

Jumping out of bed, I rush to the kitchen where I find a stranger cooking something unappetizing and green. He is tall and muscular, with brown, curly hair, just like Sawyer's. When he turns around, he looks exactly how I envision Trigger.

"What are you doing in my kitchen?"

"Getting ready to kill you." He smiles and brings his skillet toward me, a sizzling, disturbing mess.

The next thing I know, I'm sitting up in my bed, breathing hard. It's dark in my bedroom and my phone says it's five-thirty.

"Cos?" I call. Nothing.

Lanie Anders-Hill isn't one to give in to fear.

There is absolutely no reason to stay in bed. *What am I going to do, hide under the covers like a child until my husband arrives?*

I throw them off and tiptoe cautiously to the kitchen. When I find it empty, I breathe a sigh of relief. "Dreams aren't reality, Lanie."

"Only if they involve a hunky baker."

I whip around so fast Cos jumps back, startled. "I was just kidding! You don't have to hurt me!"

Quickly I gather him in my arms and hold him tight. "You feel so good," I murmur.

The time hasn't been right to tell him about Sterling Truth's death. Tonight, it must be done. I'm frankly quite surprised he hasn't already heard.

"If I'd known this was my reception, I would have come home hours ago." Cos kisses the top of my head. "Now, can we talk about why you haven't answered your phone all afternoon?"

I scroll through and find six messages. "I guess Vem must've turned my ringer off. I took a nap."

"Well, Gladys Petrie tried getting ahold of you, and when that didn't work, she called me. So of course, I tried calling you and you didn't answer, so—"

"I'm sorry, Cos. I didn't mean to frighten either of you. I'll call her back tomorrow. You're probably starving and I haven't done anything about dinner."

He releases me and points to the table, where he's placed two plates, a pizza and a dozen roses.

"When I couldn't reach you, I decided you were sleeping, so I took the liberty of making dinner."

"What did Lanie Anders-Hill ever do to deserve this?"

"Oh, and you don't need to worry about calling Gladys back. She insisted I come see her. I've got the goods on your mystery man."

"Don't leave me in suspense, Cos. What did she say?"

"Well, for starters, he worked for the Truth Corporation for five years."

I don't know how I'll explain this to my husband. He'll be very upset that I was researching someone connected to his sister. "Tell me everything and then I'll explain."

He gives me the "what have you gotten yourself into now?" look before continuing. "Our friend, Trigger, was fired for his violent outbursts, which left others uncomfortable. That's when things get really interesting."

He motions for me to sit at the table, and a part of me wonders if he's setting me up for a big lecture about how I shouldn't snoop in Cedar's business. *Nonsense, Lanie. He loves you.*

When I'm seated and he has placed two slices of veggie pizza with a nice addition of chicken breast on my plate, Cos continues.

"Trigger, who I'm assuming is NOT an animal of

any kind, goes off the radar for two solid years after he's fired. Nothing. Nada."

"Hm."

Chewing away on the cracker-thin crust and perfect blend of sauce and toppings, I start to wonder what Trigger knew.

"The reason he was MIA for so long was that he was in prison, for extortion."

Did he come here to blackmail Cedar too? Is that his game?

"Mrs. Hill? Are you going to tell me why you're researching someone who worked for my sister's ex? Someone whose name is most definitely made up?"

"I...can't. Not yet, anyway. Please trust me, Cos. I'll tell you everything just as soon as I can."

He nods and my heart sinks. I hate keeping secrets, so it's time to release a big one.

"The other day, when Cedar, Vem and I were having lunch at the bakery, there was a big commotion. When I went to see what it was, I discovered—"

"The body of Sterling Truth." Cos takes a large gulp of his wine and smacks his lips, like he doesn't have a care in the world. "Boysie's morning coffee group jawed about it nonstop. There is talk our serial killer—who I decided to call The Spoonful Serial— took his anger out on the poor dude."

I don't know what to address first. "Cos, why aren't you more upset? And please, please don't tell me that my perfect husband entered that awful contest!"

Cosmo shakes his head and squeezes my hand. "I didn't enter the contest, babe. But I can't help myself; with a constant chatter in the bakery all day, I had to make my own name."

"And?"

"And, the fact that you recognized Sterling's face means Cedar didn't kill him. He would have been nothing but shark food by now if she'd killed him. It's obvious the guy kicked the bucket more recently."

Chapter Twenty-Eight
Lanie

"Did you ask for some time off? I can certainly speak with Andy if you'd like. I'm sure there is some sort of bereavement policy."

When I heard that her sister had been murdered, my heart went out to Meea. Wendell told me she was still working, despite her loss. I put together a gift basket filled with self-care items like soap, bath salts, candles and chocolates.

Meea was overcome with emotion when I presented it to her. "This wasn't supposed to make things worse," I say worriedly. "Why don't you take a break and we can sit and talk?"

She nods through her tears as I text Wendell:

Need a fill-in hostess at Chez Pine
while Meea takes a break.

> Tell her to go ahead. I'll be down to take her place.

"Can I buy you a late lunch?"

"My sister loved the chicken nuggets," she says, fighting through more tears.

"Then we'll have two orders of chicken nuggets in Aurielle's honor."

We stop at the kitchen to place our order before seating ourselves at the very back table of Chez Pine. It's mid-afternoon and there are only a handful of customers.

"Tell me about your sister. Did she look like you?"

"No, not at all. Ari had long, brown hair and was...um—"

"Just say it," I urge. "No judgement here." She has glopped her makeup on again. I wonder if she's unaware? Today is not the day to point out problems with her appearance, I tell myself.

"She was built heavier than me. It's not a bad thing. She took after our mother's side of the family and I was lucky to have my father's great metabolism." Meea smiles for the first time since our conversation began. "She was younger than me by one year, which meant we were into the same things at the same time. We played dolls together from morning till night and kept each other's secrets. But that all changed when we were in high school."

Meea takes a drink of the orange soda today's

chef brought her. I think he's got a thing for her, but now isn't the time for me to say anything about that either.

"In our family, she was the smart one and I was the pretty one. I don't say that to sound vain."

I shake my head. "No, you're just telling me a story. Go ahead."

"I was a cheerleader and the next year, she was going to try out too. The day before tryouts, she broke her foot. All of our plans of riding the bus together to out-of-town games and going to cheerleading camp together went out the window."

The handsome young chef brings our chicken nuggets to the table, along with another dish. "I remembered how much you liked the artichoke dip, so I made that too. Watch out, the pan is hot."

He sets a miniature cast iron pan in front of Meea and smiles at her.

"Thanks, Clint," she says, unaware that he is gazing admiringly at her.

When she has watched until every part of him disappears into the kitchen, she continues her story. "After cheerleading didn't work out, she started hanging out with a rough crowd. Because she was so smart, she helped them with their stupid things, writing notes when they skipped school. All sorts of stuff."

She pauses to take a chicken nugget and dip it in ketchup mixed with honey. Quickly, I do the same and we clink our nuggets together. "To Aurielle," I say.

"To Aurielle," Meea repeats before sticking her nugget in her mouth.

"Mm! These are good!" I say with enough gusto to convince her.

Meea wipes the corners of her mouth and continues. "She skipped school more than she went and barely graduated. I went to college—I got a theatre scholarship—and Aurielle stayed home and dated a series of criminals. Eventually, she found out about a prison pen pal program. That's where she met her current boyfriend."

Meea takes another nugget and dips it in ketchup. "Aurielle wrote to this guy for three years. He was a career criminal and should have spent his life behind bars, but he had friends in high places and got early release."

"Is he the reason you moved out here?"

She nods. "When Aurielle wanted to move with him, I asked her why this specific town and she refused to tell me. Warning bells went off in my head. That's the moment I knew I couldn't let her move without me."

"You wanted to protect her!"

"Oh, I almost forgot." Meea digs in her tiny pink purse and pulls out a folded note. "When the cops told me she'd been killed, I went home and searched all of her stuff. I didn't want them to find a surprise. In her most recent pair of jeans, I found this."

Carefully, I open the note. After reading it, I look up in shock.

"This is my sister-in-law's handwriting!"

Glancing down once again, I read the words out loud:

"'You're in way too deep, young lady. You'd better call me. Soon.'"

Chapter Twenty-Nine
Piper

"Piper? Piper? Are you there?"

Obie's friend, the off-duty deputy who was charged with watching her place, would be here soon, she told herself. The bag placed over her head smelled like...her own bakery.

Had they snuck into her home before now and stolen her flour sacks?

"Where are you taking me?" she screamed. "You're never going to get away with this!"

Instead of menacing threats, she heard laughter, which enraged her.

"Do I know you? This isn't funny. I have a million things to do!" Piper fought to loosen the restraints placed on her wrists. Though she'd taken many self-defense classes, she was no match for this surprise attack. One thug pulled a bag over her head and the other tossed her over his shoulder.

She heard a car door open and she fought against being removed from her property. "Never, ever let them take you to a different location!" November warned at the beginning of every class.

There were two sets of hands shoving her into the car like a pair of sweats that don't fit in the dresser drawer. She fought as hard as she could, but ultimately, the door was shut. They jumped in the front seat and sped away.

"Is it money you want? I'm not wealthy, but I know people who will chip in to get me out of danger."

Silence.

Piper thought hard. She needed to kick the door. In one of her self-defense classes, the instructor said that it was possible to curl your toes under the handle and release the door.

Leaning sideways, she maneuvered her feet around until they were resting on the door. Why had she worn her trekking shoes today? They were stiff on the bottom, making it impossible to loop them around anything.

The car came to an abrupt stop, causing her to fall forward into the seat in front of her. Because her hands were tied behind her back, Piper had no way of moving the sack away from her face.

"I'm suffocating!" she gasped.

This might be it. Lanie always told her not to leave anything undone. "You never know when the end is coming. I almost missed out on the love of my life and it's been a lesson I take to heart."

Obie. He was good and kind, and—

Piper took shallow breaths, trying to extend her life for as long as possible. She realized at that very second that he was her heart. She'd been so foolish to send him away when all he was trying to do was offer protection.

The door flew open and someone began tugging on her body, as if they were pulling a large item from the box store out of the car and not a living, some-what-breathing human. Someone took her shoulders, someone who'd consumed a full garden of garlic, while another person carried her feet.

"Where are we supposed to put this?"

"I'm not a 'this.' I'm a person!" Piper yelled while simultaneously trying to catch her breath.

She squirmed in hopes of being dropped.

"Stay still!" Garlic Breath hissed. "Otherwise, we'll have to truss you like a turkey. Is that what you want?"

I want you to use some mouthwash.

A door squeaked and suddenly, they were inside. Somewhere dark, noisy and— what was that smell? It was popcorn.

Her body was dropped on a thin mattress, thin enough she felt the full impact of the fall.

"Ow!"

Garlic Breath pulled the hood off and she

relished the cool air. Now that their faces were visible, they both seemed familiar. Both had ruddy, pock-marked faces and an evil glint in their eyes.

Her mind flashed back, two weeks ago. It was a slow, rainy day and she was about to close up early and curl up on the couch with a good book. The bell over the door rang and when she looked up, two very unfriendly-looking men appeared.

"We'll take whatever's left in your case." It was Garlic Breath. She wished she could open a window.

Piper glanced at the glass case. It was completely full. "That's...a lot of baked goods. Are you sure?"

He looked at his buddy, who nodded.

It took her half-an-hour to box up everything. There was a large, four-layer red velvet cake missing two slices sitting on top of the case. "This too?" she asked, half-jokingly.

"Everything."

When she'd cleaned out her case, she offered to help them load everything into their car, but they quickly declined. Not only did they pay full price, they gave her a one-hundred-dollar tip.

Piper was both pleased and bummed. Their large purchase meant her steamy romance book would have to wait. She would be baking until late into the evening to replenish the case.

Now, as she studied their faces, she noticed the same tattoo etched onto her brother's neck, the numbers 3,3,8,4 with one change. The last number on his neck was a seven, not nine like Sawyer.

"What's that?" she asked, jutting her chin toward Garlic Breath's numbers. Just as her brother had done his first day in town, he slapped his neck.

"When we join—the women's circle—each of us carries the code. We're giving a phone number and when we find another member, we text that series of numbers. Then we get our first orders."

He glanced at his partner, who clucked his tongue. "Doubt you were supposed to tell her."

Piper leaned forward, ready for the biggest performance of her life. "These ties are so tight. My hands are falling asleep." She grunted several times and scrunched her face in pretend agony. "I'm not kidding, if you are going to use me as labor, my hands may not be functional." Piper squirmed and grimaced.

"Too bad, little gal. You're not moving."

So much for that.

The two men turned and walked away, giving her time to take in her surroundings. It had to be the old popcorn factory on Cheezler Drive. In one corner, a large blue cloth was attached to the wall. Men and women were lined up, waiting for their photo to be taken.

"They're making fake IDs!" she whispered to herself. "Just like the ones Sawyer had in his drawer!"

In the center of the large warehouse, at least ten

hairdressers—both men and women—were hard at work, coloring and cutting hair.

There was another area where clothing was being distributed. If she wasn't sitting there, restrained, she might think it was a place to help those who were down on their luck to start over.

Two oversized warehouse doors opened and she squinted at the bright natural light. A vehicle of some kind was entering. When her eyes adjusted, she was shocked. It was the Cosmic Bakes delivery van backing into the warehouse.

The driver's door opened and Sawyer jumped out. Instead of the surly demeanor he maintained with her, his face looked calm, and...was that happiness?

Immediately, he began ordering people to unload the delivery van. The doors swung open and she could see large, white bags.

Sawyer pointed to an unused corner, where men and women began unloading the seemingly heavy bags.

Piper giggled softly. Those bags looked like flour. These people were trafficking in flour.

Garlic Breath walked over to Sawyer and whispered in his ear before pointing to Piper.

Sawyer's demeanor immediately changed. He punched Garlic Breath so hard that he fell to the floor. A hushed silence overtook the noisy warehouse. Even the hairdressers stopped what they were doing.

Sticking a finger above his head, Sawyer made circular motion and turned in a circle. As soon as the factory returned to its previous buzz, he stormed over to his sister.

The way he was walking, swinging his long arms angrily, made her tremble with fear. She'd seen his surly side, but never this authoritative one. When he stopped inches from the dirty mattress, he placed his hands on his hips. She released the air she was holding. At least he wasn't going to hit her. Yet.

"What are you doing here?"

Piper laughed at the absurdity of that statement. "Your goons kidnapped your sister. If it were up to me, I'd be in my kitchen, where I'm the happiest. I have six-dozen Martian Mango scones to make for the UFO—"

"This was a mistake. These weren't their orders."

She studied her brother's face. "Because they were supposed to 'dispose of me?' Like all the people who've died recently?" The pieces were starting to fit together. Sawyer was the head of some kind of smuggling ring.

"Now I'll have to figure out what to do with you," Sawyer replied dismissively, ignoring her question. He had no feelings for his sister at all, just concern for his own well-being.

"What have you been hauling in our van?"

"Glitz." Sawyer answered without reservation. Now she was positive he was going to get rid of her. She'd seen his illegal operation.

"You have to know that Obie's had an off-duty deputy watching my place. The cops will be here any minute." She was relieved that at least Obie still cared about her.

"Oh, you mean Charlie?" Sawyer turned and pointed to a familiar face, who was unloading boxes. "We pay much better than the cops." Sawyer grinned.

Piper gulped.

"Okay. At least tell me what's going on here, Sawyer. You owe me that."

Sawyer dropped his body beside her. She drank in his familiar scent: Freshright soap and cheap musk. It used to be her olfactory connection to a sweet, innocent kid.

"You probably want me to start from the beginning," he began. "I was sputtering around after my grandparents rejected me. I had no one in my corner."

"You had me!" Piper protested.

Sawyer shrugged before continuing. "I spent my last five bucks on the washer in the laundromat. That's where I met this guy, Ribeye. He was a funny-looking dude who reminded me of a bagel with feet, but he bought me breakfast and we talked for like an hour. He could tell I was a good guy, and he offered me a job working at a liquor store."

"That was nice."

Sawyer nodded. "It wasn't long before he trusted me as his right-hand man. I looked the other way when guys came in for something other than booze. Once he saw I wouldn't rat him out, he introduced me to his boss."

"Filet?" Piper joked.

"Glitz was taking over the drug scene in California," Sawyer continued, oblivious to her attempt at humor. "Guys who sold the quality stuff were pulling in ten-grand a month."

This was not the Sawyer she knew. It was Olivene all over again.

"Ribeye wanted to bring Glitz to the Midwest, except there was a guy in California running most of the country. That's when we came up with this idea to not only start our own Glitz trade, but take over his too."

"That would take more than just the three of you."

"Yeah. We had some help. Then things got messed up. Ribeye had me driving a truck in exchange for us using one of his fields to grow our crop. His daughter caught wind of our plan and threatened to go to the cops."

"So you killed her." Piper's words fell with a thud to the floor.

"Nope. She joined us after some persuasion." Sawyer chuckled at a joke only he understood.

"Is this the woman who supposedly was the love of your life?" she asked sarcastically.

"Sorry, sis. I made that up."

She could see very clearly that he wasn't sorry at all.

"The boss told me to make nice. She'd bring in the younger crowd. I found out later, he and her sister were dating." He rolled his eyes. "The whole dynamic changed after that. We had the teens, the early twenties, but we didn't have the prisoners from the state pen. I agreed to take the fall for a murder I didn't commit in order to connect with our guy on the inside. Ribeye's partner, Trigger was doing a nickel for extortion. I don't know how, but Ribeye was able arrange for us to be cellies. After we started up the Glitz business in prison, we had a good flow of ex-cons who were willing to do anything for us, in order to keep up their habit on the outside."

"I'm still not understanding how you expected to take over the entire country? Ohio is just one state."

It should have made her feel better that he hadn't actually murdered anyone, but something in her knew there was more to this story.

Sawyer grinned. It was a wide, sickening grin. It made her stomach flip. "You're right about that. We needed someone on the inside to bring the California dude to his knees." He knocked on the until-now-unseen glass window behind them. Piper got on her knees and peered through the window. It looked like a regular office, where six people were busily typing, filing and squinting at the computer.

One person stood and waved at Sawyer. When she saw Piper's face, her own turned completely white.

Piper gasped. "Aunt Cedar?"

Chapter Thirty
Lanie

"I know that look." Cosmo eyes me over the top of his black-framed readers. It's the middle-aged way of flirting with your spouse, I decide.

"You're up to something, Lanie. Whatever it is, just lay it out for me now. I've got book work to finish before the end of the day."

I'm leaning against the door frame to his office with my arms crossed. "Cos, I've been thinking. What if Sterling actually followed Cedar to Piney Falls?"

He huffs. "With his girlfriend? How was that gonna work?"

"Maybe his girlfriend is a part of this too. Vem and I have been tracking Cedar's movement." I move inside the office, shutting the door.

"Why wasn't this discussed over breakfast?"

Cosmo's voice is high-pitched and tense. "We could have saved time by talking about Cedar's life instead of November Bean's new surveillance equipment."

"If you give your blessing for me to follow your sister, I'll disappear and you won't see me again until dinner."

Cosmo chuckles and runs his hands through his thick, salt-and-pepper hair. "The last thing I want is for you to disappear. Come here."

He turns his chair away from the desk and motions for me to sit on his lap. While I'm not usually the "lap-sitting" sort, it feels appropriate today. Carefully, I lower myself to his legs and wrap one arm around his neck, kissing him gently.

"That's more like it." Cosmo smiles up at me. "Now, I want you to tell me all about your investigation, and why my poor, grieving sister needs to be followed."

"That's just it, Cos. She's not grieving at all. Don't you find that odd? Following her will give me an idea of where she's spending her time. I want to know you're on board, in case it ends badly."

Cosmo nuzzles my neck while he whispers, "If I promise to ask him today, can we continue this formation when I get home this evening?"

An abrupt knock at the door startles us both, causing me to jump to my feet. I feel like a silly teenager who was making out with her boyfriend under the bleachers. Caught by the science teacher.

"Goodness me. The way we did it in my day was to put a sock on the door handle, so's to warn others not to enter." Doris's arms are crossed as she cocks one hip to the side. I can't tell if she's disgusted or amused. Either expression on her face is the same.

Cosmo clears his throat. "Did you need something else, Doris?"

"Just got a call from the Saucy Seagull in Blackberry Cove. They didn't receive their order this morning."

"That's odd. Did you call Sawyer and ask him about it?"

Doris nods. "He didn't answer."

"Cos—"

"I know, I know." He puts one hand in the air, attempting to pause my actions and my thoughts. It doesn't work.

My chest makes an ugly thump as I think about what may have happened. And I'm deeply concerned for Piper's safety. "There's probably a good explanation for all of this. We'll laugh about it over dinner."

His weak smile tells me that he is worried too. My phone rings and I'm surprised by the caller. "Truman? Now isn't really a good time."

"Never a good time to catch an intruder, Lanie," he grumbles.

"Who did you catch?"

Cosmo mouths, "Put him on speaker!"

When I do and set the phone on Cos's desk, Doris decides to stick around, much to my chagrin.

"Truman, you're on speaker now. Cos is here too."

"What's up, buddy? Did you catch another bear?"

"No, friend, not a bear. An FBI agent."

There is a stunned silence.

"Are you sure?" I say when I've gotten hold of my senses.

"That it isn't a bear? Quite, Lanie. In the words of our first president, 'remember that it is the actions, and not the commission, that make the officer.' Hardly worth the agent's title when he stepped on my trap the first night I set it."

Cosmo stifles a laugh with a strong clearing of his throat. "Now that you've caught yourself an FBI agent, what do you intend to do with him?"

"He keeps insisting that he needs to talk to you."

"Me?" Cosmo frowns as he stares helplessly at me.

"No, not you. It's Lanie he wants to speak with."

"Can you put him on the phone, Truman?"

There is muffled conversation as I'm trying to imagine a serious man wearing his dark blue FBI jacket and reflective sunglasses. He's trussed up like a Thanksgiving turkey, waiting for Truman to release him, but instead, Truman wants to play presidential trivia.

"You have to come to us, Lanie."

Grabbing my purse off the desk, I say, "heading your way now."

When Cos hangs up, I'm afraid to look at him. Instead, I say to the desk, "We can talk later. Don't we think Truman is in trouble?"

He shakes his head decisively. "No we don't. After you and Bean found that trail leading through Truman's back yard, he fenced it off right away. Hasn't had any problems since. You got him upset for nothing at all."

"Almost forgot what brought me in here," Doris muses.

"I brought my nephew's old fishbowl. Going to put it on the counter, since your tiny box wasn't big enough."

"Are you having a drawing?" I ask eagerly. "I could supply something from the Fallen Branch."

Doris shakes her head. "It's for entries in the name-the-serial-killer contest."

My head snaps toward Cos, who frowns and give me the "we'll talk about it later" look.

"That's fine, Doris," Cos replies as I call Piper's number.

After Doris has left us, I place my phone back in my purse. "Her phone is off. "The hairs on the back of my neck are standing straight up. "I'll drive, Cos," I say as he nods knowingly.

Chapter Thirty-One
Lanie

"So now..." Vem touches her fingertips together like a villain plotting her next move. "Now you're out of options and you thought, 'well, Bean over there looks bored. Maybe I'll see if she needs a hobby?'"

My eyes roll almost to the back of my head. "You know better than that, hon. Can we get to the matter at hand? We've only got a few minutes before Cosmo gets upset. You have new information on Trigger Jarvis? We need to get out to Truman's place ASAP. Can we focus on that?

Without further conversation, she spins around in her fancy office chair and begins typing with the fury of an angry pianist.

"Hm. Very interesting."

I lean over her shoulder to see just what's captured her attention, but she bats me away. Vem's super-human strength is enough to push me back against her door.

"Vem! Stop it! This is childish."

She rubs her chin and continues scrolling down the page. When she's finished, she spins around again to face me.

"Trigger is a member of the Starfish Syndicate, a group of people who distribute drugs. He and someone named Ribeye were running it until—"

"Until what?"

I can hear Cosmo honking the horn. He came home to grab a clean shirt and that's the only reason I'm here at all.

"Hurry, Vem!"

Today's ensemble is a fluorescent yellow jump-suit, headband and glasses frames that reflect in her computer screen. I can also see her expression and determine she's still out of sorts with me.

"Here's a newspaper article I found, sister-friend," she singsongs. When a newspaper article flashes up on the screen, I attempt to lean over her shoulder, but before I can, an arm blocks me.

"An arrest warrant was issued for Trigger Jarvis, age 39, Del "Ribeye" Winterkorn, age 50, Aurielle Chard, age 26, and Meea Chard, age 27. All are considered armed and dangerous."

"What did they do?" I don't have time for shock over Meea's association with this group.

Cosmo isn't even bothering to take his palm off the horn now. "Quickly, Vem!"

"Murdered a city councilman. He discovered they were dealing Glitz in the nightclubs and the prison. The police chief is implicated as well. They think he tipped the Toots off."

She whirls around again, this time with dizzying speed that would make any lesser human sick. She takes my hands in hers and holds them tightly. "We're going to keep this between us for now, at least until we've got some reason for them to be together in Piney Falls. We should probably contact Boysie."

"You're absolutely right! I've completely left him out of this equation." Glancing toward the door, I say, "We need to get to Truman's place. Come over for dinner and we'll figure this out."

"Oh, I'm going with you," Vem says matter-of-factly.

"No, Vem. This isn't—"

"My presence was requested, Lanie. I'm going."

Chapter Thirty-Two
Piper

"I can't believe it," Piper whispered, as she slid back down the wall.

"What? That your brother is number two in the Starfish Syndicate Crime Syndicate, or that Cosmo's sister helped us take out the West Coast Flower?"

"I'm assuming there is an alternate meaning for that word?"

"Oh, that's what we called him. He came up with the idea to sell Glitz to people from a dating app." Sawyer pulls a small mirror, like the one I found in his room, from his pocket. "You've heard of Truthfully Yours?"

Piper nodded, though she'd never actually used a dating app. Lanie would have a fit if she knew her daughter was on there.

"Everyone who pays for six months gets one of

these in the mail. Once you turn it on," he flipped a small switch on the side of the mirror, "it emits an odorless Glitz gas that causes the user to become addicted within three uses. Brilliant, really."

Piper turned her head away, hoping she wasn't smelling it right now. "Sterling Truth started all of this? And he hired you?"

"Nah. I was hired by Ribeye, like I said. We decided—Trigger, Ribeye and me— to take over the west coast syndicate. That's when your aunt approached us. She suggested we look here in Piney Falls for an out-of-the-way place to run our operation."

Piper was certain her mouth was hanging open, but at this moment, she didn't care. "Cedar is making the decisions for your organization?"

"Just that one. Once we moved everyone out here, she just did office work. Oh, and I guess she did alert us to the fact that Ribeye was stealing from us. She arranged for his exit. Proved her loyalty to us right there."

Piper shuddered. Her aunt couldn't possibly have killed a gangster. That wasn't the person she knew, the person her father adored almost as much as Lanie.

"I'm trying to get this straight in my head. Your first murder was our delivery driver, so that you could use our truck, right?"

"No, not the first. It was more important to clean

house. There was a guy in Tellum who worked for Sterling, and another in Blackberry Cove. They were before Sterling."

"What about Aurielle? Did you kill her too?" Something about his killing a female around her age was even harder to take.

Someone came up and whispered in Sawyer's ear. He nodded. "I'll be there in a minute." He turned back to Piper with the same icky smile on his face. "Where was I? Oh yeah. Aurielle was dating Trigger. When he met her sister, Trigger decided he liked Meea better. That's when the two of them came up with the idea to get rid of Aurielle. She'd already blabbed about our operation to her neighbors in the apartment complex, so it was a good hit."

"Shot and strangled," Piper replied mournfully. "And what about the pretty woman they found? Harmony something?"

"Gregory." Sawyer scoffed. "She wasn't mine. Trigger sent his girlfriend on that job."

Piper's mind raced. "And you killed Mr. Truth?"

A short, round man with a pock-marked face approached them. "Sorry, boss. This can't wait."

Sawyer stood and wiped the dust from his pants. "Guess you get to breathe a few more minutes," he said to his sister.

Though she was relieved he was gone, the thought of never seeing the people she loved again was too much. Tears fell from her lavender eyes and she had no way of wiping them away.

She felt a presence behind her. "If you're going to...kill me," she sobbed, "just be quick about it."

"I'm going to get you out of here, sweetie."

It was Cedar's gentle voice.

"I don't understand how you could be a part of this!" Piper cried as Cedar undid the zip ties.

"There's no time to explain. I set up a diversion to get Sawyer out of here, but he won't be gone more than a few minutes. Here, I'll help you up."

Cedar placed her hands under either armpit and helped Piper to a standing position. "Let's go!"

As Piper stepped off the dusty mat (which she was relieved to see wasn't a mattress at all) her legs buckled.

"Cedar!"

Her aunt turned around, and understanding her distress, put one of Piper's arms around her shoulder. They moved quickly and unseen, out the same door her captors used to bring her in.

They stopped in front of Cedar's rental car and Cedar handed her the keys. "Do you think you can drive?"

Piper nodded. "My legs are feeling much better."

"Good. You're going straight to that boyfriend of yours. Tell him to contact the FBI and give them this location. I'm sorry I don't have time to tell you more now."

Cedar glanced from side to side.

"Won't you get into trouble for letting me go?"

"That's not for you to worry about. Go!"

Her aunt opened the car door and pushed Piper inside. The pedals were too far away, but there was no time for adjusting. With shaky hands, Piper started the car. She sank down low in the seat so she could reach the gas. As she was pulling out of the warehouse parking lot, she looked in her mirror, hoping to catch one last glimpse of her aunt. Cedar was already gone.

All the way back into town, Piper tried processing what had happened. After all of her guilt about not seeing her brother, he wasn't here to catch up with his sister anyway. He'd murdered people, lots of people. Probably more than she knew.

Sawyer needed connection. That was the problem all along. Unlike her, Sawyer never found a place where he felt at home. That's why, after the Broken Branch Cult fell apart, he sought another one. This time, it came in the form of a drug-pushing gang.

As she pulled into the first space in front of the police station/library, Piper realized she'd been gripping the steering wheel so tightly that her fingers were numb.

Jumping out of the car, she almost ran over Boysie.

"Where are you headed in such a hurry, Miss Moonlight Hill?"

She studied his concerned and kind face and without warning, an avalanche of tears and emotion came flowing out. Boysie pulled her in against his chest and patted her shoulder. "There, there. It can't be as bad as all that."

"I'm so sorry. For everything." She pulled away and wiped her eyes with the back of her hand, thankful that she had the ability to move her arms again.

"I wish I had the time for a good heart-to-heart, but I'm headed out on a call." He pivoted toward the building and then back to her. "There are other folks who might be able to help."

She nodded. Her silly feud with Obie wasn't important. At least not right now. As she waved goodbye to Boysie, she thought about what a good man he was. And it didn't end there. His sons were good people too.

Once she reached the front desk, Piper scanned the busy room.

"What can I do you for, Miss Moonlight Hill?"

It was the creepy guy who'd asked her out before. Larry or Barry. "I'm looking for Obie. Is he here?"

He took his pen and pointed vaguely behind him. "In his office. You're going to crush a poor guy's heart like that?"

"What do you mean?"

"I thought maybe you were here to see me!"

She didn't bother responding. When she reached Obie's office, her stomach did a little flip. He was typing ferociously away on his computer, chewing on his cheek the way he did when he didn't like what he'd written.

"What did the computer ever do to you?"

Obie looked up with surprise. "Pa-Pa-Piper? What are you doing here?"

In his attempt to reach her, he stumbled over his chair and fell right into her arms. His closeness made Piper long to hold him.

"Sorry about that." Obie stood and brushed his uniform, taking time to pat each of his shoulders three times.

"What brings you in? Aren't you busy with that conference out at the convention center?"

She was touched he remembered her calendar, given the way she'd left things.

"Obie, I'm sorry. I'm stubborn and sometimes that gets in my way." She stared at the floor, forcing back tears. "There's never been anyone who understands me the way you do. Love is like a rollercoaster ride. It's terrifying and thrilling, and sometimes you end up throwing up your cotton candy, but then you get back in line and do it all over again. You're my ride or die."

Instantly he moved in and hugged her. "I love you too, Piper Moonlight Hill. You're a very passionate person and I knew that when we met. But next time, let's talk things through. No throwing up cotton candy. Especially if we're riding again in the same outfits."

She grabbed his face and brought it to hers, kissing him passionately. It was exactly how their first kiss had happened so long ago.

"Now, I'm assuming you didn't come just to apologize?"

"Why would you say that?" Piper asked, half-teasing.

"Because when you walked in here, you were as white as a ghost. Something serious is going on. Fill me in."

Chapter Thirty-Three
Lanie

"**B**uddy, do you think it might be a good idea to let Mr. Goins down?"

The FBI agent Truman had trapped with an elaborate net and motion-sensor system was hanging from the light pole in his yard.

"I s'pose so," Truman replied begrudgingly. He untied the pulley he'd constructed and lowered the man to the ground.

Quickly, Cos and I fight our way through the netting to release him. He smiles at us appreciatively when he's firmly on the ground.

I hand him a bottle of water and a chocolate chip cookie. "What else can I get for you?"

After consuming the entire cookie in two bites, he shakes his head. "Nothing. This hit the spot."

"And now you're going to tell Mrs. Hill why you trespassed onto my property," Truman orders him.

"Would you like to sit down? Truman has a lovely patio," I say, ushering him to the back yard. Truman and Cos stay in front. I can tell my darling husband is doing his best to keep Truman occupied. His surly demeanor wouldn't make for good conversation. Once we're seated, Agent Goins clears his throat.

"We'd been looking for a way into the Glitz market for some time. The west coast market is booming, unfortunately. We knew who was in charge, but he had so many smart people around him, it was impossible for our agents to become a part of his inner circle. That's when the perfect person fell into our laps."

I'm very curious why he's telling me all of this. Does he think I'm involved somehow in the drug trade?

"Mr. Goins, this is very interesting, but I'm afraid I don't understand."

"Please, be patient," he says, clearing his throat again. "I was up in that infernal net, screaming my head off for so long that I've got a tickle in my throat now."

Instinctively, I reach into my purse and pull out Vem's remedy. "As soon as we're done, I'll heat up some water. This stuff is miraculous!"

He nods with uncertainty, but continues his story.

"We did our research, trying to find someone who would help us infiltrate this organization."

"You mean someone you could blackmail? I've watched enough crime shows to understand your lingo."

Once more, he nods, but this time his body moves in his seat.

"Did I touch a nerve, Mr. Goins?"

Leaning forward, he clasps his hands together on the table. "Mrs. Hill, sometimes my job stretches to the boundaries of my morality. This experience was one of those times."

This confession is most surprising. Though I know FBI agents are people who have feelings just like the rest of us, I've always thought of them as a superior breed who've been conditioned to shut off emotions.

"We combed the books of many companies who did business with Mr. Truth. The man we'd recruited was ready to move forward, but as much as he tried, he couldn't get a moment alone. It seems Mr. Truth was smitten with a woman who was attending the event. A Miss Cedar Hill from the Sleepy Sounds Corporation."

I expected this news, but it still makes me gasp. "What did you do to my poor sister-in-law to force her into this undercover work?"

FBI Agent Goins looks down at his rapidly moving

thumbs. "I told you there are things we do that bother me. We presented her with a false series of emails. They all had her work address and each one referred to the budget for the marketing department." He clears his throat again. This time, it's very clearly nerves.

My blood is boiling. "You made my sweet, sweet sister-in-law think she'd somehow misappropriated her marketing budget, didn't you?"

When he doesn't respond, I bang my fist on the table. "Admit it! You've forced her into this dangerous world by making her think she is a criminal too!"

"Mrs. Hill, we don't have time for this. If you want to take out your anger on me later, that's fine. Right now, I need you to listen carefully."

Taking deep breaths, I lean back in my chair and cross my arms. "Go ahead."

"Cedar far exceeded expectations."

"Of course she did!" I snap. "She puts her all in everything she does!"

"Yes, well, she'd convinced Mr. Truth to open a large facility here in Piney Falls. It was perfect—we'd be able to fit the building with surveillance devices before they opened. But then your sister-in-law had an unfortunate encounter with Mr. Truth."

"She found him with his girlfriend. Harmony Gregory."

"Yes. And then she got drunk in the bar and told the bartender everything. Luckily, he was one of ours. He slipped something in her drink to make her forget everything."

I can hardly breathe. "You set everything up to make it look like she'd murdered him! Just when I thought you couldn't get any lower!"

"It was necessary to keep our agents safe. Once more, we blackmailed her by making her believe Mr. Truth met a violent end. We convinced her to come up here and set everything up before the Ohio group arrived.

No wonder she's looked ill ever since she arrived. "Poor Cedar. She thought she killed Sterling." I glance at Mr. Goins. "Who did kill him?"

"Someone from his organization. We're not sure yet. There's a large faction of ex-cons and fringe people who moved from Ohio. Sterling and Ms. Gregory's deaths were a power play. And Cedar ingratiated herself with the Ohio organization without our approval. She's off-script, so-to-speak."

"I'm trying to figure out how I'm going to tell my husband."

"The reason I came to you, and not him directly, is because our local operative we hired insisted you be a part of the extraction operation, to remove Cedar."

"Really? Who would—"

"Sister friend! Now the party begins!"

Chapter Thirty-Four
Piper

"And that's when my aunt gave me her car keys and told me to leave."

Obie sat next to Piper, holding her hand.

"This is, wow. I can't believe how close I came to losing you forever."

He leaned over and kissed Piper. Again.

"What do we do now, Obie? She's in real danger, especially because she let me go."

Obie pursed his lips. "Dad's on his way out to Mr. Coolidge's place. Something about an FBI agent stuck in a net? I don't know. I'll text him and ask him to contact me right away when he's done there."

Piper nodded and smiled at her boyfriend, feeling pleased that she could call him that once more.

Obie texted his father and then stood. "I think I

should get together a team while we're waiting for Dad."

She jumped up and pulled him in close. "What? No! Obie, you can't go out there, it's too dangerous! I just got you back!."

"I know, Pips," he uttered softly. "But from what you've told me, your aunt is in real trouble, and a crime syndicate won't think twice about getting rid of her if they think she betrayed them."

She nodded. Piper understood his words, but her heart thought differently. "What I don't understand is how she's involved with these thugs anyway. And my brother? How did she connect with him?"

"Don't worry. We'll figure it out. Right now though, I need you to stay put."

"Obie, no!" she begged.

"It's okay. This is what I'm trained for. Please trust me when I say I know what I'm doing."

She kissed him one more time, then waved goodbye. It occurred to her that she'd missed all of her orders today, and that Sawyer never made any deliveries. She dialed her father's number.

Before Cosmo answered, she hung up. "He'll be really upset that he misjudged Sawyer."

"Miss Moonlight Hill?"

It was an officer Piper only knew as Rubins.

"Yes?"

"I've got a bottle of water and homemade brown sugar oatmeal cake. My wife's special recipe."

"Thanks, Rubins!" The last thing she felt like doing right now was eating.

"I offered to bring you coffee, but Officer Lumquest said you'd prefer water. Let me know if you need anything else."

"I will."

After he was gone, she tried calling her mother. It went straight to voicemail. "Hi Mom! This is me, Piper." She giggled, though she didn't know why. "Just wanted to let you know that there is an...interesting reason I missed the deliveries this morning. I'm going to call everyone who expected them and explain. And when you're done with whatever you're doing, give me a call. It's too much to tell you in a message. Okay. Love you!"

She stared at the cake. It was decorated very fancy, with swirly tan piping on the side and the remnants of a message on top. "Ha..Ru."

Any other day, tasting the work of another baker would intrigue her. Not today.

Her eyes traveled around the room, coming to rest on the desk once more. Only this time, she saw Obie's phone.

He did tell her to wait here. But the lack of communication could put his life in danger. She grabbed the water and stood. There was no time to waste.

Chapter Thirty-Five
Lanie

"Vem? You're...an FBI agent?"

Of the fifty unlikely things I might encounter today, this was not even on the list.

"Yes indeedy," she replies proudly. I should have known something was up when she appeared with her hair pulled back in a bun. That's not the normal Vem look.

I've never actually seen her face without frizzy hair around it, and now that her features are prominent, I'm stunned by her beauty. Her face reminds me of a painting I saw in the Chicago Museum of Art. She has very high cheekbones and an oblong face with full, salmon-pink lips. Our Ms. Bean could be a model.

Vem's flawless complexion is a result, assuredly,

of her crazy face concoctions. "Like a baboon's behind, Lanie. You should try it."

"We swore Ms. Bean in last week, after she called us with information about your sister-in-law." Mr. Goins scratches the back of his neck. "My boss was hesitant until he learned of her extensive collection of equipment."

Vem beams. I'm quite sure it's never occurred to her that they're using her for her gadgets. We'll keep it that way. "And I blackmailed him, don't forget that," Vem says proudly.

"Yes, that's true." Agent Goins turns to face me. "Ms. Bean used her high-powered surveillance equipment to catch our boss in a...let's just say it wasn't where he was supposed to be."

Vem opens her mouth to explain, but I shake my head. This isn't information I need.

"I wish you would have told me, Vem. Instead, you let me go on and on about Cedar."

Vem opens her mouth to speak again, but Agent Goins starts first. "Ms. Bean signed a contract with us. She's not allowed to sue us if anything goes wrong. And my boss was very firm about her silence."

"They know things, Lanie," Vem whispers, as if no one else can hear.

"Our plan was to raid the compound in three days, but we've received intel that your sister-in-law may be in danger, so we have no choice but to go now."

My heart drops. Poor Cedar.

"There are three agents in the area. Along with you and Ms. Bean, who will play minor roles, you have to understand," he stares pointedly at Vem, "we're hoping to make the extraction quickly."

I gulp. I'm used to dealing with one criminal at a time. "I'm ready."

"Ready for what?"

Cosmo and Truman have joined us. "Bean? What are you doing here? Not enough whacky moaners to keep you busy?"

"Cos, she's been—"

"I'll have you know, Cosmo Hill, that I've been an undercover operative for the FBI. One of their most valued agents. I've been promised a jacket."

He chuckles before glancing at our long faces. "What? You can't be serious! Lanie? What's going on?"

After I've given him a quick update, he and Truman say in unison, "You're not going after her without me."

Agent Goins rolls his eyes. "You're just going to get in the way," he pleads. "Besides, it's likely these people are all heavily armed. Considering you don't have weaponry or training, the likelihood is high that you would get yourself killed."

"Au contraire, my turtle-shelled friend," Vem

replies, patting his bullet-proof vest. "I have enough easy-to-use weapons for all of us. And I've already given Lanie instruction on more than one occasion."

"It's true," I concede. "Two afternoons of weapons and wontons."

Cosmo stares at me with a look of wonder and I shrug in response. Most of the time when I tell him I spent the afternoon with Vem, he doesn't want to know what we did.

"Your only job is to provide backup," Agent Goins reiterates. "As soon as my crew arrives, we'll head out. I'm going to confirm they're on the way. Excuse me."

When he has removed himself to the other side of the patio, I prepare for Cosmo's blow up. He won't be pleased that we both deceived him.

"Before you say anything, I just learned about Cedar's undercover work."

"Lanie, I don't know what to say." The tears in his eyes are even harder to deal with than the expected dressing down.

"Babe, it's all right. There are more FBI agents on the way. Those drug dealing thugs are no match for these trained professionals."

"Actually, there's been a change of plans." Agent Goins has returned from the other side of the patio. "My men were called in at the last minute for an armed stand-off in Tellum. We'll go in later this evening instead. We won't need your back up after all." He grins, obviously relieved to be rid of us.

"Later this evening? My sister could be dead by then!"

"Cos, it's okay," I say, trying to soothe him.

"No, Lanie, it's anything but okay!" he shouts.

I pivot toward Agent Goins. "Could you give us a few minutes of privacy?" At the same time, I direct a head-tilt towards Vem. When she's in tune with me, she understands this as a "keep him occupied" signal. There are other times when she believes this means I'm ready to join her in a full-throated yodel. Luckily, today she gets my drift.

"Did I tell you about my experience as a world-record holding moaner?" she says as she locks arms with the agent, guiding him away from us.

"Cos, we're still going in, aren't we?" I whisper.

"What?" This experience has him so worked up that he didn't think it through. In an instant his crystal blue eyes light up. "You bet your bonnet we're going in! We've got Bean's weaponry, your smarts and my muscle."

"And mine," Truman adds, a new addition to the conversation.

"How do we get rid of him though?" I ask, shrugging and tilting my head toward the corner of the patio, where Vem is gesturing wildly in between duck walks.

"Leave that to me," Truman says, pivoting toward

the theatre taking place across from us. "Officer? Could I have a minute?" He calls, motioning for Agent Goins to join us.

Agent Goins practically runs from Vem. "Thank you! One more story and Ms. Bean would end up on the watch list. She's got too much weaponry and too many strange ideas to be safe."

"My assumption is that you'll be using my property for a staging area?" Truman asks.

The agent nods.

"And I assume as well that you want us to carry on with our normal activities in the meantime?"

He studies our faces. "Provided those activities won't draw attention to the former popcorn factory location."

"Agent Goins, as an employee of our proud government, I'm shocked that you haven't recognized this auspicious occasion."

After an appropriate silence, he continues.

"It is the knowledge that all men have weaknesses and that many have vices that makes government necessary. James Monroe, our fifth president." Truman smacks his lips with satisfaction. "Have to celebrate the man's birthday for that quote alone, don't you think?"

"Um, okay, sure." Agent Goins's face is blotchy and he looks as though Vem and Truman may have done him in.

"My dear friends and I planned a nice barbecue

in honor of President Monroe's birthday. Since my place will be otherwise occupied, Cosmo and Lanie have graciously offered theirs. Would you allow us to host our party? We'll be in constant contact, rest assured."

I hold my breath, hoping that this story works.

"Yeah, that would be really helpful!" he replies cheerily. "Mr. Coolidge, if you don't mind, my team and I will assemble right here, on your patio. We'll be very careful so nothing else is damaged."

Something occurs to me. "Agent Goins, is that what was going on when tire tracks were found behind Truman's property? You were meeting with someone?"

He stares out across the pasture land. There are still tire tracks leading to the Sassy Lasses Winery.

"Yes, Mrs. Hill," he says, as if reading my mind. "Cedar met us in the middle of the field. She assured us it was private. We had no idea we were being followed."

Chapter Thirty-Six
Piper

Piper cranked her radio. Her windows were down and she jammed to Azure Whirlygig, her favorite steampunk group. She pounded on the steering wheel as she sang at the top of her lungs, "Our mechanical hearts beat to a clockwork beat, We're the band of merry misfits, the masters of the street."

When they were kids, Olivene had no patience for music or children who let go and sang nonsense at the top of their lungs. Piper remembered the times her parents left them alone. The very first thing they did was crank up the radio and jump on the bed while they sang along.

Sawyer was a sweet, thoughtful boy who looked up to his big sister.

Her heart sank as she thought about the twisted man he'd become. *Was part of this her fault?*

She turned down Cheezler Drive and shut off her music. Just like her brother, Piper had a job to do.

In the distance she could see law enforcement in a staging area. They were parked just off Cheezler Drive, on Daisy Drive. There were so many large pine trees, their presence would be hard to spot if you weren't looking.

Slowly she drove onto Daisy Lane. At least a dozen policemen turned in unison, staring at her like she was the enemy. Piper cowered in her car, wondering if this had been a mistake.

She heard Obie's quick footsteps before she saw him. He didn't bother knocking on her window, instead he threw the door open and leaned inside. "Pa-pa-Piper, what about, 'stay here,' didn't make sense to you?"

Piper hadn't seen him that angry before. His face was almost purple. Instead of frightening her, his demeanor had the opposite effect. She burst out laughing. "I'm so sorry. It's just that, well, you look like an evil blueberry!"

Obie bit his bottom lip and gave Piper a moment to collect herself. "You shouldn't have come, Pips," he remarked in a softer tone. "I know you're worried about your aunt, but—"

"I brought your phone. I thought you might need it." She reached over to the passenger seat and handed it to him. "Didn't mean to interrupt anything."

Suddenly, there was a loud boom, causing the officers to move behind their vehicles. Everyone but Obie. He jumped in Piper's car, shoving her to the passenger side. Obie placed the car in gear and sped to the far end of the street.

Piper looked at her over-dry baker's hands. They were shaking. "What do we—"

"Get down!" Obie ordered. He didn't bother waiting for her to obey. Instead, he pushed her head into her lap, barely missing the dash.

She could hear the sound of his gun cocking and the rhythmic sound of his breathing. The longer they sat, the calmer he became. Obie had nerves of steel.

There were more pops and Obie remarked all-too-calmly, "They're moving this way. I've got to get you out of here!"

Piper wasn't sure if she should sit up, or if staring at her feet was a position she should maintain.

"There's a dairy farm at the end of this street, if I remember correctly. We're going to do a little off-roading. We'll see if those new tires I bought you are worth the hefty price tag."

"You used your police discount!" Piper protested. It didn't have as much meaning when she was looking at the floor. "Can I sit up yet?"

"No, Pips. It's not safe. I'll let you know."

She felt the car lurch forward on uneven ground. The familiar scent of cattle relaxed her, strangely enough. Her cattle neighbors had become a great source of peace. Finally, the car rolled to a stop.

"Okay, it's safe to sit up now."

When she lifted her head, everything spun around. "Obie, I'm going to be..."

Instinctively he reached over and opened her door moments before she got sick. Now she felt justified in leaving the oatmeal cake untouched. After she caught her breath, Piper realized the world was no longer spinning and they were parked behind a barn.

Obie handed her a water bottle that she'd forgotten in the car after their last hike together.

"Now that you're going to live, I have to tell you again, coming out here wasn't a good idea." His voice wavered. "Your life isn't worth my phone."

"I know," she replied with the gravelly voice of someone who just upheaved. "I'm sorry. You have to admit, though, if I hadn't shown up when I did, you'd be right in the middle of that gunfire."

His face was devoid of color. "Pips, there may be mass casualties back there. I'm going to take you home and have Dad call for the Blackberry Cove tank."

"They have a tank? It's a tiny town, smaller than ours!"

"We all have our weaponry," he replied slyly. As Obie put the car in gear once more, Piper caught sight of a large vehicle approaching them at a high rate of speed.

"Obie! Behind us!" She screamed, before her car was hit. The airbags thrust both Piper and Obie back in their seats. It felt like being hit by a stuffed animal, if it were traveling at 90 mph. As the car became airborne, Piper smelled the scent of something burning. Because she couldn't see or hear anything, time stood still. When the car finally landed, it came down with a hard thud. Her ears were ringing and everything around her was spinning."Obie?" she called weakly.

"I'm fine, Pips." He took her hand and squeezed it. Slowly, she began opening her eyes. Her face hurt, like it had been drug across the floor.

The passenger door opened and large hands reached in, pulling Piper out. They shoved her into the back seat of another vehicle and soon, Obie was beside her.

Two men sat in the front seat, one with a distinct odor: garlic.

"Thought you got away, didn't you, little pixie?" he taunted.

"You're never going to get away with this. The entire west coast will be looking for their missing officer," Piper warned, fighting the nausea that was overtaking her.

The goon slapped his driver. "Gerry, would you look at that! We've got ourselves a cop, along with the little pixie. It's like a two-for-one coupon!"

Obie grabbed Piper's arm and shook his head. She realized the force of the airbag had given him a black eye.

The next thing she did was throw up.

Chapter Thirty-Seven
Lanie

"I'd argue with you people, but I just got word there was a showdown with our officers and the police we'd assembled to go in."

Boysie looks as though he might pass out. I can't say as I blame him, given he's just been informed that his son and his fellow officers have been involved in an altercation. I'd like to ask more questions, but time is of the essence. "We're ready, Boysie. Vem's got us armed to the teeth."

"What about our FBI friend?" Cosmo asks. We'd been rushing to load ourselves into Vem's gigantic vehicle when Boysie pulled in. No one had given a thought to Agent Goins since.

"I'll communicate with him on the way," Boysie says with urgency. "Let's roll!"

Before today, I'd never sat in the back of this thing, but to my amazement, it looks like the five of us could stretch out and nap without touching one another.

"It will take us thirty minutes to reach Cheezler Drive," Boysie begins. "In that time, we need to decide how we'll extract your sister." His radio beeps and we fall silent, waiting to hear the fate of the police officers.

No one has been injured, she says. "What about my son? Sounds like something he'd put himself right in the middle of."

"He wasn't there, chief."

"Ten-four. We're headed out to the factory now."

"You have to be so relieved!" I say, stating the obvious.

"Yes and no. I'm still very concerned about your sister. What is your plan to get her out?"

Vem crosses her arms and gives Boysie one of her know-it-all smirks. "We've been talking, and since Truman practiced with the Boom Boom, so he'll create a diversion once we're in place."

"The what?" Boysie asks.

"Bo-oom bo-oom," Vem enunciates unnecessarily. "It's a neat trick I picked up at the big military discount sale last winter. It's like a gigantic firework. Shoots pink sparkles fifty feet in the air."

Boysie chuckles. "You can't be serious. How will this help?"

"We're assuming some will come out to see what

the heck is going on. That gives Bean a chance to deploy her next goodie," Cosmo says.

"Wait till you hear the name of the next one," I say. Though it's not a time for humor, the look on his face is priceless.

"With the air full of pinkness, Lookie Lucy will appear. It's a bee-sized camera that can enter the building and show us where Cedar is being held, exact coordinates and all that. It moves at a pace of 20 miles per minute, so it should be in and out before they even realize it's there."

"Meanwhile, I'll be waiting for whoever comes out."

"Phase three, Cosmo Hill," Vem reminds him.

"Yeah, whatever. I've got a Woozy Wanda. That's something similar to a gun that will render the bad guys so dizzy they can't stand."

Cosmo finally gets to use it.

"Phase four is Nightie Nellie. It's three tiny canisters of a powerful sleeping spray launched through a quiet rocket and into the building. We'll use the coordinates gained from Lookie Lucy."

Boysie looks as though he's about to burst. "I can't take it anymore." He starts laughing so loud and hard that it startles all of us. "The next weapon you're going to tell me about is Shooting Shelly, right?"

November frowns. "Just good old-fashioned gas masks, Officer Lumquest. Geez. Do you think I'm some kind of a nut?"

We've reached the designated drop-off point for Truman. He steps out of the vehicle and Cos hands him the rocket. "Just like the Fourth of July, buddy," he reminds his friend. "I'll be a phone call away if you run into trouble."

Truman shakes his head. "There's no reason to worry. I've never let you down before."

Vem takes a left, curving around to an area that is a safe distance from the back side of the building. When she puts the car in park, it occurs to me that Boysie, our police chief, has been given no role in our rescue plan. We only have four gas masks and the plan is to put one on Cedar.

"Boysie, what will you..." I pause. It seems silly to tell a seasoned officer what to do.

"I'm going to plant myself by the back door," he replies, as if reading my mind. "That way, I can catch anyone who thinks they'll get away. Will this mist of yours, Ms. Bean, keep them knocked out for a while?"

"Forty-five minutes, give or take."

"We're short on manpower after the incident earlier. I'll call my son and see if he can meet us there."

Chapter Thirty-Eight
Piper

"You really hurt me, sis." Sawyer used his gun to scratch his forehead, oblivious to the suffering in front of him and the danger to himself.

"How so?" Piper asked, the taste of vomit still prominent in her mouth. Her entire body ached from the accident and she still smelled something burnt. She could only imagine how bad she looked.

Piper realized the longer she kept her brother talking, the more time she and Obie had to formulate a plan. They were tied, back-to-back, on the same dirty mat she had been seated on earlier in the day. Every few minutes, she squeezed Obie's hand for reassurance. He squeezed back without any concern for the cleanliness of her fingers.

"Well, for starters, you and boyfriend here." He

pointed his weapon at Obie and Piper held her breath until Sawyer found something else in the room to capture his attention. "You guys invited all sorts of cops to our party. I didn't give you permission to bring guests, sis."

"I'm...sorry about that, Sawyer." She wondered if all of the officers survived? "That must've put a real crimp in your productivity for today."

Piper wiggled a little, trying to find a comfortable position in which to place her body. There wasn't one.

"I've got fifteen injured. At least one dead." Sawyer clicked his tongue. "Not good, sis. Not good for you at all."

"Sa-sa-Sawyer, why don't you let your sister go? She's got all of those orders to get out and those customers will start asking questions real soon. Keep me here. If you need a bargaining chip, a cop is the person you want."

Piper squeezed his hand. Obie Lumquest was the bravest person she knew.

"Nah. I'm going to get rid of both of you. Now that our location has been compromised, we're going to pack up and move along."

"You're in charge of this? All of the Glitz production on the west coast?" Obie asked with surprise.

Sawyer bent down so close to Obie's face that their noses were almost touching. Piper could feel

Obie's pulse quickening. Her brave boyfriend had serious issues with personal space. *Just put all of your energy in my hand, Obie.*

"Copper boy, I sensed doubt in your voice. Don't you think I can run this by myself?"

"Sawyer!"

He stood and whipped around so fast, his gun hit Obie's already swollen face. "Trigger! What are you doing here?"

For the first time today, Sawyer's voice wasn't dripping with arrogance.

Piper noticed that everyone in the building had numbers tattooed on their necks, just like Sawyer. It was another way her brother could feel like he belonged, she reasoned.

Trigger, a man with more muscles than anyone Piper had ever seen in her life, walked with purpose to the mat and slapped Sawyer across the face. Her first instinct was to comfort her brother, but she bit her lip and kept quiet.

Sawyer grabbed his bright red cheek. "What was that for?"

"You've messed up everything we've worked for. Didn't I tell you to wait for my instructions before taking hostages?"

"I'm—"

"We got rid of Truth and his girlfriend in order to run this organization ourselves. I brought the ex-cons from Ohio. Then you had to go and make friends with a cop and this chick."

Piper frowned as she thought about that statement. Didn't this Trigger know she was Sawyer's sister?

"Sorry."

"Yeah, you're sorry all right," Trigger barked. "Eight of my best men are gone. Now it's gonna take another three months of re-building. Are you happy with yourself?"

Sawyer was silent.

"Ribeye told me you'd been acting weird, ever since we got here. I should've listened to him."

"Cedar said she caught Ribeye stealing a shipment, remember?"

"Mr. Trigger?" Piper asked. "What happened to Cedar Hill?"

"Babe, I'm ready!"

Piper couldn't see whoever this was. Her voice was familiar though. Someone close to her age.

"Thanks, Meea." *Kiss. Kiss.*

"Are you Meea from Chez Pine?" Piper asked.

She moved into view and bent down close to Piper, squinting. "Do I know you?" She displayed numbers on her neck as well.

"Probab—"

"You don't know her," Sawyer interjected. "Just tell me what you want me to do next. It won't be long before the place is swarming with cops."

"Meea, didn't you have a sister named Aurielle?" Obie asked, baiting her.

"Why would you ask that, copper?" she snarled.

"You know that there was video of the crime scene. The apartment building you live in has the highest quality cameras."

"What?"

Piper squeezed Obie's hands again. "Not only that, we found your DNA and matched it to the other murders. It won't matter if you get rid of us, there will be more cops soon."

"When she was found dead, there was DNA all over her body. It was your boyfriend's. They confirmed with the staff at the Fallen Branch Hotel. Your DNA was all over that room."She was improvising, but Piper sensed their window of opportunity was closing.

"I work there, you idiot," she snapped. "Of course my DNA was found. Is that the best you can do?"

"Did your boyfriend tell you that it was his plan all along to get rid of your sister?" Piper continued.

"No, it wasn't. It was my idea."

Piper marveled at Obie's calm.

" spent months planning everything. How they'd lure both of you out here after Aurielle sent him all of her savings. That's when they'd convince you to get rid of her, right Trigger?" Piper paused, letting it all soak in. She hoped.

"Babe?" Meea's confident voice was beginning to fade. "You love me more than her, right?"

"We talked about this. She wanted out. Don't let these idiots convince you otherwise.

"Meea, I wasn't born yesterday, but you certainly had me fooled."

Chapter 39
Fifteen minutes earlier
Lanie

"It looks like Cedar is being held in this storage room." Vem points a camouflage-colored fingernail at the screen. Sure enough, it is a crystal-clear image of Cosmo's sister.

I lean in close and squint, wishing I had quick access to my reading glasses. "I can't tell, is she moving?"

"Here, let me," Vem says, grabbing her tablet. She takes two long fingers and stretches them across the screen. "There. Cedar is not only alive and breathing, she's trying to get out of her restraints."

"What does the label on those boxes say?"

"Gemfinder. No time to explain now, Lanie."

"I know what it's for." My heart breaks. Cedar's been through so much already. "Are we ready for phase three?"

Vem nods and brings a walkie talkie to her face. "Lummie and Hillie, are you ready for Nellie?"

"Yes. We caught six guys when they ran out. Boysie is finishing trussing them like turkeys." Cosmo chuckles. "And Bean, if you call me 'Hillie' again, you'll be in a world of hurt."

"Cos, we've got eyes on Cedar. She's in a storage area. It's in the opposite end of the building from where you're stationed. We've counted four other people in the building. They seem to be standing in a large room. Well, and two who may be sleeping on the ground. We were in a hurry and didn't take time to look."

"Thanks, babe," he says in the soft voice that makes me weak in the knees.

"Vem and I are about to shoot the rockets. Put your gas mask on and give us six minutes. Vem says it will take that long for the gas to take effect. We'll meet you where Cedar is being held."

"What? That wasn't part of the deal. Is this Bean's nutty idea? You guys are the lookouts."

I grab November's arm and shake my head. Now isn't the time for her to be triggered by my husband.

"Vem found two more Woozy Wandas. We'll be perfectly safe."

"Lanie, you're not going in. Stay outside and have the car running. We don't know who else might show. It's more important to have a getaway driver."

"Okay. Love you!"

I set the walkie talkie down and stare at Vem. "He does have a point."

Vem shrugs. "We'll move the Veminator closer, so no one will have to run too far."

She knows my thoughts on running.

We settle on the hilltop and Vem shoots the first Nellie. In her neverending supply of...well, supplies, she digs in her pocket and pulls out a miniature set of binoculars. "Target hit. Launching rocket number two."

"Lanie? I hope you can hear me!" Cos is whispering into the walkie talkie, scaring me.

"I'm here, babe! What's going on?"

"I saw the rocket coming in. Nothing happened. There's no sprinkle at all."

Vem opens her box of rocket launchers and studies a Woozy Wanda. "Oopsie. They expired two years ago." She sighs. "You can't trust the government to do anything right."

"Now what?" I ask. We no longer have that safety net.

She takes the walkie talkie from my hands and turns it off. "We're going in."

Chapter Forty
Lanie

"Meea, you had me fooled."a woman's firm voice repeats.

Piper gasps. "Mom! Don't come in! This place is full of booby traps!"

"Piper? What are you and Obie doing here?"

"I caught them. Not real smart for a policeman," Sawyer says with sarcasm.

Ignoring Piper's dire warning, I rush to the other side of the large warehouse. "Lanie! Not yet!" Vem yells. There's nothing Vem or anyone else can say that would keep me from my daughter.

I've almost reached her when Sawyer rushes me. Instead of knocking me to the ground, he bearhugs me and attempts to grab my weapon. As we struggle for control, the gun discharges. Sawyer stumbles backward until he hits the wall and falls to the ground.

"Cool toy," Trigger says with amusement as Sawyer writhes in pain. "I'll have to order some of those for myself."

Pivoting toward this loudmouth, I fire with gusto. As he drops to his knees, I continue firing. There is something to be said for gaining control over someone so evil.

As soon as it's clear Trigger isn't going anywhere, Meea dashes over and attempts to throw her arms around me. Impulsively, I pivot to the side. I don't trust anyone in this room that hasn't eaten in my home.

"He...killed my sister!" she sobs. "He forced me to go along with everything!"

"She's lying, Mom!" Piper shouts.

"Oh, I know." I shove Meea's body away from me and observe her tearless face. "You attempted to cover your tattoo with makeup, which should have been my first clue."

She is staring at me as though I'm speaking in French.

"But then I remembered that you mentioned attending college on a theater scholarship. This— everything since you came to town—has been one big performance."

In an instant, Meea grabs my gun and attempts to hit me over the head with it. Luckily, I've got November Bean in my corner.

Vem yanks my weapon from Meea's hands and

shoves her to the floor with less effort than it takes to brush her hair. As she stands astride Meea's squirming body, she calls to me, "Lanie, find something to restrain her!"

My eyes scan the cavernous space.

"There should be some zip ties over by the conveyor belt, Ma-ma-Mrs. Hill," Obie says.

I don't understand how Obie can see those small things from such a distance, but we're lucky he can.

As Vem is tying Meea's arms, I turn my attention to Piper and Obie. For the first time, I really look at them and I'm shocked by their appearance. Piper has scratches and what looks like are rug burns all over her face and arms. Obie has a black eye and is bleeding on the top of his head.

"Did Sawyer do this to you? I'm so sorry, hon. We'll get you to the hospital right away." A picture forms in my head of my sweet daughter and her boyfriend being brutalized. It's too much for my already weary mind to handle.

"We got in an accident. The airbags went off in our faces. We're fine, but my car..."

"Don't you worry about your car, sweetie. That's tomorrow's worry."

"Mom, Aunt Cedar is —"

"I know. She's been working with the FBI all along. She's so brave."

"Lanie! Watch out!"

I turn my head just in time to see Trigger, who

has inexplicably risen. He stands behind me holding a standing light used for photography. His actions appear in slow motion as I freeze, waiting for the impact.

Instead, both the light and his body fall to the ground. Cedar, Cos and Truman have all used their Woozy Wandas to subdue Trigger. This time, he is out cold..

I rush to my husband, hugging him tightly. "Cos! That was close!"

"I distinctly remember telling you two that we would handle it!" he says after kissing me.

When I enter Room 112 of Piney Falls General Hospital, I'm surprised to see Urica in the sitting position, wearing her favorite pink and orange robe. Her long grey hair, normally in braids or pulled back with a pretty clip, is wound on top of her head.

"Lanie! I'm so glad you came!"

I kiss her cheek and set her favorite peanut butter bars beside her bed. "Piper sends these along with her best wishes. Only with your doctor's okay," I warn. "Though, after what you've been through, your doctor should be okay with anything."

"It's about time, toots!"

I don't know how I missed Gladys sitting on the other side of her bed.

"Yes, I should have come sooner. You're looking great though, Urica!"

She nods enthusiastically. "I'm going home tomorrow. Wouldn't it be grand if the three of us could enjoy lunch at the public records building?"

"It would be quite grand, Urica. I'm going to fill in for Doris for the next two weeks, though. She's been away from for funerals and vigils and now she's got a taste for time off." I wink at Urica, who nods my direction.

"Cos booked her a cruise to Alaska. He figures with all of the vacation time she's never taken, he owes her."

"I'm sure Boysie's been to see you, but—"

"What Lanie's trying to say so clumsily is that she'd like a complete rundown of your injuries and how you got them," Gladys interrupts. "Did I get that right, toots?"

"Yes, Gladys."

Urica glances over at her best friend with love and extends her hand. When Gladys takes it, they share a mutual gaze of admiration. Vem and I will be just like them in a few years. But will I be the Gladys, or the Urica?

"Well, my next-door-neighbor asked me to walk his dog while he was in Seattle for his grandson's graduation," Urica explains with her usual energy.

"Since I like taking walks, I thought it would be a good excuse for more exercise."

"This walk was different though," Gladys says. "You were walking over by Denver's place when you saw some no-goodniks, up to no good."

"That I did, Gladys, that I did." Urica nods in agreement.

"Sawyer and his friends killed Denver and were in the process of taking everything in his home that connected him to the Starfish Syndicate Crime Syndicate. You must've interrupted."

"Yes, Lanie dear, that's exactly what happened. The next thing I know, I'm on the ground and one of them is saying, 'First, we shut you up, then we put a bullet through ya.'"

I reach over and take her free hand. "This is so hard to hear. How did you get away?"

"I took November Bean's self-defense course, so I knew to put my knee right where—"

"Right where the goods are," Gladys interrupts again.

"Yes, that's right. It gave me time to get up. I thought I'd gotten away from them, and I could hear sirens in the distance."

"That must've been when Piper called Boysie to come because the street was blocked."

"She saved my life. Instead of just conking me over the head, they would have finished the job."

Chapter Forty-One

"Cedar, after all of that ugliness, we didn't want to make you relive your experiences. But now that we've put some distance between us and those memories, can I ask you something?"

We're seated in the Piney Falls City Park, listening to the local band, Sea Fungus play songs they wrote themselves. Boysie insisted on a ceremony to honor those who showed tremendous bravery.

"Sure, Lanie. Anything."

"We found blood on your seatbelt, as well as on the jacket behind Truman's home. Where did that come from?"

"I was meeting the agents every night. We chose different times every day in order to prevent the gang from figuring out what I was doing. Somehow,

Ribeye found us. He'd followed me from the warehouse, I guess."

"Oh."

"I didn't do anything, Lanie. There was a struggle, and, let's just say, he didn't have the opportunity to rat me out. No one was to blame."

"Cedar, you are the bravest person I've ever known."

The band mercifully stands up and Boysie motions for Cedar to join local dignitaries and Vem on stage.

"We appreciate your selfless service to our community, to rid us of the scourge of Glitz," Boysie says, as he pins a small gold medal on Cedar's chest. She blushes, still the humble woman I first met in Piney Falls many years ago.

Boysie moves to the person standing beside her. "In honor of one of our bravest citizens," Boysie begins, readying himself to pin an impressive medal on Vem's chest.

"THE bravest," she corrects him.

"Yes, the bravest. Were it not for your selfless acts and donations of powerful weaponry in the former popcorn building," Boysie's voice quivers, "many precious lives would have been lost."

"Don't forget my generous donations today, too!" Vem whisper-yells.

"I forgot, she bought these lovely medals and a few other things for our celebration today too.

November Thursday Bean, you are hereby recognized as the Bravest Citizen in Piney Falls."

He moves her FBI jacket aside and pins the oversized bright green medal on her chest. When he finishes, he turns to the small but enthusiastic crowd and says, "Let's give these gals some applause."

Cosmo whistles loudly as I applaud. My hands are at a forty-five degree angle and are slightly cupped. November made me practice. Several times.

"Thank you, thank you, Chief Lumquest," November begins, when the applause dies down and she's performed six curtseys. "I didn't think about myself that day. Of course, I have a history of bravery and selflessness. If you come to my newest moaning class, Moaning for Heroes, I'll tell you all about it in the sixty-minute warmup video."

I make a twirling motion with my finger and mouth the word, "Cake."

"Agent Goins, would you like to say a few words about me?"

The other person on the stage appears very uncomfortable but he stands up anyway, not bothering to use the microphone. "Yes, the government is most grateful to these two women for their service in the drug war." He turns his back to the audience, but luckily I'm close enough to hear what he says next:

"The chief wants me to watch while you destroy your surveillance of him."

Vem shoves him aside so that she can finish with

a broad smile and her best cupped-hand wave. People are getting up to find the refreshments when Vem calls out,"I have one more thing to say!"

I make a slicing gesture across my neck and hope she gets my point.

Boysie yanks the microphone from her hand before she can begin the lengthy speech she prepared as backup. "I've been asked to announce the winner of the Name the Serial Killer contest."

Cos squeezes my knee. We are equally appalled.

"The winner was to receive a plaque with their name on it, a year's supply of Cheese With Your Burger coupons, a free sunset cruise on the Flanagan Fair Weather, dinner extra, and three thousand dollars cash."

Boysie pauses and our gazes meet. *Is that a twinkle in his eye?*

"There's been a change of plans though. Piper, could you come here for a minute?"

She and Obie are serving the cakes she made for the occasion. Her dark head pops up and she points to herself with cake-covered hands. "Me?"

"Yes, you my dear. Bring that beau of yours too."

Wiping her hands on her Cosmic Bakes apron, she takes Obie's hand before walking to the stage. She still bears evidence of her battle wounds—a large area on one cheek that was injured by the airbag and a seven stitches on her forehead. Though healing, Obie still sports his black eye as well.

"Two more unsung heroes from the warehouse violence. Let's give 'em a hand, shall we?"

Both of them blush and keep their eyes trained on each other as Cosmo whistles in between outbursts of, "yeah! That's my kid!"

"For the folks that don't know, Miss Piper Moonlight Hill's car was totaled as she and my boy, Obie were trying to escape the Starfish Syndicate. We couldn't let that bravery go unnoticed. We talked to folks around town and decided there was a better use for our funds than that contest. With the help of Ms. Bean and local businesses, we've purchased a brand new car for you!"

Piper's mouth drops as she looks from side to side.

"Where is it, Boysie?" Cosmo asks.

At that moment, flashing lights appear. Both police cruisers and two more from Blackberry Cove are escorting a shiny new deep purple car down the street.

We all venture over to the street to admire Piper's new car, complete with a big, red bow on the hood.

"Did I do good, Lanie?" Vem asks. "I had it painted her favorite color."

"Perfect, Vem. I can't believe you kept this a secret!"

"Never underestimate me, Lanie Anders Hill."

"What happens the next time there's a shooting? Will I get a car?" Someone jokes.

"Nothing is going to happen any time soon," Boysie replies with confidence. "Piney Falls is peaceful from here on out."

Cos, Lanie Piper and I all exchange glances before we erupt in laughter.

Acknowledgments

Thanks as always to my wonderful worldwide family. Your strength and love has given me the inspiration to do what I love. The Keder Readers are an important part of my team and I appreciate you! Molly Burton, you're always upbeat and ready to create, no matter how things are going in your world.

About the Author

Joann Keder is a USA TODAY Bestselling author who has won numerous awards. She spent her formative years (over 40) living on the plains of Nebraska. When she and her husband chose to make a move to the Pacific Northwest, she came to an agreement with her soul that it was time to start writing.

Today, she creates stories about strong women, their quirky sidekicks and the paths they choose. When she's not writing, she and her husband enjoy nature, a good chocolate and spending time with family. Not necessarily in that order.

Also by Joann Keder

Piney Falls Mysteries

Welcome to Piney Falls

Saving Piper Moonlight

Tales of Naybor Manor

Lavender's Tangled Tree

The Twisted Stitch Society

Kinundrum

Charming Mysteries

Oceanberry Blues

Tangerine Troubles

A Lime in Time

Emory Bing Mysteries

The Case of the Half-Baked Bing

The Case of the Rootbeer Bungle

The Case of the Fudged Features

The Case of the Chunky, Funky Monkey

The Case of the Clairvoyant Carrot

The Case of the Vegan Vixen

The Case of the Cream Cheese Caper

Pepperville Stories

The Story of Keilah

Secrets and Sunflowers

Franniebell and Purple Wonder

Be the first to hear about new releases! Sign up for my newsletter here:

http://www.joannkeder.com